NATION OF THE STARS
By HR Moore

Titles by HR Moore:

The Relic Trilogy:
Queen of Empire
Temple of Sand
Court of Crystal

In the Gleaming Light

The Ancient Souls Series:
Nation of the Sun
Nation of the Sword
Nation of the Stars

http://www.hrmoore.com

Chapter 1

Talli looked out of the window of the small, shaking airplane, taking in the snow, the buildings, the sea … the bitter winter. She and Christa were here for a prominent climate scientist named Belle Christie-Richardson, and they probably weren't the only ones after her interview on the BBC. Who could have missed those eyes …?

Ira, of the Holy Star, had sent Belle's full bio, detailing everything from her impressive academic record to her efforts as a climate activist. It was a wonder she'd stayed under the radar for so long, but she was a private person, with no social media accounts, very few friends or relations, and no evidence of a romantic partner.

'Ready?' said Christa, taking Talli's hand as they landed in Nuuk, Greenland's capital.

'I hate the cold,' said Talli, adjusting her scarf.

'Yes, that's exactly what I meant,' said Christa, giving Talli a scathing look.

'Other than that,' said Talli, doing an action jump, 'I was born ready.'

'Good, because I need you prepped to fight.'

Talli took Christa's hand. 'I know.' She kissed Christa's lips. 'And you, don't do anything stupid,' she said, lightening the mood as she ducked through the door into the frigid air.

They pulled their coats around them, glad of their sturdy footwear and thermal layers, then climbed into a waiting car.

'It's so … depressing,' said Talli, as the car drove along snow-covered roads.

'I think it's beautiful,' said Christa.

'The electricity pylons and streetlamps against the snow feel wrong. The worst of humanity against the beautiful wild … the stamp of destruction littered everywhere.'

'What has got into you today?' said Christa, taking Talli's hand.

'I don't know … I guess our woes seem so pointless in the face of Earth's destruction. Belle has spent her whole human life trying to do something about it, and we're about to convince her to leave that fight … and for what?'

'To stop people dying,' said Christa.

Talli shrugged. 'It feels wrong. Selfish.'

'But if we don't get her to help us, another nation will recruit her,' said Christa.

'I know,' said Talli, 'so we'll do it, but that doesn't make it any better … everything's so fucked up.'

They pulled up outside a nondescript box of a hotel building and climbed out of the car. The lobby was like any other, and Talli wanted to run screaming … the soullessness of it was somehow more evidence of everything bad about humanity. She squared her shoulders and told herself they would be out of here soon.

'We're here to see Ms. Christie-Richardson,' said Christa, smiling her most charming smile at the receptionist. 'She's expecting us.'

'Who should I say is here?' said the woman.

'We're friends of her research partner, Mr. Pickering.'

The receptionist smiled stiffly, clearly unhappy at not having a name, but not wanting to push further. 'Thank you,' she said, picking up the phone receiver. 'Please take a seat.'

The elevator doors opened, and Talli watched as its contents spilled out. She inhaled sharply, making a strangled sound. 'Christa,' she said, grabbing her arm, 'we have a problem ...'

Christa followed Talli's gaze. 'Shit,' she said, then jumped to action without another word.

Christa made for the entrance, intercepting Belle, and Jamie and Tamsin who flanked her. It was no surprise the Templars had got here first; they were closer.

'Belle!' said Christa, nudging Tamsin out of the way. 'I need just one quick word.'

Jamie took hold of Belle's arm, refusing to let Christa pull her away. 'No,' he said.

'I didn't realize you spoke for her,' said Christa.

Talli came up behind them and tapped Belle on the shoulder. She turned, brushing off both Christa and Jamie's hands.

'This is going to seem very strange,' said Talli, 'as you don't know any of us, but to go with those two is a big mistake.'

Jamie tried to interrupt, but Talli kept talking.

'I'm not sure what they told you, but the organization they represent doesn't even acknowledge climate change exists, and I'd be concerned for your safety if you went anywhere with them … they're not the most savory of individuals.'

Belle stepped away from them all. 'And who are you?' she said suspiciously.

'I'm Talli, of the Pagan nation,' she said, looking into Belle's eyes, into her soul. 'You are a very great demon, I believe …'

'What are you talking about?' said Belle, taking another step back.

'The Sphere? The Nexus? This …' said Talli, showing Belle the symbols Christa had drawn in henna on her hand.

Belle's composed features turned suddenly unsure. She sat on the arm of a chair, shaking her head.

'Enough of this,' said Jamie. 'She's already agreed to come with us. We're funding her research … very expensive research.'

'So you can use her to improve the profile of your corrupt, dispassionate organization?' said Christa.

'Stop with the act,' said Jamie. 'She'll find out the truth when she wakes.'

'What act?' said Christa. 'You *are* corrupt and dispassionate, and your profile's in the gutter!'

'And what of your lying, thieving nation?' hissed Jamie. 'Are you going to tell her how you *stole* my daughter?'

'She's not your daughter,' said Christa, her voice full of venom.

Jamie's face flushed, and Talli prepared to step in between them, to knock Jamie on his ass if need be …

'Jamie,' said Tamsin, her voice urgent. All three of them swung their heads to look at her. 'Belle … she's gone …'

Jamie and Tamsin ran for the door with Christa hot on their heels. Talli hung back, picked up the scarf Belle had dropped as she'd fled, and stuffed it in her bag. Belle's demon soul was awaking, and with eyes like hers, she'd use her magic to give them the slip in no time.

Belle had been surprisingly easy to wake, and now they had to hope she wanted to be found, because if she went to ground and used magic to hide, the Pagans knew of no demon left in the world who'd be able to find her.

The plane ride back to the U.S. was not a pleasant one. Tamsin had failed him again and needed to be punished. Why could no one do their fucking job?

Raina wouldn't have let Belle slip away … but at least the Pagans had lost her too.

Jamie had gone back into the hotel when it had become apparent Belle was lost, deciding that killing two Pagans would be a suitable second best. But the two Pagans had gone, so the trip had been for nothing … a total waste of time.

'Don't unpack,' said Jamie, as they reached the open-plan living space in his loft in lower Manhattan.

Tamsin looked forlorn … wary.

'You're going back to the West Coast.'

'Wha …'

She started to protest, but Jamie held up a hand to silence her.

Raina's words taunted him … words she'd spoken when she'd been about to join the Templars: *They've set up a stronghold right under your nose, and no one can get in …*

consolidate in North America, or you'll always have a threat at your back.

'You will go to the West Coast, infiltrate, and find a way to bring them down.'

Tamsin paled. 'Jamie …'

'Or we will always have a threat at our backs.' He would show Raina. He would bring down the West Coast. How much of a threat could they really be anyway? And he would prove that he was fit to be king. He would rule, and then Raina would have no choice but to come crawling back. The whole demon world would lie at his feet.

A quiet cough interrupted him, but Tamsin was nowhere to be seen; he hadn't even noticed her exit. 'Ah, Sir,' said one of his henchmen.

'Yes?' said Jamie, his tone a snap.

'This woman …'

'Pixie,' said a woman, as she stepped around the henchman.

'Pixie,' repeated the man. 'She says she's here to see you.'

'I have information about the Slayers I am sure you will find useful,' said the blond-haired, blue-eyed beauty. Her stature lived up to her name. She was short and slight, but she had something about her … energy … pluck.

Jamie raised an eyebrow. 'And who are you?' he said, his gaze brazenly travelling down and then back up her body. She didn't seem to mind. In fact, she dropped a shoulder and cocked a hip.

'I'm Noah's wife,' she said. 'You know, the old Grand Master … the one you did away with? His son. He's Grand Master now … a meteoric rise by anyone's standards …'

'Is that so?' said Jamie, slowly. 'And if that is the case, why are you here? Shouldn't you be lording it over all the other Slayers as the new Grand Master's wife?'

'Well, you see,' she said, moving around the loft on confident legs, exploring his personal space, a look of mock distress on her pretty features. 'He never wanted to marry me. His father forced us together because I was the best student in their … breeding program.

'The old Grand Master deemed me most likely to provide him with a strong, healthy, worthy grandchild … an heir.' She waved a hand around as she spoke, apparently unconcerned about the threat to her life being here presented. 'His intention was to pack me off to a breeding camp to be pampered, caged, and ridden … a brood mare … my myriad potential lost.'

Interesting. Jamie waved away his henchman, now alone with the petite Pixie. 'Tell me more about what made you worthy,' he said, offering her a seat.

'I'm strong, healthy, intelligent, strategic, fertile, good at pleasing my husband in every way …' she said coyly.

Jamie smiled. Sometimes the universe dropped gifts in your lap, and this was a gift he wanted to unwrap. But she wasn't finished …

'I'm ambitious, ruthless, willing to do what's necessary to get what I want …'

'And what is it you want, exactly?' he said, leaning into her space.

She didn't flinch. 'To rule,' she said. 'To take the Slayers in a new direction. To move them into this century. They'll never wipe out the demons … a stronger race.'

'A stronger race?' said Jamie, delighted.

Her eyes flicked up to his, their faces so close he could see every line on her creamy skin.

'You reincarnate,' she said, 'we cannot. You have experience, resources, time … we should work with you, not try to kill you. Based on our past performance, we'll never be successful. And it's all for what? Death and destruction? I want to be great … to build something great, and the Slayers are headed for ruin, especially now Noah's in charge.'

'Why did they pick him?' said Jamie, placing a hand on her thigh. She barely seemed to notice.

'His father changed the succession rules. He wanted to create a dynasty.'

Jamie couldn't fault the ambition …

'Does Noah want to pack you off to your gilded cage now he's in charge?'

'Noah's a child,' she said, 'he doesn't know what he wants, and he certainly doesn't know what to do with me.'

Jamie assessed her for a long moment. 'And if we did … collaborate?' he said. 'How would that work?'

She smiled. 'I'll give you the Slayer organization and all their resources.'

'And in return?' he said casually, tracing a circle on her leg.

'From what I hear, you're ambitious too … have vision, and the determination to see your plans through. You're the kind of man I was trained for … a man worthy of my skills … a king.' She looked into his eyes, no trace of hesitance to be found. 'And I want to be your queen.'

Chapter 2

The fire crackled as Raina and Caspar watched Callie play. This was all Raina had wanted for hundreds of years ... her own child ... the three of them together. If only Callie wasn't stuck here at Maltings. It had been fine to start, Callie exploring the outbuildings and fields, but she wanted to go further, to run free, to explore the woods and streams that stretched out towards the horizon.

If only they could bring the war to an end. If only they could disband the Templars ... but that would mean more killing ... more devastation. It would get worse before it got better.

Caspar leaned in and dropped a chaste kiss on her lips, seeming to sense her dark thoughts. Callie's eyes flicked up to take in the spectacle. 'Mum!' said Callie, turning away. Raina smiled and kissed Caspar again.

Callie had been so wary of Caspar, but she was coming around, thank the Gods. All it had taken was kindness. Jamie, for all the presents he'd bought her, had never given Callie that.

A draft sucked the warm air from the room, and Raina turned to find Christa and Talli entering, Talli brandishing a scarf. 'Where's Zahora?' said Talli.

'Upstairs, asleep,' said Raina. 'Keeping the protection up around this place is draining her dry ...'

'I'll get her!' said Callie, jumping up and racing from the room.

'Be gentle!' Raina called after her.

Callie and Zahora had developed a strong bond ... maybe it was because they were both trapped here ... had both been through a lot ... were still going through a lot.

'How was the trip?' said Raina.

'Same as always,' said Christa.

Talli shrugged and sat in a chair. 'Fucking awful.'

Raina looked to Christa. Christa shook her head ... apparently Raina shouldn't ask Talli what was up.

Zahora plodded down the stairs, rubbing her eyes, while Callie bounded ahead. 'Hey,' Zahora said wearily. 'You need me?'

'Can you find someone using this?' said Talli, handing over the scarf.

Zahora rubbed the scarf between her fingers. 'Is Alerac here?' she asked, sitting heavily in an armchair.

'Not yet,' said Raina, guilt flooding her as she took in Zahora's diminished form. When she'd first met Zahora, she'd been a firecracker, full of life and guile. Now she was a zombie, barely able to hold up her own head.

'Maybe Alerac can help us on his own?' said Caspar, obviously seeing the same thing.

'And take shifts maintaining the barrier,' said Raina. 'You're working too hard ...'

Normally, Zahora waved away any suggestion she couldn't cope. This wasn't the first time they'd tried to lighten her load ... but she didn't do that today. She nodded. 'I think that would be good,' she said, her voice little more than a whisper.

Callie sat half next to and half on top of Zahora, and threw her arms around her. Zahora leaned in and closed her eyes, falling instantly asleep.

'I'm here,' said Alerac, entering the sitting room, Meredith a few paces behind. He looked more sprightly than he had in weeks—more like he should, considering he wasn't even yet forty—his dark hair glossier, even the ink across his skin somehow more vibrant.

'Can you track the scarf by yourself?' said Raina, nodding to where Zahora slept, Callie stroking her hair. Talli and Christa had called ahead, so the request wasn't a surprise.

'No,' said Alerac, his usual blunt self. 'I can't travel around the Nexus … I can only send across it. I get glimpses and snippets. Zahora gets a front-row seat to the entire show; it will be far more effective if she does it.'

'Then we'll do it in the morning,' said Raina.

'But …' said Alerac.

'I know, it's a risk,' said Raina. 'But the Templars don't have magiks of their own.'

'They could have recruited some,' said Alerac.

'It's possible,' said Raina, 'but unlikely. We don't think they took anything belonging to Belle, which means they're not being advised by a magik.'

'Fine,' said Alerac, turning for the door, 'but don't say I didn't warn you. Call me when you deem her fit to start …'

'For Zahora to rest, you'll have to maintain the barrier tonight,' said Raina, stopping him in his tracks.

Alerac looked like he might argue, but his eyes flicked to Meredith, who watched him like a hawk. He gave a curt nod, then left. Meredith followed him out.

'What was that about?' said Talli, not caring they probably weren't out of earshot.

Raina and Talli shot each other knowing smiles.

'I don't know,' said Caspar, 'but I want to find out.'

Rose took a breath. This meeting was the most important in … well, probably half a century or more. She didn't worry about messing up—this wasn't her first rodeo—but she did worry about the irrationality of her allies. She turned over ways to get through to them, had researched the Pagans' records, and drew up from her memory the things each of them cared about, things they were vain about, past relationships, grudges …

Rose had a good memory for such things, but it was impossible to know everything about the past … even one's own. Brains could only hold so much, and records were notoriously subjective.

She was staying with Malcom—the Pagans' representative at the Registerium—in a large house on the Registerium's estate. Most of their allies were here too, no one allowed to stay in the castle during the inquiry, aside from members of the Registerium itself. Representatives from the other nations had been housed in various houses around the estate.

Rose pulled her shoulders back as best she could … this body was getting old … and walked confidently into the drawing room, where the breathtaking view of the loch through the wall of windows stopped her in her tracks. She took a moment to savor it before getting down to business.

When she tore her eyes away, she found every demon in the room watching her. Vikings, Wakan, Buddhists, Shindus, and The Holy Star had all put stakes in the ground as the Pagans' out-and-out allies. Rose still had hopes for the Egyptians, Aboriginals, and Animists, but it would be foolish to approach them ahead of time ... experience told her they wouldn't appreciate it.

'Thank you for joining me,' said Rose, lowering herself into a tartan armchair. 'It goes without saying, but I will say it anyway ... the Pagans appreciate your support and friendship. We are proud to call you friends, and share your values of freedom, equality, and peace.'

'And we are honored to call the Pagans friends,' said Sofie, Queen of the Vikings.

Rose inclined her head in thanks as the others agreed with Sofie's sentiments.

'And thank you for meeting today,' said Rose. 'The outcome of this inquiry will have far-reaching effects. Our way of life is at stake ... our freedoms ... the checks and balances that have long served us well ...'

'Whatever happens, the Shindus do not want war,' said Eka.

'Neither do we,' said Rose.

'What about Raina?' said Tsering, the Buddhist leader. 'Has there ever been a time when she didn't want war for some purpose or other?'

A ripple of agreement spread across the room.

'War is not a dirty word,' said Sofie.

Rose cut across them before they disappeared down one of the rabbit holes that divided them. 'The Pagans do not want war,' she said firmly. 'Raina does not want war. She has a family now ... has only just got her daughter to safety ... she wants peace.'

'Jamie says the girl is *his* daughter,' said Eka, 'and she is a registered Templar.'

'She is,' said Rose. 'The Templars took advantage of the child. Manipulated her, terrified and coerced her, and now they say they *own* her, like she's an object they can play with ...' Rose let the words sink in, meeting their eyes, daring them to defend the archaic practice. 'Once this inquiry is over, when we have clarity around the future of the Registerium, my nation will petition for a change in the rules.'

Several demons shifted uncomfortably in their seats ... presumably because this was precisely the type of talk that could lead to war ...

'It is barbaric for nations to hold members hostage for an entire lifetime. If a demon wishes to change nation—for whatever reason—they should be free to do so. Raina and Caspar's daughter—for despite the rumors spread by Jamie, she is Caspar's—was registered under duress. She is five years old, in only her third lifetime, and in none of her lives has she ever lived to be a teenager.

'She is a child, kidnapped by the Templars, and forced to register in secret, with no understanding of what that registration meant. And now she suffers, because Jamie invokes painful magic to try and force her back to his side. Tell me, are those the actions of a father?'

The room went silent.

'If what you say is true,' said Tsering, 'Jamie is in the wrong. But I will reiterate ... we Buddhists don't want war. We're losing many as it is ... we cannot lose more.'

Tsering's words brought Rose up short, and she looked into his eyes for a long beat, the cogs in her brain trying to make sense of his words. 'What do you mean, you're losing people?'

'You're not?' said Tsering.

Rose shook her head.

Tsering looked around the room. 'What about you?'

'We are,' said Eka, with a grim look on her face.

'Us too,' said Sofie. 'Not many, but a handful.'

'Not us,' said the representative from the Holy Star.

'I would have to check across our nation,' said the Wakan. 'We are fragmented … we don't keep a close track of our people.'

'Where are they going?' said Rose.

'We don't know,' said Tsering, 'but we must find out … and for that, we need stability.'

'Does anyone know more?' said Rose.

The others shook their heads. 'Our people disappeared in the middle of the night,' said Sofie. 'No signs of a struggle.'

Rose nodded, troubled by the news. 'Believe me, we want stability too, but the only way to get it is to cut out the corruption at the Registerium's heart. When that is done, I pledge to you, the Pagan nation will help you find your missing demons.'

Chapter 3

Noah sat in his father's office in New York, trying to focus on the reports in front of him. It had been days since his father's death, and the funeral would take place today, in the chapel at the center of the Slayers' building. It was his duty to say goodbye to the man who'd raised him, but after that … what? Stay and try to reform the rotten organization, or flee, find Zahora, and be happy?

Staying was fraught with danger … but it was a chance—a unique opportunity—to bring about real change. Although he would most likely wind-up dead, or be discovered as a demon …

He turned his eyes back to the reports and reread the same sentence three times, still not sure what it said. What was this report about? He checked the title. Oh … his father's death.

A knock sounded from the door—a welcome distraction. 'Come in,' he said, but his shoulders slumped when he saw who it was. 'Pixie.'

'Husband,' she said, eying him speculatively. 'You haven't come to see me since your return …'

'No,' he said, tracking her approach. She was very attractive, with striking eyes and an air of strength, but she reminded him of a beautiful monkey—a creature liable to turn ferocious in a heartbeat.

'So I took matters into my own hands,' she said, pouting a little, 'and came to see you.'

'How can I help?' he said, as she came round to his side of the desk. She perched on the edge and crossed her legs, her skirt riding up, exposing most of her thigh.

Noah's eyes flicked to the exposed skin, and a seductive smile spread across her lips.

'Oh, no, my love,' she said, 'I'm here to help you. In … whatever way you require. As your wife, the perks of both my mind and my body are open to you, and I want to be of use.'

It took everything Noah had not to kick her out. Entertaining Pixie for a moment longer felt like a betrayal of Zahora, but she might be able to tell him something useful. He looked down at the report on his desk, words from the executive summary finally sinking in.

'Do you think the Templars were behind the attack? That they killed my father?' he asked.

Pixie stiffened the tiniest bit, but met his gaze. Noah could see her mind working.

'Almost certainly,' she said at last. 'Who else but demons would attack us? And this is Templar territory, after all.'

Noah nodded. She'd followed the same logic he had.

'We must strike back,' she said, putting a hand over his, 'before they strike again.'

Noah pulled his hand away and straightened the report, refusing to look back into her eyes.

'What's your plan?' said Pixie, her tone almost mocking ... he'd wounded her pride. 'I'm assuming you have one?'

'I'm still considering my options ... it would be foolish to rush.'

Pixie barked out a laugh. 'You have no idea what to do ... do you? We must defeat the demons once and for all, and then move this ancient organization into the twenty-first century.'

Noah's eyes flicked back to hers before he had time to think. 'How do you mean?'

'We have colossal resources, powerful connections, and an army. We could do anything ...'

'Like?'

'Build our empire, and live happily ever after, ruling over our people.' Pixie shuffled along the desk, pushing the mouse, keyboard, and report out of the way. She put her feet either side of his legs on the chair, her skirt riding all the way up.

'Pixie ...' he said, looking away.

She took his head in her hands, forcing him to look at her.

'Don't you see?' she said, shaking him. 'This has all happened for a reason. God has put us here, now, joined in matrimony, to serve his higher purpose. We are supposed to rule together. Your father was supposed to die at the hands of our enemies. We're being tested ... we must show God we're worthy ... serve him ... live a life devoted to him and each other ...' Pixie moved forward off the desk, sliding into his lap.

'Pixie ...' Noah said again, averting his gaze.

She kissed him, and something in Noah broke. He'd been unfaithful to Zahora once before, because of this woman and his father; he would not do so again.

'Take what is yours,' she whispered into his ear.

Noah pushed her away, lifting her back onto the desk. 'You are not mine,' he said. 'I never asked for you, don't want you, and my position is the only reason you want me. We don't even know each other …'

'God has put us together.'

'No,' said Noah. 'My father put us together, after training women like you to serve men in any way they desire. You're better than that.'

'I serve the Lord,' said Pixie. 'He moves in mysterious ways … it is not for me to question his will.'

'Have you heard yourself?' said Noah. 'My father was not God.'

'Your father served the Lord, as do I.'

'Look, Pixie, I don't know what bullshit Dad forced down your throat, but he served nobody but himself.'

'And what about me?' she said. 'What if I want you?' She dropped a hand to his leg and slid it towards his crotch. Noah caught it and pulled it away, then forced her off the desk.

She stood, embarrassment flushing her cheeks, but her features were set into a murderous stare. She looked at him for a beat, then turned for the door.

'Lord,' she said, 'I tried.'

The funeral was a long, somber affair. The Knights of the most righteous Order of the Hospi donned their armor, long swords held double handed in front of them, tips to the ground. The scene was creepy, Noah thought, as he clunked towards the circular altar, where his father's body rested in a marble coffin. They would intern the body in the Slayers' crypt, along with every grand master since the order began. Would Noah's body rest there one day too?

It was a stupid question driven by nostalgia; Noah had already decided to leave. Pixie had reminded him—in stark detail—just how devout the order's followers were ... how unlikely they were to change.

Noah knew this, of course, had grown up around these people, but he hadn't seen a display like Pixie's in a while. Those at the very top, like his father, had a certain contempt for the rules ... bent them when it suited, but most Slayers didn't operate that way.

Changing this place, convincing the order's most fervent sticklers not to be so rigid, would take years ... decades ... if it was even possible, and Noah's heart wasn't in the fight. His heart was with the demons, with Zahora.

Noah laid a hand on his father's coffin and said the necessary words. The priest droned on—Noah had no idea about what—and then, finally, it was over ... at least the first part. They processed out in order of seniority, into a large room with tables laden with drinks and elaborate platters of food. A string quartet filled the air with somber tones.

Several of Noah's fellow knights clapped him on the shoulder, telling him his father would be missed, that Noah would make a fine Grand Master, that his father would be proud. Noah could do little but nod in return. If he said anything, they would surely see through him, would know his plans, would kill him there and then.

After twenty minutes, Noah excused himself, saying there was much to do. The knights didn't try to dissuade him. 'Just like his father,' one said. 'So dedicated, even at a moment like this.'

Noah didn't tell the man the real reason his father always left gatherings early was because he had no interest in anyone but himself. Maybe that meant Noah *was* just like his father …

With any luck, they would get drunk, and no one would look for him until dawn, because by then, it would be too late.

Rays of morning light crept in through the kitchen window. Zahora sipped a cup of steaming tea, feeling worlds better than she had in longer than she cared to remember. She'd slept for the best part of twenty-four straight hours, and even though she'd happily return to bed, sleep didn't tug so hard at her eyelids.

Conversely, Alerac looked beat as he entered the kitchen, like he hadn't slept at all, which, Zahora knew, might well be the case. Zahora should have asked him to share the load before, but she'd worried the others would think less of her … think her weak. If anything, asking for help had made her feel more like she belonged … like part of their team.

'How does this work?' Zahora asked Alerac, as he accepted a cup of coffee from Meredith.

'We use the scarf to locate its owner,' said Alerac with a shrug. 'Usually, it's an inexact science, but with your skills, maybe not …'

'Why didn't you tell me about this before?' said Zahora, her brain finally rested enough to think coherently. 'I could have tracked Noah.'

Alerac shrugged again. 'Thought you knew ...'

A burst of anger shot through her, and she slammed down her mug. 'You're a terrible liar.'

Alerac gave her a long-suffering look. 'No good will come from tracking him. If and when he wants to return, he will.'

Zahora would have pushed the point further, but Talli and Christa entered the room. 'Ready?' said Christa, looking from Alerac to Zahora. 'Everything alright?'

'Fine,' said Zahora. At least there was something she could do now ... she would track Noah as soon as she could.

'Then let's go,' said Christa. 'We need to be back in time to bolster the shield.'

'Which gives us what?' said Talli. 'Four hours?'

'Five at a push,' said Alerac.

'Where are we going?' said Zahora.

'To the nearest standing stone outside the shield,' said Christa. 'It's not far; there are many in this area.'

'Give me a second,' said Zahora. She rushed upstairs to grab a t-shirt of Noah's and shoved it in her bag.

The standing stone was in the corner of a field at the top of a hill, exposing them to the howling wind and driving rain.

'Could have picked a better day for it,' said Meredith, turning her back to the wind.

'Let's be quick,' said Talli, handing Belle's scarf to Zahora.

'What do I do?' said Zahora, looking at Alerac.

'Connect to the Nexus through the stone and press the scarf against the rock. From there, you'll have to see what the magic gives you, but try to follow the connection to its owner. I'll warn you, it's not as straightforward as it sounds …'

'Fine,' said Zahora, keen to get this over with … keen to replace the scarf with Noah's t-shirt. She sank onto the waterproof mat Meredith had thought to bring, pressed the scarf against the standing stone, and connected to the magical web using the Pagan wheel for protection.

She concentrated on the scarf, impatient for the magic to do its work. When it did, it showed several threads, but it encouraged her along one pointing east. She went willingly, throwing every ounce of intention into the task; she had to get this over with quickly. She flew across the Nexus, barely noticing as she traveled across half the world to a building in India.

It was strange. The magic showed her a child sitting on the floor, surrounded by many other children. They were … they were making scarves. *Shit*. Maybe she should have paid more attention to the options.

She looked at the child, took in the smudge of dirt on his face, his bright smile, his … he looked suddenly upwards, right at her, and she recoiled with a gasp. She slammed back into her body at such speed she fell back onto the wet grass, winded.

She clutched her chest, desperate for air, trying to force oxygen into her lungs. Alerac hovered over her. 'Anything we should worry about?' he said.

Her lungs finally complied, and she shook her head, drawing in deep breaths.

'What happened?' asked Talli, crouching at her side, helping her up.

'I followed the wrong thread. I went to a sweatshop in India … one that makes scarves.'

'Ha!' Alerac laughed. 'I told you it wasn't an exact science. Maybe the magic considers the child to be the scarf's owner … they probably weren't paid properly for making it …'

'Does that mean the scarf's useless?' said Christa.

'There were other threads,' said Zahora. 'I can follow another.'

'No need,' said a voice Zahora didn't recognize.

She looked around, finding the others similarly confused. 'Did you hear that too?' said Zahora.

'Yes,' said Christa and Meredith together.

'Who is it?' said Zahora.

'We should get out of here,' said Meredith. 'It's a threat …'

'No need to panic,' said the voice again, but this time it was attached to a woman clad in jeans, boots, and a thick jacket approaching from the bottom of the hill. Where had she come from?

'Oh, good!' said Talli, with a beaming smile. 'How did you find us?'

'I followed my scarf,' said the woman. 'More successfully than you did …'

Zahora didn't listen to whatever they all said next. She cast aside the scarf and pulled Noah's t-shirt from her bag. She pressed it to the stone. This time, the magic connected immediately, and there was only one thread. She flew across the Nexus without conscious thought, towards New York.

The magic jolted Zahora to a halt outside the Slayers' building, holding her there for several beats. Then it took her inside, through the walls, into a living nightmare.

The building was under attack, and everywhere Zahora turned, bleeding bodies were strewn on the floor. Slayer bodies. Zahora's pulse rocketed as she searched frantically for Noah. But her mind couldn't process fast enough. Swords … armor … blood … battle cries … terror … pain.

Zahora's eyes found a painting of Noah's father. Someone had slashed it across the middle with a knife. Zahora's chest constricted. Noah was the new Grand Master. Whoever was behind this attack wouldn't leave without him.

She cast around again, calling to the magic that had brought her here, using the connection with Noah's t-shirt. *Please show me where he is ...*

The magic spun her around, then pushed her forward until she stood in front of a wood-paneled wall. She searched feverishly, until her eyes found a panel near the bottom that was open the tiniest fraction. She shot forward to see Noah crouched inside, clutching a bag to his chest.

'Noah,' she said out loud, stroking a hand down his face.

Noah jumped, turning his head wildly in the small space.

'Noah, it's me ... Zahora,' she said. 'I'm using magic.'

'Zahora?' he whispered. 'I was on my way ... to you ... but the attack ...'

'It's okay,' she said, 'but you need to move, or you won't get out of here alive ... the fighting's dying down.'

'If they catch me ...'

'They won't; I'll guide you.'

Noah nodded, and Zahora went ahead to make sure no one was coming, that no one would harm him. Luckily, the Slayers' building was vast, and most of the attackers had moved to the upper floors.

'They've got people on the front door,' said Zahora.

'There's another way, through the basement,' Noah whispered.

They crept along a corridor, then through a door that hid stairs. They descended into the pipe-filled basement, and Noah didn't hesitate when they reached the bottom, striding across the underground space to the far side, where he climbed the steps that would lead to his salvation.

'Wait,' said Zahora, rushing to check the exit, but she was too late. A young, overweight woman appeared, blocking his way, a short sword in her hand.

Shit. Shit. Shit. 'Noah, she's a demon,' said Zahora, urgently. 'She's not the easy target she might seem.'

'I know,' said Noah, searching for a weapon. A hammer lay on a nearby workbench, and he lunged for it, narrowly missing a swing from the woman's sword.

'Who are you?' said Noah. 'Why are you doing this?'

'You know who we are,' said the woman, stalking him.

'Templars,' said Noah.

'Knights,' said the woman. 'Just like you.'

Noah shook his head. 'Not any longer,' he said, heaving a tin of paint at the woman's head. She ducked, and he rushed her, knocking her over, then ran for the exit.

The woman was on her feet in a heartbeat, racing after him. 'No,' said Zahora, aiming her magic at the woman, reaching for her.

The woman heard her, spinning to face the new threat, her features turning fearful when no one was there.

'That's right,' said Zahora. 'You should be scared.'

'Who are you?' said the woman.

But before Zahora could answer—or figure out how to do the woman actual bodily harm—a force pulled her away, back across the Nexus, back to her body.

'We've been over this,' said Meredith. 'We had to return for the shield, and you looked like you were in trouble …'

'So you let a total stranger yank me back?'

'We didn't have many options,' said Christa.

'She could have killed me!'

'Doubtful,' said Belle.

'I passed out …'

'I used a little too much force, that's all. I'm rusty …'

'Noah was in trouble,' said Zahora, pacing back and forth across the sitting room at Maltings. A fire raged in the hearth, perfectly matching her flaming mood.

'Tell us,' said Meredith, who had asked several times for Zahora to share what she knew. 'We want to help.'

'Ira called,' said Caspar, entering the room with Raina. 'The Holy Star picked up a disturbance at the Slayer building.'

'Zahora was there,' said Meredith. 'She's about to tell us all about it …'

Meredith looked expectantly at Zahora. Zahora sneered.

'The Templars attacked the Slayers,' said Zahora. 'The building was in chaos. I was helping Noah get to safety when Belle pulled me back … I don't know if he made it out alive.' Tears stung her eyes as she vocalized the painful words. 'I have to go back to the stone ... to find him.'

'You can't,' said Meredith. 'I'm locking everything down. This could be part of something bigger ...'

'I have to go,' said Zahora.

'I won't put everyone in danger,' said Meredith. 'Not to satisfy your curiosity.'

Zahora whirled to face her. 'You can't stop me.'

Talli sucked a breath through her teeth. 'She can, Zahora, and believe me when I say she will.'

'She absolutely will,' said Christa. 'We've all tried, over the years.'

'No one's ever succeeded,' said Talli.

'Except that one time,' said Caspar, shooting a knowing look at Raina.

Meredith scowled. 'Try that trick again, and I swear to all the Gods ...'

'Oh yeah,' said Talli. 'Munster, wasn't it?'

'In Germany?' said Belle.

'Twelve sixty-six,' said Raina, 'if I'm not mistaken. We only wanted to go to the fair.'

'There was a war on,' said Meredith.

'But we didn't die,' said Raina. She sat next to Caspar on a sofa, bringing her legs up and leaning against him. 'It was such a lovely night.'

'Fried mushrooms to die for ...' said Caspar, stroking her arm.

Zahora shrieked in frustration. 'I don't want to talk about fried fucking mushrooms! My boyfriend is in danger.'

'Alright,' said Talli, 'no need to shout.'

'You're not going out there,' said Meredith. 'And by now, there's nothing you can do. He was either caught or he wasn't, and if he wasn't, there's a good chance he's alive.'

'How will he get back to us? If he tries to use a plane, the Templars could intercept him,' said Zahora.

'If he's that stupid, he deserves to die,' said Alerac, who'd been sitting so quietly in the corner, Zahora had forgotten he was there. She was about to give him both barrels, but he looked tired, large black circles under his eyes. He must have bolstered the shield again …

'Look,' said Meredith, 'my team's scouring all the intelligence we can get our hands on, as is Ira's team. When we're sure there's no immediate threat, we'll go back to the stone. Not before.'

'When will that be?' said Zahora.

'When it's done,' said Meredith, her features set.

Zahora sat, bowed her head, and grabbed handfuls of her hair. What else could she do?

'We'll ask Ira to keep a lookout for Noah,' said Caspar, kindly. 'He would be an asset to our nation, and he's important to you … we want him to return safely too.'

'If you'd just let him come here in the first place, none of this would have happened …'

'We questioned his loyalty,' said Raina, her hands spread wide, 'but now it looks as though he has little option but to be loyal to us.'

'And he is a demon,' said Talli.

'Unless the Templars have got to him,' said Meredith.

'He would never do that,' said Zahora. 'He's coming back to us … he's loyal to us … to me. He was leaving anyway, even before the attack.'

Meredith raised an eyebrow, like Zahora was naïve. Zahora stormed out, because the only other option was throwing something at Meredith's head, and she really didn't need to have her ass kicked on top of everything else today.

Raina watched Zahora's retreating back and sighed. She felt for her … she was going through so much, and working with the leadership was so new to her …

'That was a joy to behold,' said Belle dryly. 'Can't say I've missed the drama of nations.'

Raina looked the Adept up and down, wondering if they'd met in a previous life, wondering if she bore grudges against the Pagan nation …

'Why did you seek us out, Belle?' said Raina. Beating around the bush with this woman would get them nowhere.

'My name isn't Belle,' she snapped '… it's Amelina. Ame to my friends.'

'My apologies. Why did you seek us out, Ame?' said Raina.

'You sought me out first,' she said, drumming her fingers on the arm of her chair. 'I'd like to know why.'

'The Templars sought you out too,' said Christa. 'Why not go to them?'

'I have roots in Europe. And you two,' she said, looking at Christa and Talli, 'seemed more … like my kind of people. So, what do you want?'

'Times are turbulent,' said Raina.

Ame laughed. 'When are they not with you people?'

Raina cocked an eyebrow and smiled. 'Fair point, but we'd like your help to put an end to it.'

'There will never be an end,' said Ame. 'The cycle will continue until the end of time. Our natures are not so different to humans as we would like to think …'

'That may be the case,' said Raina, 'but the Templars have corrupted the Registerium. We want to put an end to that, at least.'

Ame stood and walked to the window. She perched on the wide sill. 'How?'

'We were hoping you could help with the details,' said Talli.

'We want to change the magic underpinning the Registerium,' said Raina.

Ame turned to look at Raina. 'Why?'

'They've abused the power the nations gave them,' said Raina. 'They've gone against their founding principles. They no longer serve us as they should.'

Ame looked harder, into Raina's soul, a look that contained venom. 'No. The real why.'

Raina locked her lips and looked away. Could they trust this woman? Who was she? What were her allegiances? Although, they had nothing to hide … the Pagan's reasons were public knowledge anyway …

'Our daughter was forced to register as a Templar,' said Caspar. 'The Templars do not let their demons leave. They're using magic to hurt her, to force her back to them. We want to change the magic so we can transfer her without the Templars' permission.'

'But that's not the only reason,' said Raina. 'The Templar leader, Jamie, wants to rule the demon world. He wants to be king. If he controls the Registerium—and he's getting close—his path to dominance is … more leisurely.'

Ame took a deep breath. 'And why is your cause any more or less just than his?'

'Nothing is objectively just or unjust,' said Raina. 'But the Pagan nation is not trying to expand. We want to live our lives peacefully, in our own territories. The Templars want world domination.'

'And what is you want from me?' said Ame.

'We're hoping you can help us understand the Registerium's magic,' said Talli.

'So you can change it?' said Ame.

'An inquiry is underway into the Registerium,' said Raina. 'Assuming a majority of nations agree to the changes we've proposed, we want to be prepared to make those changes happen.'

'And right now,' said Talli, 'we don't understand the magic.'

'And if they disagree?' said Ame. 'You'd like me to help you steal your daughter back anyway?'

Raina stayed silent; she wouldn't deny it.

Ame shook her head. 'You don't need me for the first part; the Registerium's own magiks will make your changes.'

'They don't have anyone capable,' said Caspar.

Ame frowned. 'Have they requested help from the Nation of Stars? To train up new magiks?'

Raina's mouth went dry. 'The Nation of Stars hasn't been seen for hundreds of years.'

'Why?' said Ame. 'What the hell happened?'

Jamie stood in the Grand Master's office, looking down at the Manhattan streets below. Finally, they were his and his alone … no one left to stand in his way now he'd destroyed the Slayers.

'My King,' said Pixie, with a coy curtsy. She'd changed into a demure dress straight out of the nineteen fifties. It was absurd, given the carnage she'd helped him unleash. 'We have secured the building, killed or captured all knights, and contained news of the attack.'

'Good,' said Jamie, watching with interest as she prowled towards him. He could do with a distraction now the battle was over.

'My team's already scouring the files,' said Pixie, 'determining the locations of all Slayer cells.'

'Excellent,' said Jamie, taking hold of her waist, running his hands over her curves. 'They trained you well.'

'You have no idea,' she said, reaching for the bulge at the front of his pants.

Jamie exhaled as her fingers made contact. She freed him, then he spun her, bending her over the desk, lifting her dress. No underwear … they had trained her well. He slid into her with a grunt, then moved with harsh, brutal thrusts.

She cried out, but pressed back against him. He lasted barely a dozen thrusts, coming hard on a string of expletives.

He pulled out, and she turned to face him, perching on the desk, a mischievous smile on her lips. Jamie moved to stand between her thighs. 'You are surprising,' he said, then kissed her. She kissed him back, matching him move for move.

'The wives …' she said, as he moved his lips to her neck, 'they want to marry demons.'

'Why?' He took her face in his hands, caressing her skin.

'Because they trained us to serve the best, the strongest, the most impressive of men, to create the finest children … the future of our cause. And demons are superior to our own breeding stock in every way.'

'Demons rarely have children,' said Jamie. 'Believe me, I've tried.'

'But what if? What if we could find a way to maximize the chances?'

'Human women are beneath us.'

Pixie scoffed. 'Have I not already proven you wrong? Human men may be a lost cause, but believe me, we women are not.'

Jamie gave her a skeptical look, although, he had to admit, this woman had delivered all she'd promised and more … far more than any of his demons.

'Don't worry, my King, I will continue to show you.'

The work *King* sent a fresh bolt of desire down his spine, a need to possess, but footsteps approached.

'Urgent news,' said a curt demon from the office entrance, barely blinking when he took in the scene— Jamie between Pixie's legs, her skirt up around her waist. Nor did Pixie blink, looking expectantly at the messenger … looking every inch the queen she wanted to be.

'Yes,' said Jamie, his voice clipped.

'The Grand Master … the kid … he got away.'

Chapter 4

A hunter, Jamila, had been selected to chair the Registerium's inquiry. She had no affiliation to any nation—never had—and was known for impartiality when it came to selling leads on new and sleeping demons.

'I call this meeting to order,' said Jamila, casting her gaze around the clearing, to where each nation's representatives sat on low stools in a circle around the standing stone.

Rose stole covert glances at her nation's enemies, and at those whose allegiance was uncertain. Janet—the Templar representative—sat alone, her face giving nothing away. Malcolm sat beside Rose, and she was glad of the company, the support, the extra pair of hands … her body was getting too old for all this …

'I will read the charges against the Registerium,' said Jamila, 'which form the full scope of this inquiry.'

They had all seen the list ahead of time, had already suggested additions and amendments.

'The accusations against the Registerium are:

One: supporting false, covert, and illegal registrations of demons to the Templar nation.

Two: favoring one nation—the Templars—above all others, by providing information and access to records that were not available to all, and by backing them in the current war without first carrying out appropriate due diligence.

Three: allowing the new West Coast nation to grow powerful, with no formal investigation or invitation to join this institution.

Four: failure to maintain sufficient magical skills.

Five: failure to appropriately investigate complaints, for example, the recent disappearance of demons from a number of member nations.

Do all here present agree to the scope of this inquiry?'

Each nation agreed in turn.

'Do any here present have additional scope they would like to add to this inquiry?' said Jamila.

Each nation confirmed they did not, except the Templars. 'I have something to add,' said Janet.

All heads swiveled to look at her. Typical of the Templars not to abide by the etiquette …

'We would like to propose that the inquiry considers the disbandment of the Registerium entirely,' said Janet.

The faces around the circle remained stoic, and none of them made a sound; they were too old, too experienced, too clever to betray their emotions openly to this audience, regardless of the size of bombshell Janet had dropped.

'You should set that forth as a motion after this inquiry concludes,' said Jamila. 'It is not an allegation that requires investigation.'

'It could and should appear in this inquiry's recommendations,' said Janet, undeterred.

'The cart before the horse …' said Rose, eliciting snickers from her allies.

'I'm merely making our objective plain, for the purposes of transparency,' said Janet. 'Never let it be said we were clandestine.'

'Noted,' said Jamila. 'We shall vote. A reminder that a two-thirds majority is required. All those in favor of the original scope of inquiry say aye.'

All but four nations said, 'Aye.'

'Those against, say nay,' said Jamila.

'Nay,' said Janet.

'And three abstentions,' said Jamila. The Egyptians, Aztecs, and Persian Zorros. 'The scope is agreed. We will reconvene tomorrow at sunrise.'

Zahora returned from bolstering the shield and could think of nothing but falling into her warm, cozy bed. She was so focused on it that she almost walked right past Ame, who sat outside Malting's back door … almost. She stopped dead in her tracks when her limbs caught up with her eyes.

'Can I help with something?' said Ame, her head cocked to one side in a look of amusement.

'Um, hi,' said Zahora, willing her brain to concentrate. It was hard, given how much energy she'd expelled on the shield. 'I … just … wanted to properly introduce myself.'

'Hello,' said Ame.

'You're an Adept, right?'

'Right.'

'Can I ask you some questions?'

Ame shuffled along the bench, making room for Zahora, who sighed in relief when she took the weight off her feet.

'The shield's taking it out of you?' said Ame.

'Yes.'

'There are ways to make it easier …'

'How?' said Zahora, hope kindling in her chest.

'By getting the others to give some of their magic, their energy.'

Zahora's shoulders slumped. 'Oh.'

'You don't think they will?'

'They have important work to do; I can't ask them to do my job for me.'

'It's not their job to keep Callie safe too?' said Ame.

'It is … just … in other ways.'

'Don't be a martyr,' said Ame, in an overly bright tone. 'It never ends well.'

'I'm …' Zahora trailed off.

'What did you want to ask me?' said Ame.

'Can you help me understand my magic? The Proficients tried—Marla and Alerac—but … I'm not compatible with their teaching methods.'

Ame barked out a laugh. 'What is it you want to know?'

'Everything,' said Zahora.

Ame chuckled. 'Give me your hand.'

Zahora complied without a second's hesitation. Ame took it, then almost immediately dropped it, jumping to her feet like Zahora was a live wire.

'What did you do?' said Ame, her face full of fear.

'I … don't understand,' said Zahora.

'How did you do it?'

'Do what?'

'Don't play with me. Magiks have tried for millennia … have died … you're a child! How did you do it?'

40

'Do what?'

Ame went still, assessing Zahora anew. 'You really don't know, do you?'

'Know what?' said Zahora, angry now and not afraid to show it.

'You have the power of the Sphere … inside you … running through your veins. But it was not yours to take.'

Jamie looked down at the unzipped body bag his security team had pulled in off the street. It had been left on their doorstep in the middle of the night.

'Who did this?' said Pixie.

'The West Coast,' said Jamie, crouching next to Tamsin's lifeless body. He couldn't bring himself to feel regret, only anger that she had failed him, that Raina had been right in her disdain of the young demon all along.

'Who dropped her?' said Pixie. 'Are we tracking them?'

'Four demons … they disappeared,' said Jamie, bitterly. What would Raina say about their enemies getting so close to Templar headquarters without consequence? She would mock him. And rightly so.

'What's your plan?' said Pixie. 'How will you retaliate?'

She was right … just like Raina had said. He had to do something about the threat at his back. 'How many Slayers do you have?'

Pixie and her team of wives had recruited many of the Slayers who'd survived the attack. The young ones had been easy to manipulate, most turned by a few devout lines and a quick fuck, with promises of prominent roles in the new world order. Few of the older Slayers had survived the attack, and those who had were trickier to deal with … most had been shot.

'We're still working through them,' said Pixie, 'but it should be near four hundred. Your people did a good job of containing news of the attack … few of the smaller outposts knew of it. I've been acting under my poor lost husband's authority …' Her look turned sharp. 'Have you found him yet?'

'No,' said Jamie, 'but he can't have gone far. Rally who you can … we're going to war.'

Rose sipped her smooth, heathery whiskey, and listened to the others talk. The sun was setting over the loch, a fire crackled in the colossal hearth, and if she tried hard enough, Rose could imagine she was back in the seventeen hundreds. It would have been blissful, had they not been at war, and had she not been in a room full of bickering demons.

'It went well, for the most part,' said Tsering—the Buddhist's leader. He referred to the first full day of the inquiry, where they'd heard evidence on a number of counts. 'I can't see how anyone could refute what we saw today.'

'They don't need to,' said Sofie, with a chuckle. 'Not if the Registrar wants to disband … he is in the Templars' pocket, after all.'

'And what then?' said Eka. 'Anarchy?'

'Survival of the fittest,' said Sofie, a wishful gleam in her eye.

'You just want a fight,' said Rose, with a wave of her hand. 'You wouldn't care for the administrative overhead that came after a disbandment.'

'That's the whole point,' said Sofie. 'No administration …'

'That would be chaos,' said Rose, 'and you know it.'

'Yes, yes,' said Sofie, reluctantly. 'You're right … I do want a fight. It's been so long … I envy Torsten.'

'I'm sure death at the hands of the Aztecs can be arranged, if you so wish,' said Eka.

'I'd rather fight that snake, Jamie,' said Sofie. 'Then we could end this particular administrative overhead and get to the good stuff.'

'Which is?' said Tsering.

'Changing the stick-in-the-mud Registerium,' said Sofie.

Rose tensed. The idea of change divided their allies, both the concept and content.

'I've long suspected that's the true motive behind this circus,' said Tsering.

'You know that's not true,' said Rose, sitting up straighter in her seat. 'You said yourself, your own people are disappearing … and what has the Registerium done about it?'

'But you have no missing demons,' said Tsering. 'What you have is possession of a demon who belongs to another nation. You want to change the rules only because it is *Raina's* child.'

'Will you ever let go of your grudge against her?' said Rose. 'It can't be good for your progression to Nirvana.'

Tsering scowled. 'That woman is evil.'

Rose waved a frustrated hand. 'She's just a woman. A clever, capable, ferocious woman who's not scared of going after what she wants.'

'Which is?' said Tsering.

'To protect her family and her nation,' said Rose.

'But that is not what I want,' said Tsering.

'No?' said Rose, looking him in the eye. 'What is it you want, Tsering? To exact revenge on Raina for stealing Caspar away?'

'Can't you see she caused all this?' said Tsering. 'Courting Jamie, then pushing him away? Toying with all our lives like we are mere pawns in her game.'

Rose put down her whiskey and leaned forward in her chair. 'I sent Raina to the Templars, ordered her to court Jamie. They have always wanted our territory, and I received intelligence that they were planning an invasion. Should I have sat back and done nothing?'

'There were other ways,' said Tsering.

'Like out-and-out war!' said Sofie with a grin, raising her glass.

'You, leader of the Buddhist nation, would have preferred me to choose war over diplomacy?' said Rose.

'Seduction is merely war by another name … dirty and demeaning,' said Tsering.

Rose scoffed. 'Don't be obtuse. You know how the world works … and if I had to make the same decision again, I would.'

'What of Caspar?' said Tsering. 'You care so little for the hurt you caused him?'

Rose threw up her hands. 'Caspar and Raina weren't even on speaking terms when Raina went to the

Templars ... which was as much his doing as it was hers.'

Tsering looked away, bristling.

'It might suit your narrative to paint Raina as the villain, and Caspar as her victim, but I assure you, Caspar knows how to hold his own ... and he's done his fair share of damage.'

Zahora sat on the edge of the ring of light cast by the bonfire, Callie leaning against her, both of them wrapped up against the late autumn chill. Zahora's eyes kept darting bitterly to the happy couples: Raina and Caspar, Talli and Christa, and there even seemed to be something going on between Meredith and Alerac ... they sat close, talking quietly.

Zahora felt the loss of Noah acutely in that moment, Ame her only respite from the onslaught. And Callie, of course. She squeezed her tightly. Callie looked up delightedly, squeezing back.

'Why did you call us all here?' said Meredith, looking to Ame for an answer.

'You want to know about the Registerium's magic ...' said Ame, 'and I have decided to show you its origin.'

A trickle of excitement pooled in Zahora's stomach. She leant forward, willing Ame to start.

'You set the wards?' said Ame.

'Round the perimeter, as specified,' said Alerac.

'Good,' said Ame, turning her focus to the fire, 'then we shall begin.'

Ame threw a handful of something into the fire, and the flames turned green.

Zahora caught a movement out of the corner of her eye … Raina taking Caspar's hand. Their eyes met, and held, like they were the only two in the world. Zahora's guts clenched in jealousy … she sent a prayer up into the sky, begging the universe to return Noah to her soon.

Ame began chanting, her eyes closed, hands outstretched towards the flames. The fire grew hotter, now a raging inferno. Zahora wondered if she should move Callie away … but no one else seemed concerned …

Ame's chanting grew louder, fiercer, wind spinning around the fire, causing the flames to whirl in a corkscrew. Zahora shrank from the spectacle, scared, but the others looked delighted, Talli's hands clasped as she leaned forward in glee. And then, suddenly, and at exactly the moment an image appeared in the fire, the wind, the chanting … it all stopped.

Every one of them leaned forward, including Zahora, whose fear had evaporated along with the wind. They watched the swirling image in the flames as it grew … a wheel, spinning, faster and faster, growing out of the fire, too big now to be contained.

The image rose to the top of the bonfire, slowing as it hovered above the flames. The Pagan wheel, Zahora realized, her jaw dropping as it stopped entirely, zooming into the section representing Yule. It took them through the wheel, to a scene Zahora didn't understand.

Seven figures sat around a fire, six on mats and one elevated on a stool. They wore cloaks pulled tightly around them, hoods up, hiding their faces.

'We can't do it,' said a woman, getting to her feet.

'Measures will be put in place to keep us safe,' said the man on the stool.

The woman scoffed. 'It is impossible to keep us safe. You would tie us to this new social experiment forever?'

'This *social experiment* is the only way to keep the nations from tearing each other apart.'

'What do we care if they do? We left them for a reason,' said the woman, prowling around the circle, the others fidgeting uncomfortably.

'It's true,' said a voice from the floor. 'We left because we don't want all this drama … the confrontation. I wish to live my isolated life in peace. I wish to continue with the freedom to do what I want when I want. I have no wish to be tied to this new organization.'

'We will control this organization,' said the man on the stool. 'We will control the magic that underpins their very existence.'

'Let them kill each other, and keep us out of it,' said the woman on her feet. 'You sound just like them … speaking of power … of control. I want no part in this.'

'We will put in place the magical structure, that is all,' said the man.

'And who will maintain the magic? Or make changes?' said the woman, making a sweeping gesture with her arm. 'Few are capable of such a feat.'

'We will train more,' said the man.

The woman laughed. 'Where will you find these magiks to train?'

'Then we will be enough,' said the man.

'And when it is our time to sacrifice ourselves?'

'We won't all sacrifice at once,' said the man, bristling with obvious fury, although his voice stayed steady. 'We can choose when we do so.'

'We don't know for how long we will be away …'

'Enough,' said the man, exploding to his feet. 'We will vote on it, and that is that.'

The woman returned to her place on the floor and said nothing further.

'All those in favor,' said the man.

Three figures stood.

'Against?'

The other three rose.

'Then we shall do it, because I vote in favor also.'

The cloaked figures departed, all but the woman who'd spoken out. 'Come, child,' she said, a young girl scurrying into her arms. 'Alas, we must stay. You must learn here … we have no other option.'

'Why can't we leave?' said the girl.

'I am sworn to the Nation of Stars.'

'Why?' said the girl.

'Because without them, you and I would be dead.'

The scene turned to smoke, disappearing into the night.

'Those magiks have had control of the Registerium all along?' said Raina, her tone accusing.

Ame shrugged. 'They could have, if they'd wanted to. But they never used the power, at least not to my knowledge. They merely wanted a trump card, should they ever need it.'

'Why would they need it?' said Zahora.

Ame turned her gaze on Zahora, and she shrank back. 'It's not only humans who are terrified of difference,' said Ame. 'Demons too can be irrational and bigoted. That group of magiks were unreasonably powerful, and the world persecuted them for it. They left their nations and banded together, hiding away, protecting each other … until those establishing the Registerium came knocking.'

'So they did it?' said Zahora. 'They set up the Registerium's magic?'

'They did,' said Ame, her features darkening. 'Registrations for member nations were funneled through a single stone … transfers too. The stones were becoming unreliable, even then, their connections to the Sphere not always properly maintained.'

'And each nation set out their own terms,' said Christa. 'Specifying their rules on transfers and the like.'

Ame nodded. 'The leader of each nation has magical control. Many leaders these days don't know what that is, or what it means. They can change the rules of their nation as and when they please, if they can find a magik capable of helping them.'

'Would the Registerium breaking their own rules weaken their magic?' said Zahora.

'Possibly,' said Ame. 'But seeing as no one has been maintaining the magic, it's a wonder anything is still in place at all … perhaps that's how they were able to break their rules in the first place …'

'It's maintained every ten years …' said Caspar.

'By whom?' said Ame. 'One of the charges in the current inquiry is that the Registerium has poor magical capabilities … and you told me the Nation of Stars is gone.'

'But we've been probing it,' said Zahora. 'It's solid.'

'How have you been probing?' said Ame.

'I flew across the Nexus, right to the stone, and felt for weaknesses,' said Zahora. 'I pushed and pulled, but nothing gave an inch. But … I'm not experienced. Maybe I was doing it wrong?'

'You were,' said Ame. 'The magic spirals, circling for many miles before it connects at the stone. Even if the magic were about to fall apart, you could never tell by hitting it from the outside. You must travel with the magic, to the center of the spiral, to the bonds themselves.'

'How?' said Zahora.

'I will show you.'

Chapter 5

Gemma and Elliot approached the double doors that led into the West Coast nation's amphitheater. Aphrodite had asked them to come and had sent Gemma a flowing dress. The fabric swishing around her legs buoyed her, lightened her step.

Elliot took her hand and pulled her to a stop not three paces from the door. She turned towards him, and he bowed to her. 'Goddess,' he said, his eyes on the floor.

'Elliot!' Gemma hissed, her light mood tumbling to the ground. 'Get up! What are you doing?'

Elliot raised his head, his smoldering eyes meeting hers. 'Telling you,' he said, 'you're a goddess.'

'Elliot …' Her heart pounded. He didn't believe it. He thought she was crazy for entertaining Aphrodite's proclamation that she was the Goddess of Spring. But the intensity shining in his beautiful blue eyes made her pause … reconsider. Had he changed his mind?

He crowded her, putting a hand on her stomach to push her against the wall. The move was possessive, savage, and it released a shot of burning desire into her blood. 'Elliot,' she breathed as his lips met hers.

'Goddess,' he purred between kisses.

A shiver ran up her spine at the word. He believed her … that she truly was a goddess … that she was worthy of such adoration … such love.

'I love you,' she said, as his lips moved to her neck, sucking her skin in a way that made her pulse with desire. 'I want …'

The doors to the amphitheater opened, and Elliot pulled slowly away. He placed a last kiss on her lips, then moved his mouth to her ear. 'I love you too,' he said. 'I am yours, and you are mine.' He nipped her lobe then released her, leaving her disorientated, wanting more.

'Although carnal pleasures are only to be rewarded in my eyes,' said Aphrodite, leaning seductively against the door, 'you are late, Goddess.'

'Sorry,' said Gemma, straightening her dress.

Elliot leaned in. 'Goddesses don't apologize,' he murmured, taking her hand, entwining their fingers.

Gemma squeezed his hand; he was right. She squared her shoulders and strode into the amphitheater, unsated desire still running hot in her veins.

'Say hello to our newest members,' said Aphrodite, waving an arm around the amphitheater.

Demons—maybe two hundred of them—turned to face them as they entered.

The new recruits bowed and curtsied. 'Goddess,' they said as one. But they weren't looking at Aphrodite … they were looking at Gemma.

Gemma flushed, and Elliot leaned in. 'They want to meet you, my love.'

Gemma dropped his hand and walked into the crowd, and they flocked around her.

Caspar held up the phone, Rose's face filling the screen.

'How's it going?' said Raina, taking a large bite of toast laden with marmalade.

'Middling,' said Rose. 'Today was more of the same—hearing evidence on the charges—but something's shifted. The mood is more hostile towards us, and the Persians even suggested the whole inquiry had been set up to further your ulterior motives.'

'Why would they think that?' said Raina. 'I've done nothing to …'

'Let me see …' said Rose. 'There was that time in the twelve hundreds when you stole an entire goat herd and sold it to the Holy Star …'

'That was a bet … it was just a bit of fun,' said Raina.

'Or maybe because of the time you traded the life of a prominent Egyptian, which led to their death at the hands of the Aztecs.'

'I did that out of necessity,' said Raina, scowling. 'You know that.'

'But Heba was swayed, given the recent kidnap of her son by the Templars while you were with the Templar nation.'

'I was being held against my will!'

'Heba is a mother who recently lost her son. You think she cares?' said Rose, really getting going now. 'What else? Ah, yes, you cost the Shindus a colossal quantity of rice because of the deal you set up with the Buddhists in the seventeen hundreds.'

'I was trying to convince Tsering to like me,' said Raina, indignantly.

'Well, it wasn't worth it, because Tsering is still convinced you cast some kind of spell on Caspar to make him leave.'

'Ridiculous, impossible, irrational man,' said Raina.

'And of course, the Templars are adding fuel to the suspicions with grievances of their own. They say Callie is Jamie's, that you went back on a deal with them, that you were working with the British monarchy during the first bid for American independence …'

'Well, that one is at least factually accurate,' said Raina.

'We have to win them over,' said Rose. 'Remind them why you're an asset as an ally … why they like you. Most haven't seen you in decades … lifetimes.'

'Because I was trying to prevent war with the Templars,' said Raina. Caspar stiffened. 'At great personal cost.'

'I know that,' said Rose. 'I sent you there, and I've told them that, but they've forgotten who you really are … they're beginning to believe the legend. Show them Callie is your only priority. Show them you couldn't care less about taking over the world.'

'I've never tried to do that!' said Raina.

Rose furrowed her brow. 'You two must make the other nations believe you care for nothing but Callie.'

Rose hung up, and Caspar wrapped his arms around Raina. 'I quite like it when people don't like me,' said Raina. 'It means I don't have to send them Yule cards.'

'When have you ever sent anyone a Yule card?'

'I sent you a few …'

Caspar stroked her hair. 'I don't think I count, and they usually contained secret messages, if I correctly recall.'

'It was more fun passing information before the internet age,' said Raina, with a sigh.

'Yule games,' said Caspar.

Raina pulled back and looked at him. 'Here?'

'Why not? We've got plenty of space, and it would keep Talli occupied for a few days … she's driving me potty.'

Caspar was right. Talli had been irritating everyone with her pent-up energy. Maltings had too many demons with not enough to do, and it was sending everyone round the bend. Most hid it better than Talli, but it was there, bubbling beneath the surface.

'Yule games,' Raina agreed.

Zahora entered the domain Ame had commandeered for herself in one of Malting's many outbuildings. She'd fixed the holes in the aluminum roof, cleared out all the rusting bits of metal, and swept the cobbled floors. It was almost cozy, with herbs strung up along the rafters, and makeshift shelves laden with interesting looking bottles.

It was cold, however, and Zahora pulled her coat more tightly around her as she watched Ame—in nothing more than a thin cotton dress—crush leaves in an enormous pestle and mortar.

Ame looked around at the sound of Zahora's shuffling feet. 'Ah, good. Pass me those,' she said, waving her hand at a pile of leaves on a lopsided wooden chair.

Zahora scowled at her tone, but did it anyway, watching Ame's movements with fascination as she added the leaves to the bowl, rubbing the pestle around the edge a few times. She poured a clear liquid over the top, then put down her tools, the smell of alcohol wafting up from the bowl. 'That can be left to steep,' said Ame, dusting her hands.

'You asked for me?' said Zahora. She followed Ame to where two low wooden stools and a table stood, inside what must have once been an animal stall.

Ame pulled a flask out of a canvas bag and poured two mugs of tea. Zahora took one gladly, cradling it for warmth.

'You have questions, I'm sure,' said Ame, blowing on her tea, 'as do I. So, tell me ... what do you want to know, Sage?'

Zahora ignored the nickname, not a clue what it meant. 'Where do you think they went? The Nation of Stars, I mean.'

Ame shrugged. 'Impossible to say ... Maybe they're all dead, in hiding, or maybe the magic demanded their sacrifice ...'

'As payment?' The Pagan magiks followed a similar practice.

'That group took a great deal over a very long time ... eventually the magic demands something in return, in quiet, incessant ways. If that is what happened, it's impossible to say how long it will keep them ... if indeed it ever lets them return.'

Zahora shuddered. 'I take it that will that happen to me? The magic demanding payment?' She hated how unknown it all was … not to mention having to kill herself in a ceremony of sacrifice first.

Ame fixed her with a penetrating stare. It was almost sinister, and Zahora had to fight the urge to turn away. 'With you … you didn't just use what was freely offered, you took that which was not yours. You *stole* from the Sphere. Who knows what the magic will do to you …'

'I …' Zahora shivered, trying to clear the fog of exhaustion from her brain.

Ame leaned forward. 'How did you do it? How did you survive?' Curiosity shone in her eyes … no, more than that, she looked like … an addict craving a drug. Zahora recoiled in alarm.

'I don't know,' said Zahora, looking away. She inhaled deeply, getting her spiking pulse under control. Ame felt … dangerous somehow.

'I touched the Sphere when I shouldn't have,' said Zahora. 'I didn't even know that's what I was doing …' She tried to think, but her perpetual exhaustion made everything that much more of a struggle. She looked at her hands as she collected herself, then met Ame's gaze once more.

'The magic has always called to me, but my Pagan teachers held me back. They'd already frustrated my efforts for an entire lifetime, and I was bored, angry, and grew reckless.

'One day, I threw caution to the wind and connected to the magic. I had no idea what I was doing and went straight to the Sphere. I didn't know to stop in the Nexus … I didn't know anything really … still don't.'

'You *touched* the magic?' said Ame. Her face crinkled as though she were trying to force together two pieces of a puzzle that didn't quite fit. 'It didn't carry you away? Burn your soul?'

'It tried, but I clawed my way back … wouldn't let it take me.'

'Unbelievable,' said Ame. 'Unheard of. There were no side effects? It had no impact at all?'

Zahora gave a sarcastic laugh. 'I caused a shock-wave that spread across the world. But other than that, nothing.'

'But you took from the Sphere. I can feel it in you … your magic must be stronger now than before?'

Zahora shrugged. 'My teachers never let me *do* anything, so how could I know? I don't feel any different … but if you say I took something, maybe my power's increased …'

'No one has ever touched the Sphere and survived … there are legends, yes, but ...'

'Not that you know of,' countered Zahora. 'Would they have told you? Would they have told anyone?'

Ame raised a concessionary eyebrow. 'True, although, I've never heard of a shock-wave like the one you described …'

Zahora put down her tea a little too hard. She didn't care about legends, or what should or shouldn't be possible … she'd touched the Sphere, and that was the end of it. 'Can you train me or not? And help me test the Registerium's magic?'

'I can,' said Ame, not batting an eye at Zahora's tone.

'Will you?'

Ame inhaled loudly. 'I suppose you're the most interesting—if naïve—student available to me … and I suppose I don't have anywhere else to be, given the Nation of Stars is missing …'

'You were the girl, weren't you?' said Zahora. 'The one in the fire?'

'I was,' said Ame. 'My mother was a member of the Stars, but she died ... they threw me out before my training was complete.'

'No ...' said Zahora, a pang of sympathy swelling her chest.

Ame shrugged dismissively. 'It was probably for the best. Power is corrupting, and they were powerful—unbelievably so—but they wanted more, especially the leader. He wanted to be a Sage, like you ... although he never found a way.'

'A Sage?' said Zahora. Not just a nickname then ...

'One who can take from the magic, rather than merely accepting what is given.'

'Maybe the Sphere gave willingly ...' said Zahora, 'if it gave me anything at all ...'

Ame looked at her for a long moment, considering her words. 'Maybe,' she said, 'but that seems unlikely. Now ... you wanted to probe the Registerium.'

Ame rose from her stool and headed for the door. Zahora followed, glad of the modifications Ame had made to the shield. Zahora didn't understand exactly what Ame had done, but it was less draining to maintain than it had been before, which at least meant she didn't have to sleep all the time.

They reached the stone circle, and Ame placed her hand on the nearest stone, gesturing for Zahora to do the same.

'I thought we couldn't use these stones,' said Zahora. 'The shield ...'

'Yes, well, we should be fine if we follow your bond out.'

'My what?'

Ame rolled her eyes. 'My goodness. You know nothing, child.'

'Yes,' said Zahora, hotly. 'I've been trying to rectify that for two lifetimes, but no one seems overly inclined to teach me anything useful.'

'Very well,' said Ame, removing her hand. 'When you ally yourself with a nation, you bond yourself to them, magically. Because most registrations now take place at the Registerium, bonds are generally tied to their stone. I'm assuming yours was?'

'Yes,' Zahora confirmed.

'Which means we can follow your bond right to their stone, within the spiral of magic, rather than trying to push against it as you've been doing until now.'

'Okay,' said Zahora, still not fully understanding, but keen to get going. 'How do I do it?'

'Connect to the Nexus,' said Ame, 'then find your bond, and use it to guide your sending. Follow it all the way to the Registerium.'

'Sounds easy enough,' said Zahora, placing her hand on a stone. She looked at Ame, expecting her to tell her to wait, or be careful, or twelve things she should make sure not to do.

Ame did none of these things. Instead, she gave her an impatient hand wave, encouraging her to get a move on. 'It may take some time, and I don't have all day,' she said pointedly.

Zahora smiled; finally, a teacher she could work with. She did as she was told and found the bond almost immediately, then followed it towards the Registerium. But to her astonishment, as her soul flew up into the sky, she saw not only her bond, but an endless, enormous spiral of bonds hundreds of miles wide. Countless strands fanned out across the world, each one joining the spiral, circling with the others, presumably connecting to the stone at the core.

Zahora couldn't believe she'd never noticed this before … all these strands crisscrossing the world. But then, she'd never known to look for them, and had always had another pressing purpose in mind.

She followed her strand, which circled in a wide arch away from her destination, towards the North Sea. Ame wasn't wrong ... this would take hours. Zahora's mind filled with an image of the Triskelion. She wished she'd inked the symbol of perpetual motion on her skin ... it would speed things up for sure ...

But by merely thinking of the symbol, of holding it in her mind, her speed increased, her stomach lurching at the pace. She laughed and willed herself onwards, the Triskelion spinning in her mind's eye. She urged it faster until it was nothing but a blur.

She turned her attention back to the strands, elated, but ... the standing stone ... how was she here already? She looked frantically to her left and right, but the strands were so tightly packed, she could see nothing but their dull blue glow. She dismissed the Triskelion, desperately trying to think of a symbol that would slow her down. But she couldn't think of anything ... and anyway, the stone was coming at her too fast ... much too ... *shit.*

Meredith heard the shouts first. Nothing hysterical, but urgent all the same. 'Zahora! Zahora! Wake up!'

She ran toward Ame's voice, towards the stone circle. Alerac put down his shovel and ran too.

Meredith took in the scene as she approached, Zahora lying on the ground, still as the dead, Ame at her side, shaking her.

'What happened?' said Meredith, dropping to her knees, feeling Zahora's neck for a pulse. She found one and breathed a sigh of relief. 'She's alive ... her pulse is strong.'

'Her body's alive ... I just hope ...'

Zahora opened her eyes, hazy and unfocused. She tried to sit, but fell back to the ground, clutching her head. She rolled to her side, crying in pain.

'What happened?' Meredith said again.

'She was probing the Registerium's magic,' said Ame. 'She was gone for hardly any time, and then she collapsed.'

'I went ... too fast,' said Zahora, still clasping her head. 'Way too fast.'

'What did you see?' said Ame.

'It was all a blur. Stands of magic ... so many ... spiraling into the stone. Then ... I think ... I crashed.'

'How?' said Ame.

'She doesn't send,' Alerac said, his voice an angry growl. 'Her soul travels across the Nexus.'

'What?' said Ame. 'That's ...' She rounded on Zahora. 'You could have died!'

'Fuck off, all of you,' said Zahora, struggling to her feet.

'Where are you going?' said Meredith. 'You need a healer.'

'I'm fine. Just ... a headache.'

They let her go, and Ame turned to Alerac. 'I've never known anyone who could do that ... even the Adepts.'

Alerac shrugged. 'With her, all the rules go out the window. Assume nothing.'

Meredith pulled out her phone and messaged Rose. She just hoped, whatever Zahora had done, it didn't have consequences.

Jamie turned to Pixie as they observed the battalion of soldiers assembling below them, both demons and Slayers alike. They stood only a block from the West Coast's headquarters, which perched on the waterfront.

The night air was still, everything quiet, but despite that, Jamie knew their enemy would be waiting. Ares—the God of War—was nothing if not vigilant ... at least if their intelligence could be believed.

Jamie didn't believe for a second he was the real God of War. Most gods were human creations ... Ares was probably some crackpot who'd convinced a handful of gullible followers. Although he was a rich, influential, security-conscious crackpot ... Jamie would give the man his dues.

'Ready?' said Jamie's general.

Jamie nodded, and his general issued a radio command. Four demons stumbled down the street as though drunk; the vanguard sent to test the waters, and Jamie and Pixie watched from a rooftop, a bank of monitors set up before them.

Their soldiers made it right up to the front gate, leaned against it, then shouted and laughed, but nothing happened. They slumped to the ground, singing, while the general issued orders for teams two, three, and four to deploy.

Team two scaled the wall beside the gates, while team three scaled a side wall. Team four approached from the beach on the far side, a boat dropping them on the sand.

'It's deserted,' said the leader of team two over the radio.

'And this side,' said the leader of team four.

'No activity here either,' said team three's leader.

'Open the gates, and search the place,' said the general.

The teams did as they were told.

'No signs of life,' a voice said through the radio. 'No, wait … there's one man … approaching now.'

The computer monitors showed the obese man sitting on the floor in the middle of what looked like an amphitheater. He was stock still, his head angled towards the ground.

The hairs on Jamie's neck stood on end at the eerie sight. Something about this felt wrong.

Pixie grabbed his arm. 'Jamie,' she said. 'There's something about that man …'

'I know,' said Jamie. 'General …' But before he could complete the command, the man on the screen rose to his feet, a short sword in each hand. He looked confident, cocky even, as he began to circle, wearing nothing but a loincloth, rolls of fat jiggling.

Was this the crackpot himself? The supposed God of War, taking on an entire battalion of fighters alone? Or maybe this was a decoy, a distraction … Jamie looked up from the screens just as the last of his army entered the compound. Just as the gates swung shut of their own accord.

'Fuck,' said Jamie. 'Pull them out.'

But before the general had time to issue the command, archers appeared on the top of the compound's walls. Where had they come from? Jamie's soldiers were like fish in a bowl … about to be massacred …

'Demons aren't supposed to use bows!' said Jamie. 'Get them out. Now!'

The general issued the command, but it was much too late. The screens showed the bloodbath, the man with the short swords flowing around the amphitheater, slaying soldier after soldier with barely a check.

In a shockingly short time, the air went silent, the only sound a man's groaning as the life drained out of him. The man with the short swords filled the computer monitors, a chilling device in his hand—a Furor. He bent, using it to gouge the dying demon's eyes out.

'No,' said Jamie, slamming his fist on the desk. 'Fuck.' Furious anger filled him. He longed for a gun. He would make that son of a bitch regret his actions.

Ares threw the demon's eyeballs into a newly lit pit of fire. Dead. The true death. Jamie's soldier would never be born again.

Jamie hoped the others were already dead, or had had the sense to finish themselves off before this nation of barbarians took their eyes.

'Jamie,' said Pixie, squeezing his arm, pointing to something flying through the sky towards them.

'What the fuck is that?' said Jamie.

'Drone,' said the general, his tone urgent. 'It could be carrying explosives.'

'Are those … pieces of paper?' said Pixie.

'We need to get you to safety,' said the general, tugging at Jamie's arm. 'Now.'

Jamie picked up a spanner. He would not run like a scared animal. He waited until the drone was close, much too close for the general, who'd retreated. But Pixie remained by Jamie's side. He was … proud of her.

The drone came closer, closer, and then Jamie hurled the spanner so hard it knocked the drone right out of the sky. It didn't explode.

Pixie snatched a piece of paper from the air. 'You broke the rules first. Don't think we didn't notice,' she read, confused. She handed him the paper. 'What does it mean?'

'The bows and arrows,' said Jamie. 'Demons are only supposed to fight with knives, so we don't draw human attention.'

'But you used guns when you attacked the Slayer headquarters?' said Pixie. 'Is that what it means?'

Jamie's brain filled with other examples of how he'd broken the rules … Raina's illegal nation transfer … blackmailing the Registerium … it was impossible to tell which instance had offended the West Coast. 'Probably,' he hedged.

Ares climbed the stairs of the compound. He stood with his archers and turned his gaze in Jamie's direction. Jamie looked back at the note in his hands, feeling like he'd missed something.

The general appeared in the doorway. 'Sir,' he said, 'we should go.'

And then everything blurred. Pixie screamed Jamie's name. She threw herself at him, knocking him to the ground. A dull thud filled the air, and the general slumped to the floor, an arrow protruding from his throat.

'Fuck,' said Jamie. Pixie was on top of him, shaking, and his hands went to her face. 'Are you okay? Are you hit?'

She shook her head as another arrow landed close beside them. 'No,' she said, her teeth chattering, 'we have to go. We'll defeat them another day.'

Gemma watched as the others cleaned up the bodies. She had tried to help, but Aphrodite had scolded her, saying, 'That is not appropriate for a Goddess.'

Aphrodite had disappeared somewhere with Ares, presumably to celebrate their decisive victory. Gemma's blood was up too … it had been a while since she'd been in a battle, and she'd missed this feeling.

'You were magnificent,' said a voice in her ear. A voice that blistered with intent.

Gemma shivered. 'Thank you,' she said, then stepped away, trying to ignore his magnetic pull. She'd successfully avoided the mysterious man since their meeting in Aphrodite's apartment, but the compound was small, and tonight she'd dropped her guard.

He stepped up behind her, so close she could feel his radiating warmth. He skirted a hand down her bare arm. 'You were the Goddess of the Hunt tonight,' he murmured, his breath caressing her skin.

Her traitorous body melted. It would be so easy to tip her head back against his chest, to guide his hands to her breasts … she stepped away. It was because of the battle, that was all. 'I'm in a relationship,' she said. 'Please don't touch me again.'

Gemma returned to the room she shared with Elliot and found him on the bed. He had refused to fight … had said he was here on behalf of the Pagan nation as an envoy, not a soldier. Gemma had had none of those qualms … had relished the chance to step into the fray.

'Are you hurt?' said Elliot, coming to her, running his hands across her skin.

'No,' she said, luxuriating in his touch. She stripped off her dress—Aphrodite had told her to fight looking like a Goddess, to inspire the others. Elliot's eyes dipped to her naked breasts, peaked from the excitement of combat … and her encounter with Hades …

She stepped into Elliot's space and kissed him. He groaned into her mouth, and she pushed him back onto the bed. She had never been so bold, the surprise in Elliot's eyes telling her it wasn't lost on him either. *Good.* She didn't want to be shy, demure Gemma any longer.

Afterwards, they lay on the bed, Gemma wrapped in Elliot's arms, his fingers trailing lazy circles across her skin. Her eyelids drooped as sleep tried to claim her, but Elliot tensed, and the movement made her eyes fly open. 'Aphrodite came to see me,' he said.

Adrenaline shot through Gemma's blood. It wasn't so much Elliot's words as his tone … she leaned up on her elbow, meeting his gaze. 'What did she say?'

He played with a lock of her hair. 'That I'm holding you back … I'm not worthy of a goddess … that the Goddess of Spring is destined for Hades …'

Gemma dropped her gaze. 'What did you say?' she asked, her heart stuttering in her chest.

He paused for a beat, and her eyes flicked back to his. He pushed the hair off her face, then cradled her head in his hand. 'That I love you, and will do whatever you want me to do.'

Gemma's insides caved and she lowered her head, resting her lips against his chest. What did she want him to do? A week ago she'd been ready to send him away, but then he'd called her Goddess … shown her he believed in her. But what if she was destined for Hades? What if they were soulmates?

'I know it's not that easy,' Elliot continued. 'You're probably confused, and uncertain … I would be if I were in your shoes.'

'I love you,' she said. 'I don't want you to go. Aphrodite doesn't know you.'

'No,' Elliot agreed, 'but she will make it difficult for us.'

'Elliot …'

'I don't give a damn about Aphrodite, or Ares, or any of the people in this place. I only care about you. I'll never leave you, but … I don't want you to forever wonder what would have happened if you'd chosen Hades … if you were flying in the face of your destiny.'

'What are you saying?' said Gemma, her heart in her mouth.

'I'm not naturally jealous. I've been in open relationships before, and I know, so long as we're both truly honest with each other, I can do it again. If you want to have a relationship with Hades … to explore … I won't stand in your way. But he can't have you all to himself … he'd have to share too.'

'Elliot, I …'

He leaned down and kissed her. 'Think about it,' he said, running a thumb across her lips. 'I love you, and if this is what you need, I can make peace with it.'

She rested her forehead on Elliot's chest, focusing on the rise and fall, hiding from his eyes as she tried to slow her racing thoughts. She couldn't wrap her head around his words, his … offer. Could she do it? After everything she'd been through … everything men had put her through? Could she put Elliot in that position? And even if she did, would Hades ever agree?

Hades' smoky brown eyes filled her vision, his raging intensity. He didn't seem like a man who liked to share … but maybe if it was his only choice … Was she really entertaining this? Was she going to do it?

Elliot sensed her discomfort. He slid a hand into her hair and scratched her scalp. She purred. 'Roll onto your front,' he said, sliding out from underneath her.

Gemma did as she was told, and Elliot straddled the tops of her thighs. The press of his weight and feel of his skin was erotic. She purred as he leaned forward, his stomach brushing her behind as he slid his palms up and down her skin. But as he gently kneaded away her tension, her body forgot about the desire, and so did her mind, until eventually, she found the blissful oblivion of sleep.

Chapter 6

Meredith had been successfully avoiding Talli's furious organizational typhoon. Today however, Talli was lying in wait.

'I know your game,' Talli said, as Meredith tried to make a quick exit after an early breakfast. She handed Meredith a long list of tasks, told her to take Alerac with her—because he needed to do the magical parts—and flitted off to find some other poor, unsuspecting shirker.

Meredith and Alerac trudged through the driving rain, digging holes, planting clues, laying decoys, and generally complaining.

'Maybe disbanding the Registerium would be a good thing,' said Alerac, as he hacked at the ground.

Rose had called earlier with the latest from the inquiry. It sounded as though more nations were rethinking the Registerium's position.

'Especially given they're so magically weak …' said Alerac. 'Zahora crashed into their stone, doing who knows what damage, and they haven't even noticed …'

'Or they did and are keeping it quiet,' said Meredith, leaning on her shovel. 'And I for one don't want to live in the Wild West, which is what our world will become if the Registerium disappears. That wouldn't be good for anyone … not anyone who wants to live in peace, anyway.'

'And I don't trust Ame,' said Alerac, wiping sweat from his brow.

Meredith laughed. 'You don't trust anyone!'

'And you do?'

Meredith shook her head. 'Of course not, but what specifically offends you?'

'We don't know who she is or her real allegiances, and she's keeping her magical knowledge close to her chest. I've asked her to teach me, but she declines every time, for no good reason.'

'Hmmm, but she's teaching Zahora,' said Meredith.

'Which is strange … Why only her?'

'Because she likes Zahora, and you're a pain in the arse?'

Alerac flicked a clod of dirt at Meredith. She turned to avoid it, to find Zahora hurrying off in the direction of the standing stones. She seemed agitated.

'What's wrong with her?' said Meredith.

Alerac shrugged. 'She's young and temperamental … could be anything.'

Meredith gave him a scathing look. Whatever it was, she didn't want to get involved … and anyway, she didn't have time … Talli's schedule must be obeyed.

Zahora hurried to the edge of the shield, then, as she had for the last two days, slipped across the boundary. She practically ran the half mile to the hay barn she'd been using, pulling out Noah's t-shirt as soon as she crossed the threshold.

It wasn't the same as it had been through the stone … she couldn't use the t-shirt to travel directly to him. She wasn't sure she was even properly connected to the Nexus, but she could get a sense of him, of his distance away, his state of mind. She'd been guiding him as best she could through the magic, and it was working … he was close.

She clutched the t-shirt and focused on Noah, but for the first time, nothing happened. She screwed up the fabric in frustration, then held it to her mouth to muffle her scream. She inhaled Noah's scent—fading now—and breathed it deep into her lungs. The smell of him buoyed her, calmed her, gave her hope.

She inhaled again, then tried once more to find him. The magic gave her nothing but a vague sense that he was near … very near … How was he travelling? Did he have money? Was he on foot? Her heart pounded with anticipation.

Zahora completed another sending, telling him specifically about the barn. She had no idea how much of her messages made it, but she hoped he understood enough not to go directly to Maltings.

She had to get back, but she lingered, as though she might find him in the hay if she looked long enough. Tomorrow, she told herself, maybe then …

Dinner that night was insufferable. Talli went on and on about Yule … the games, the feasts, the dancing, the seasonal decorations, the hunt … Zahora couldn't care less about some stupid celebration. All she wanted was to see Noah, to know he was alright.

Callie grasped her hand, '… don't you think, Zaha?' she said, adorable puppy dog eyes turned up to Zahora's.

'Sorry, what did you say?' she replied.

'You'll read me a story tonight … won't you?' she said, nodding in encouragement.

How could she refuse such cuteness? 'Of course,' she said.

'Yay! We should start the …'

Something in Zahora's chest lurched. It was all she could do not to bend over and clutch her heart. She bowed her head and took deep breaths. What in the world was causing it? It felt like … disappointment.

'You know what,' Zahora said to Callie, 'I think I need to sleep now. Can I read to you tomorrow?'

Callie made a whining noise, but Zahora gave her a firm look, showing she wouldn't budge. 'Okay,' said Callie in the singsong way of children. She hugged Zahora's arm, then turned back to the table, seeking her next target.

Zahora left, heading to her room. She'd only made it as far as the base of the stairs when feelings pummeled her … impatience, longing, frustration, fear. What in the world? She slipped out of the house … it was time to bolster the shield again anyway. Thank goodness for Ame and her efficiencies. Zahora wasn't sure how long she could have gone on feeling like she did before, all her energy drained each time she strengthened the shield. Now it was tiring, but not debilitating.

She was so well practiced, it took no longer than five minutes for Zahora to fix the shield, and then she stole through to the other side. The strange feelings became a barrage outside the protection of the shield, and now she could feel them properly, without distortion or modulation, she knew exactly what they were.

Noah.

Zahora ran for the hay barn, nothing to guide her but the light of the moon. She reached the barn and called out for him. 'Noah? Noah, are you here?'

But the barn was silent, devoid of Noah's warm face and comforting arms. Tears pricked at Zahora's eyes. She'd been sure he would be here. She sank onto a hay bale and sent out her magic, wishing she'd thought to pick up his t-shirt.

She forced her magic out, but before it had a chance to explore, she heard his voice say, 'Zahora?'

She opened her eyes to see a shadow in the entrance. Her heart stopped, and then she jumped to her feet, rushing for the door. 'Noah?'

The figure stepped into the barn and dropped a backpack to the ground. 'It's me,' he said.

She came to a halt a pace away, taking him in, his features bluish in the moon's light. Was this really him? Or a cruel trick? An enemy in a clever, magical disguise …

He reached for her, but she stepped back, wary. 'Tell me something only you would know,' she said, feeling ridiculous.

She thought he would laugh and call her paranoid. The carefree Noah she'd first met probably would have … but he seemed changed … hardened … weary. She longed to know all that had happened to him.

He took a deep breath and looked outside, where the moon sat low and heavy in the sky. 'I first knew I loved you looking at a moon like this one,' he said. 'I was carrying you back to your hut. You were exhausted, nearly asleep in my arms, but then you stroked my face and hummed one of my songs.'

'That's when you knew you loved me?' said Zahora.

He nodded, and she ran, throwing her arms around him. She clung to him, resting her face against his chest, sliding her arms inside his coat, her shoulders relaxing for the first time in … she couldn't remember how long. Seconds ticked into minutes, neither wanting to pull away.

'You're cold,' Noah said eventually, presumably because he could feel her freezing hands through his clothes.

'I didn't stop for a coat,' she said as a gust of wind hit them, making her shiver.

'Come on,' said Noah, taking her hand. He led them to a pile of loose hay, enclosed on three sides by bales.

'We can't stay here,' she said. 'I have to get back … to …'

Noah gave her a look that made her forget words. He reached for her face, holding it in his big, warm hands, and she melted, all thoughts fluttering from her mind, blown away on his breeze. He kissed her, and she couldn't think, could only feel … sense … every part of her focused on him.

He put an end to the kiss much too soon, and Zahora made a petulant noise. Noah laughed as he pulled a blanket from his bag.

Zahora practically dove for it as he retrieved and unzipped a sleeping bag, laying it over them as he joined her on the hay. His lips found her once more as she settled into his warmth. She pulled open his shirt, his fingers doing the same to hers before yanking down her bra, baring her breasts to the frigid air. She unfastened their trousers as his lips grazed her nipple, then sucked it into his mouth, making Zahora's fingers frantic. When she finally freed them, he pulled her back to his chest, pushing his arousal between her thighs, his fingers squeezing and pinching and rolling her nipple.

She gasped as she writhed against him, seeking friction, then reached down, pushing him inside her. Noah cursed, but didn't hesitate, his hand going to her hip as he pumped his hips wildly. He slid his fingers to her core, and she moaned, then rolled onto her belly, pulling him with her until he pressed her down as he moved. She tipped her hips, allowing his fingers space to work, humming with pleasure as he slowed, pressing in and out in tantalizing movements.

Noah pulled out and rolled her onto her back, then lay between her thighs. He took her head in his hands as he pushed inside her, looking down into her shadowed eyes as he teased her with short, tormenting thrusts. She lifted her hips, trying to coax him deeper, and a smile spread across his lips.

'Noah,' she breathed, clawing at his backside. 'Don't be mean …'

He laughed as he slid in to the hilt, settling all his weight on her. 'Oh my Gods, that feels so good,' she said, tipping her hips, tying to make him move.

'Patience,' he said, nipping her earlobe.

'I don't know what that is,' she said, doing her best to buck her hips.

He kissed her until her head swam, then rolled them to the side, picking up a slow, steady rhythm, their limbs tangled together, the press of their bodies the most welcome relief after all they'd endured. Zahora's insides coiled, and she rolled on top, sitting up to take him deeper, rocking her hips, her hands braced on Noah's chest.

'Zahora,' he choked, his movements becoming erratic.

Her only response was a moan, so close to the edge, and then he came, tipping her into oblivion too, ancient, guttural noises escaping into the night.

They were woken the following morning by a dog barking in a nearby field. The sun was coming up, which meant Zahora had missed more than one shift of strengthening the shield. She hoped the others had realized she was gone … that either Alerac or Ame had done it instead. *Please, please, please let Callie be alright.*

She went rigid. She should go back and check … but …

'You don't owe them anything, you know,' said Noah, his lips against her naked back.

'I …' But she stopped. She wasn't sure what she thought of that … not really, and her body urged her to stay in the delicious heat of Noah's embrace.

'I know you feel like you do … You want to be one of them, and I get it, wanting to belong … believe me. But you have to figure out what you want, and not get caught up in what they want from you.'

She rolled over and looked into his eyes, reaching out a hand to trace the lines of his face, his neck, his collarbone. 'What happened?' she said. 'You seem … different.'

'I feel it,' he said, snagging her hand and holding it to his chest, stroking the back with his thumb. 'When you came here and left me in Wales … I was alone … an outsider. I missed you, and I felt guilty about leaving my dad … leaving all I'd ever known. So I decided, if I was going to leave him, I had to do it the honorable way.'

'I'm sorry,' said Zahora, kissing his arm. 'I didn't want to leave you.'

'I know; you felt it was your duty to come here, to help Callie … and I thought it was my duty to tell Dad I was leaving the Slayers, face to face, like a man …'

'I'm assuming he didn't take it well?' said Zahora.

'No. He threatened to kill Pixie, my … wife … I suppose technically she's still my wife …'

The words stabbed jealous shards into Zahora's stomach. She couldn't shake the pain, even though she knew it was irrational … but … he'd gone back to the Slayers …

'I'm sorry,' he said, rolling closer. 'I never …'

'I know,' said Zahora, pressing her forehead to his. 'I don't blame you.'

'I told Dad if he wanted to kill Pixie, it was on him, but it wouldn't change my decision, and then I told him I was leaving. He locked down the building to stop me … but then he was shot through the window.'

'Noah …'

The shadow of the memory danced in his eyes. 'If Dad hadn't secured the building when he did, I'd probably be dead.'

Zahora didn't know what to say ... felt helpless ... 'They're not supposed to use guns,' was the best she could come up with.

'I know,' said Noah. 'But they did anyway.'

'There's an inquiry, right now ...' She stopped. What good was an inquiry, given what he'd been through?

Noah sat up, looking out of the barn to the fields beyond, and Zahora sat behind him, wrapping her arms around his middle.

'They made me their leader,' he said. 'Dad named me his heir. That's not how leaders are supposed to be chosen ... not for a long time ... but Dad wanted a legacy, wanted *me* to be his legacy, and everyone else assumed I'd returned because I'd killed you.

'I thought about leaving right away, about slipping out in the chaos, but then ... I wondered if I could change them, from the inside out ... bit by bit.'

'So you stayed,' said Zahora, her words sounding more like an admonishment than she'd intended.

'Like an idiot,' said Noah. 'They'll never change ... not with me in charge ... probably not ever. And Pixie's power hungry; she wanted us to work together ... to rule together. All I wanted was to get back to you.'

Noah twisted to look at her. 'I'm a demon, not a Slayer, and I don't have the ruthlessness needed to rule.'

'Thank the Gods,' said Zahora, stroking his face. He smiled, and she kissed him.

He pulled her around to sit across his lap, nesting her in his arms.

'I didn't want to leave you ... during the attack,' Zahora said into his chest. 'The others yanked me out ...'

He kissed her hair. 'I'm grateful you helped me get as far as you did, otherwise who knows where I'd be right now … if I'd be alive. Dad had contingency plans in case we needed to make a quick escape. He was paranoid, always worried about a coup … I did what he told me to do in an emergency, and hid in a safe house. There were passports, money, clothes … everything I needed.

'I took a boat to Bermuda, then flew to London … then a train, a bus, and then a five-mile walk.'

Zahora chuckled. 'This is kind of the middle of nowhere …'

'Yeah … I mean, haven't you guys heard of taxis?'

She smiled. It amazed her … the way he made her feel … how he felt essential, right, like she needed him to keep her on an even keel. Zahora felt settled for the first time in her life … in any of her lives.

'Run away with me,' he said.

'What? Noah … we can't …' She tipped her head to look up at him.

'They treat you like shit. They don't appreciate you, and you have more talent in your little finger than all of them combined. You don't need them.'

'I do need them, and they need me,' said Zahora. 'I know you don't like them, or trust them, and you shouldn't after the way they've treated you, but I'm a Pagan. I tied myself to them … swore an oath I intend to keep.'

Noah rested his forehead against hers, his hand cradling her head. 'I don't want to lose you.'

'You won't. Like I said, they need me. And if they want me—which they do—they'll have to accept you too.'

He held her tighter.

'I love you,' she said.

'Then don't go back today. Just for today,' he added quickly.

Zahora blew out a relieved breath. She could do that ... wanted nothing more than to be alone with him.

'Please,' he said, looking into her eyes.

She nodded, and his face split into a broad, beaming smile that finally turned him into the radiant, carefree version of Noah she loved the most.

'Zahora's gone,' said Meredith. 'No signs of a struggle, and she didn't take anything with her. Not even her coat.'

'That doesn't make any sense,' said Raina.

'Unless we finally broke her,' said Talli. 'She doesn't understand our stunted emotional development. She probably thinks we take her for granted ... nothing but a means to keeping Callie safe ...'

'Fucking Millenials,' said Meredith.

'She's not a Millenial,' said Christa. 'Gen Z.'

'Oh, for fuck's sake!' said Meredith, swearing more than usual. What had got her so flustered?

'It never used to be like this,' said Talli, 'but we have to be touchy feely with the new ones.'

'Is the shield up?' said Raina.

'Yes,' said Meredith. 'Alerac felt it weakening and bolstered it this morning.'

'She was gone all night, and we only noticed this morning?' said Raina. So that's why Meredith was flustered …

'Yes,' said Meredith, through gritted teeth.

'Maybe we are taking her for granted,' said Raina, her stomach clenching at the thought of what could happen to Callie without the shield.

'We can give her a role during Yule?' said Talli, clapping her hands. 'I could …'

'Maybe we should find her first?' said Raina, sardonically. 'Does she have any friends or family?'

'No,' said Meredith. 'No one she's in contact with.'

'Apart from Noah,' said Talli.

'We're searching the area,' said Meredith.

'She's gone?' said Ame, entering the kitchen with Caspar.

'We shouldn't jump to conclusions,' said Meredith. 'I'm going to help with the search. I'll keep you updated.'

Caspar kissed Raina's temple, and she closed her eyes, taking comfort from his touch. 'We'll find her,' he said.

'And when you do, lock her up, or better yet, end her,' said Ame.

'What?' said Raina, rounding on Ame. 'What could possibly make you say that?'

'You don't know what she is, do you? I thought maybe Alerac had figured it out, but … no. I so hate being disappointed.'

'Ame, what are you talking about?' said Raina, losing her patience.

Ame sent Raina a scathing look, and not for the first time; Ame obviously didn't like her. She'd racked her brains, searching for a reason … had they met in the past? Had Raina done something to this woman? But her past was long and tumultuous; she couldn't possibly remember everyone she'd given reason to dislike her.

'She's a Sage,' said Ame.

'A what?' said Christa.

'No!' said Talli, clapping a hand over her mouth.

'The only one I've ever encountered,' said Ame.

'They're not real,' said Talli. 'I researched it extensively … my younger self was obsessed with the legends … but that's all they were … legends. I couldn't find a single shred of proof.'

Ame turned her contemptuous gaze to Talli. She shook her head, not speaking for several long moments. 'Zahora is a Sage.'

'What's a Sage?' said Christa, impatiently.

'Someone who draws power directly from the Sphere,' said Talli.

'No,' said Ame, with an impatient hand wave. 'Someone who *takes* from the Sphere. Zahora has unimaginable power, and right now, if she has been abducted, that power is in the hands of your enemies. It's unnatural, and too dangerous for her … for you … for the world, for someone so impulsive, so reckless, to have the free rein you've granted her.'

'So your solution is to kill her?' said Raina, appalled. What was Ame's angle? Was she threatened by Zahora? Did she have some other motive?

'Or you must convince her to give the power back to the Sphere. But with one like that, you'll never succeed.'

'We don't go around killing people for no good reason,' said Raina. 'Especially people who have gone above and beyond for the good of our nation at significant personal cost.'

Ame raised an eyebrow. 'The great Raina Halabi has qualms about such things? Wonders never cease …'

It took Meredith little more than twenty minutes to track Zahora and Noah from the barn. One of the search teams had found the patch of flattened hay, and Meredith had gone straight there. They were in a nearby wood when she found them, heading for the next village over from the demons' village of Buttercross.

They walked hand in hand, Zahora happier than Meredith had seen her in days ... weeks. She envied Zahora's uncomplicated feelings ... her certainty Noah was the man for her. Maybe it was because they were both so young, their inexorable futures stretching out before them like great yawning chasms.

Meredith had felt like that once. Full of excitement for lifetimes brimming with possibility. But now she was weary. She'd seen too much death and despair ... too much suffering ... too many soul mates torn apart by time, or jealous ex-lovers, or simply because they'd been in the wrong place at the wrong time. Would that happen to these two? Would it end like that for them?

She followed them to the village pub and decided to let them have this precious time alone together. She called a team to watch them, then called Alerac, letting him know he'd have to bolster the shield a while longer.

He lingered on the phone, as did she, and when she hung up, she found her lips were smiling.

Zahora knew they were being watched. Meredith had trained her well, and she sensed it across the ether. But whoever it was seemed bored, not hostile. Nevertheless, Zahora took precautions before they exited the pub, checking through the windows to see who waited outside. She saw Meredith and rolled her eyes.

'The Pagans are here,' she said to Noah.

'We got longer than I thought we would,' he said.

'Me too, and I'm glad they didn't interrupt our lunch … that sticky toffee pudding was to die for.'

He kissed her. 'I love you,' he said.

They left the pub, ducking through the old, low door, then blinking against the bright winter light.

'Hi,' said Meredith.

'Hi,' said Zahora, then waited for Meredith to say something, but she just sat there, leaning casually against the stone wall, watching them.

'You're here to take me back?' said Zahora.

Meredith shook her head. 'Only if you want to. I won't deny *we* want you back—you're a highly valued member of our nation—but we won't force you. I'm merely here to make sure you don't get abducted by our enemies.'

Zahora's cheeks flushed at being told she was valued … at having a bodyguard … especially one like Meredith. She looked at Noah, and he squeezed her hand. 'It's up to you,' he said.

Noah would happily skip off into the sunset, run away from all this, go somewhere remote, and exist happily with only each other for company. But Zahora had never wanted a life so simple. She wanted to be useful, to be respected, to be great ... like Raina.

'I'll come back,' said Zahora, 'but only if Noah can come too.'

Meredith's eyes flicked to Noah, and Zahora held her breath. She reminded herself that the Pagans needed her. She had to be firm ... not show weakness.

'Sure,' said Meredith, with a shrug.

Sure? After the fuss about him coming the first time? 'Really?' said Zahora. 'You're not even going to put up a fight?'

'He's no longer much of a threat ... not now he has nowhere else to go ...'

Zahora wanted to lash out at Meredith's hard words, but objectively, she knew she was right. Zahora had never once questioned Noah's loyalty, but it was Meredith's job to keep their nation safe, to weigh up the risks ... and Noah had been a risk before ... but not now.

'He'll have to register as a Pagan,' said Meredith, 'if he wants to be a fully-fledged member of the gang.'

Noah tensed beside her. 'Can I ... think about it?' said Noah. 'It's not ... I mean, I would never join another nation, it's not that ... it's just ... so soon after being a Slayer. Becoming a member of something else seems ... wrong.'

Meredith shrugged again. 'Take your time ... talk it over ... preferably once we're back inside the safety of the shield,' she said pointedly.

A pang of guilt ripped through Zahora; she'd added extra work to Meredith's plate, who already had a million other responsibilities. Babysitting the two of them was ...

'Hey, honestly, I don't mind being here,' said Meredith, Zahora's feelings apparently easy to read. 'I'd only be running errands for Talli otherwise ... but it is safer inside the shield.'

'Okay,' said Zahora, gripping Noah's hand more firmly. 'Let's go.'

Chapter 7

Sofie and Henrik were the first guests to arrive at Maltings for the Yule celebration, and Raina felt like a kid again. The two Vikings understood her in a way most others did not ... especially her savage side.

Raina rushed to embrace them, telling them how happy she was to see them. Henrik wrapped her in a bear hug, lifting her off her feet, and Raina was transported to the past, to many pasts all at once, to all the times when Henrik had done it before. When he finally put her down, she had to blink away tears.

Caspar and Sofie embraced in a similar fashion, and then they swapped.

'Raina,' said Sofie, her arms wide. They embraced, and this time Raina couldn't hold back the tears. Sofie held her, stroking her hair.

When they finally pulled apart, Raina slid her arm through Caspar's, taking comfort from the feel of his body pressed against her side.

Callie rushed out but faltered at the last minute, coming to a stop a few feet away. 'Hello,' she said, her voice confident, although her gaze kept darting sideways to her parents.

'Hallo, young Callie,' said Henrik, bending down. 'You can show us around, yes?'

Callie rushed forward and grabbed Henrik's hand. 'I cut flowers for your room,' she said, pulling him towards the door.

'We found the eggnog recipe from the thirteenth century,' said Raina, as they followed the others inside.

'No!' said Sofie. 'What was the secret ingredient?' They'd never been able to replicate the taste.

Raina shook her head. 'Believe me when I say you do not want to know.'

Jamie's mood was dark … it had been since their botched attack on the West Coast nation. He still couldn't understand how it had happened … the intelligence so badly wrong, his soldiers not reacting as they should have.

He downed the remaining whisky in his glass and slammed the crystal tumbler down.

'Another?' said Pixie, picking up the decanter.

When had she entered the room? His office was supposed to be secure … his thoughts blurred … how much had he had?

'Yes,' he said, picking up the glass, handing it to her.

She poured him one, then poured one for herself. She leant down to kiss him as she handed his over, her nightdress gaping, giving him a full view of her naked breasts beneath.

He pulled her down, so she straddled his lap. She was the only light in the darkness, the only one who understood him, who wanted what he wanted, who had ambition ... and the will to see it through. She almost made him forget Raina ... almost ... because, although Pixie was like Raina in so many ways, she was not a demon. She would last only a single lifetime by his side.

He pushed the thought away and cupped her breast. She smiled at him in that knowing way, then leaned forward and gently bit his lip. He pinched her nipple, and she gasped, then moved her lips to his ear. 'We should concentrate,' she said, stroking the skin at the nape of his neck.

'I am concentrating,' he said.

She scraped her nails across his skin. 'You know that's not what I meant.'

He pushed up her nightdress, skimming his fingers up to the dip of her waist, then pressed his thumb into the hollow under her hip. She bucked against him, and he chuckled. 'I'm concentrating very hard.'

Her lips kissed his, devouring him as she rocked her hips. Jamie relaxed back into the armchair, his mind pleasantly fogged by the alcohol, his senses pleasantly fogged by her. She tugged at the cord holding his dressing gown closed, then parted the fabric. He hadn't dressed after his shower, the chill air a shock, but then she pressed her naked skin to his, and the contrast was ...

A knock sounded at the door. He expected Pixie to move, to cover herself, but she did neither of those things. 'Come in,' she said, to his surprise.

Janet entered the room. Jamie had forgotten she was coming, the inquiry on hold for a winter recess.

Janet barely flinched at the scene. Maybe there was a hint of exasperation in the purse of her lips, but that was all. 'I can come back,' she said. 'I can see now isn't a good time.'

'No,' said Jamie, shifting Pixie so she sat across his lap. 'Come in …'

Janet nodded, helping herself to a whisky before taking the armchair in front of the fire.

'I was sorry to hear about what happened on the West Coast,' said Janet, looking into the flames rather than at Jamie and Pixie's half-dressed forms.

'A minor setback,' said Pixie. 'How is the inquiry progressing?'

Janet looked at Jamie then, asking if she should answer Pixie's question, because Janet never forgot who was in charge … that's why he liked her.

Jamie nodded, his fingers trailing lazy circles up Pixie's thigh, his hand still under the fabric of her nightgown. Pixie clamped her thighs together, and Jamie almost forgot to listen to Janet's reply.

'It's long and tedious, but nothing unexpected. The other nations were surprisingly receptive to the idea of disbanding the Registerium … we may yet achieve that outcome.'

A long pause filled the air as Jamie's fingers skirted close to the apex of Pixie's thighs.

'Will you attack the West Coast again?' said Janet, breaking the silence.

Jamie held Janet's gaze as he dipped two fingers into the v at the top. Pixie exhaled sharply, digging her fingernails into the skin below his ear.

'No,' said Jamie.

'East,' said Pixie, her words forcing Jamie's eyes back to hers.

Janet stood. 'I'll debrief you in full tomorrow,' she said, heading for the exit. Jamie barely noticed.

'The Pagans are the real enemy, and they're distracted,' Pixie breathed, moving against his fingers. 'Take back what's yours.'

The following morning, Raina woke to a throbbing headache, her body and the eggnog not happy bedfellows ... she wished she'd abstained from that fourth glass ... but it had been so much fun ... reminiscing, catching up, talking shit about the other nations.

She wished she could stay in bed all day ... maybe all weekend, but Talli had mapped out every minute of the celebration, and Raina shuddered to think what would happen if she didn't toe the line.

'You as scared as I am?' said Caspar, planting kisses along her spine.

'Yes,' she said with a sigh.

Caspar chucked.

'Don't stop,' she said, pouting.

Caspar huffed out another laugh, then rained featherlight kisses on every sensitive spot he could find. She arched her back, and he ran his finger through the curve, then pulled her naked body flush against him.

Raina hummed as he kissed her neck, then sucked at the spot above her collarbone. She tipped her head back against him and had the strangest urge to cry of happiness. She had everything she'd ever wanted: Caspar, Callie, old friends ... if only they could stop the Templars, they could live like this for lifetimes.

Her younger self would have been terrified of that thought—lifetimes of nothing but the same—but it didn't scare her now, because she knew every day would be different ... a contented adventure.

The other nations were arriving today, and Talli wouldn't hesitate to march into their bedroom and drag them apart to keep on schedule—no matter what they were doing—so they rose, showered together, then dressed in warm, practical winter clothes, and headed downstairs for bacon butties.

'Oh my God,' said Raina, taking a bite. She hadn't tasted anything so delicious since Elliot had left for the West Coast. The thought saddened her ... they still had no idea what was going on. Gemma and Elliot were usually bomb proof, devoid of emotion—on the outside, at least. That had made it all the more shocking when they'd refused to heed Rose's order to return home.

Rose, in her usual stoic style, had said she would deal with them later, because she had more pressing concerns. It pained Raina. Selfishly, she wanted everyone to be here, her whole family, so they could celebrate Yule together. They hadn't done that in ... she didn't know when they'd last done that ... the sixteen hundreds?

'Raina, are you listening?' said Talli.

'No,' said Raina, through a mouthful of food.

'Pay attention; our guests are arriving soon.'

Talli outlined accommodation arrangements, catering, and who would be required to do what and when. She even made them install an app on their phones she'd convinced Ira's team to create especially for the occasion.

'They'll be listening to every word we say ...' said Caspar, reluctantly downloading it.

'Got something to hide?' Talli countered.

'I don't have a phone!' said Callie, looking stricken.

'Not to worry,' said Talli, handing her a sheet of paper. 'I've also printed copies, which I've helpfully distributed around the site.'

Callie took the paper and studied it carefully, even though she couldn't read all the words. Raina's heart lurched with love.

The rest of the morning was a whirlwind of guest arrivals, including Eka of the Shindu Council, Heba of the Egyptian nation, Ira of the Holy Star, and representatives from both the Wakans and the Animists. Not all agreed with the Pagans' politics, but they'd come, which meant the door to convincing them was still ajar …

Most of their guests would stay in the village, in houses belonging to other Pagans. Maltings was full now Henrik and Sofie had taken the remaining spare room, and Raina was glad for the privacy.

Her younger self would have wanted everyone under one roof, would have suggested they hold the event at the Pagans' country estate, so she could more easily keep an eye on everyone. It was a shock even to herself that she was so changed. Although she'd missed Noah and Zahora during the morning's activities.

'They're on shield duty,' said Talli, when Raina enquired.

Guilt made Raina's blood rush. 'Poor Zahora,' she said. 'Will Alerac and Ame help?'

'They will,' said Talli, 'and the guests shouldn't have to come and go too much. Most of what we've prepared will take place inside the shield.'

Raina nodded … that was something. 'And you've planned for Zahora to join in? And Noah too?' Raina had been careful to involve them in everything, to make them feel at home. She knew what it was like to be kept from the one she loved, and she wouldn't put barriers in their way, not now the security threat was so small.

'Yes,' said Talli, tersely, 'as per your request.'

'Good.' They'd neglected their young demons and shouldn't have; they needed fresh blood to give them strength.

'Now, if you'll excuse me,' said Talli, 'I have afternoon tea to prepare.'

Raina entered the malt barn. They would use it for most of the gatherings over the weekend—a beautiful old stone building the size of a cathedral. Her mouth fell open. Talli had worked wonders, the whole place swathed in winter greenery, punctuated by red berries and mistletoe.

The tables were adorned with candles and dried oranges, cinnamon sticks, and fir cones. Trees twinkling with fairy lights flanked the entrances, and cartwheels hung ethereally from the ceiling, also swathed in green. Candles in storm lanterns lined the paths to and from the barn and around the stone circle, and each table contained a Yule log, ready to be lit.

It was stunning ... a dream.

Caspar came up behind her, wrapping her in his arms. 'Talli strikes again,' he said, his lips against her ear.

'And then some,' said Raina, stroking his arm.

Callie dashed in, dragging Zahora by the hand, Noah following in their wake. They seemed happy ...

smiles on their faces … and it warmed Raina's heart to see.

The Pagans spread themselves across the circular tables. Rose had been clear that it was a celebration, yes, but it was also an opportunity for them to cement alliances and gain ground with those on the fence. Each and every one of their guests would be treated like a VIP, regardless of the personalities involved.

Caspar kissed Raina's neck and then relinquished her. 'See you later,' he said, but she pulled him back for a kiss on the lips.

She hated events like this, where she had to be nice to everyone … listen to their problems and pretend she cared. She cared deeply about her true friends … friends like Henrik and Sofie … but the others barely bothered to conceal their distrust of her. They believed Raina's reputation without question, and it pained her that she had to smile at their jokes.

She sighed. 'See you later,' she said. He kissed her hand, then strode towards the Egyptians' leader, Heba.

She watched him go, her chest tight with love. He was so good at this stuff … diplomacy … making people like him … bending them to his will. Raina preferred the direct approach … probably why she felt such an affinity with the Vikings.

She looked longingly at their table, but headed for Eka, of the Shindu Council. She donned her most diplomatic face …

The room buzzed, filled with fifty or so demons. They were full of holiday cheer, helped along by the champagne Talli had plied everyone with on arrival …

Talli stood and walked to the front, her long winter skirts swishing around her legs, and the room went quiet.

'I am so delighted to welcome everyone to this special Yule gathering,' said Talli, beaming. 'We have a packed itinerary, which I hope you will all enjoy. If you have any questions, at any time, please don't hesitate to ask me, or anyone from my nation.'

Rose stood, and all eyes swung to her. Talli moved to the side, relinquishing the floor.

'Thank you, Talli,' said Rose, 'and everyone else you coerced into helping you pull all this together at such short notice …' A chuckle ripped across the room.

Talli gave an ironic curtsey, and Raina couldn't help but laugh along with the rest.

'And thank you to everyone in this room,' said Rose, 'for joining us. It means so much to have you all here … not only our staunch allies, but also those with whom we do not always see eye to eye. We hope to show you who we are as a nation, what we stand for, the values at our core. We hope after this weekend, you will understand us a little better, and that we can say the same about you.

'Yule is a most treasured time in our calendar. It is when we celebrate the turn of winter, when the darkness starts to recede and light returns, so the earth may spring to life once more.

'We view the Registerium inquiry through the same lens. We hope this is our darkest moment, and when the inquiry is done, that we can move towards the light. In that spirit, I invite you to light the Yule logs before you, then tuck in!'

Rose turned to an enormous Yule log behind her and lit the equally enormous central candle. The room erupted into cheers when she stepped back, the flame dancing.

The food came out next: great towers stacked with sandwiches, cakes, and other treats. Raina caught Callie's expression and laughed out loud, her eyes wide with gleeful anticipation. Callie barely waited for the tower to be placed in front of her before making a grab for a sandwich. But Rose sat next to her, and pulled her hand away, making her wait until the table's Yule log had been lit.

'She's a firecracker,' said Eka, watching Raina watch Callie.

'She is,' said Raina, with a beaming smile. 'Most days I still can't believe she's real.'

Eka nodded. 'It is a rare and wondrous gift for a demon.' Her eyes became sad. 'I once had a daughter of my own ...'

Raina braced herself.

'But she was a human ...'

'I'm sorry,' said Raina.

'Don't be. I'm luckier than most ... I had her for one lifetime, and a peaceful lifetime at that.'

Raina nodded, at a loss for what to say. She couldn't imagine how it must feel ... the deficit.

Christa leaned over. 'Have you tried these sandwiches?' she said, offering the plate to Eka and Raina, snapping the reverie. 'They are divine!'

Raina took one. 'Oh, my ...' she said as the flavors of blue cheese, caramelized onion, and mushroom hit her tongue. She didn't even like blue cheese ... how was this so good?

'That is delicious,' said Eka, taking another bite.

'Do you think the inquiry will lead to reform?' Raina asked Eka, helping herself to another sandwich, this one filled with beetroot hummus and grilled vegetables. It was equally spectacular.

Eka took a bite of a cucumber sandwich. 'I've never understood the point of these,' she said, 'but this is ... it's wonderful.'

Raina barked out a laugh at Eka's genuine surprise.

Eka smiled. 'I hope it leads to reform,' she said. 'The Shindu Council wants that ... and enduring peace.'

'As do we,' said Raina, her eyes flicking back to Callie, who was forcing a large piece of Victoria Sponge into her mouth.

'I believe you,' said Eka, watching Callie too.

Noah and Zahora snuck back to their room as soon as afternoon tea was over. The novelty of being able to spend time together still hadn't worn off.

They lounged on the bed, Noah lying between Zahora's thighs, his head resting on her stomach. 'I think that last piece of billionaire's shortbread tipped me over the edge,' he said with a groan.

Conversely, Zahora, who didn't have a sweet tooth, had tucked into the sandwiches, but abstained from all the cakes ... aside from a taste of a superb rhubarb crumble cake. She laughed. 'Maybe don't lie on your front then?' she said, combing her fingers through his hair.

He kissed the soft flesh of her belly, and she lay back on the pillows, letting the waves of delicious sensation wash over her.

'This is my favorite place to lie,' he said. He pushed her top higher to expose more skin, then rested his cheek against her.

'It was nice, meeting demons from different nations,' said Zahora.

'You never have before?'

'No. After they realized I was magical and sent me to Wales, I rarely left the compound. I guess I could have left, if I'd really wanted to, but all I wanted was to learn magic … not that they taught me much of that.'

'For all their self-importance, the Pagan magiks don't seem to know a lot,' Noah agreed.

'I think Marla's powerful … probably as powerful as Alerac, but she doesn't know how to teach. She certainly doesn't want to … or … she didn't want to teach me.'

'The others seem nice though,' he said. 'Raina isn't as scary as everyone says, and they're fun, in a quirky kinda way.'

Zahora laughed. 'They're certainly quirky …'

'Callie's sweet … and she loves you …'

Zahora ran her hands across his shoulders. 'She's adorable, and we're both trapped here. I guess I'm the nearest to her in age too … all the others are *so* old, it's suffocating to think about.'

'You're going to be stuck here a while longer though, right?'

Zahora inhaled. 'I'm sorry …'

He lifted his head to look at her. 'No, I didn't mean it like that. I meant, if you're going to be stuck here, that means I am too, and the people seem … nice … genuine … but they won't trust me … not unless I'm a Pagan too …'

Zahora held her breath.

'I want to become a Pagan … to register, or whatever I have to do.'

She cupped his face. 'You don't have to … if their trust is the only reason …'

'It's not,' he said quickly. He moved to lie next to her, stroking a lock of hair off her face. 'I love you, and I want to be with you. I would join the Pagans for that reason alone, but I also want to be part of something bigger than myself. I was born into the Slayers … have always belonged to their family. I like that feeling ... want it again, and the Pagans can give me that.'

'Your life won't be your own ... they'll expect you to make sacrifices ...'

'I know.'

She dropped her eyes, bunching his shirt in her fists, the steady thud of his heartbeat pulsing against her fingers.

He slid a finger under her chin, forcing her eyes back to his. 'I don't want any barriers between us, and I like these people ... could fit in here ... far more than with the Slayers. I'm one of you ... one of them ... a demon. And if you're a Pagan, I want to be one too.'

Dinner was an informal affair, again in the barn, but Talli had organized sofas and low tables around the edges to encourage their guests to relax.

Callie had finally gone to bed, Raina had diligently made small talk with Wakans, Egyptians, and Animists, and she groaned in relief as she flopped down next to Caspar on a sofa. She kicked off her shoes and lay with her head in his lap, closing her eyes as he stroked her hair. 'I'm glad that's over,' she whispered.

He kissed her forehead. 'Me too,' he said. 'Although ... trouble inbound ...'

Raina opened her eyes and lifted her head enough to see Rose, Henrik, and Sofie approaching, their hands filled with drinks. Raina made a whimpering noise. 'This body doesn't like alcohol ... I don't know if I can ...'

'Boring, non-alcoholic cocktail for you,' said Rose. She handed Raina an elaborate glass, the liquid tinted orange.

'Thank you,' she said, sitting up and leaning against Caspar's side.

'And the good stuff for you,' said Sofie, handing Caspar a brandy.

Raina looked pointedly at the two glasses Henrik held in his hands. 'And two for me,' he boomed, then laughed loudly.

They sat and sipped their drinks in silence for a moment, gentle music from a Celtic band trilling through the air.

'You heard about the West Coast attack?' said Sofie.

Rose nodded.

'And Jamie's glorious defeat,' said Henrik, a twinkle in his eye.

Raina rolled her eyes.

'A massacre,' agreed Rose. 'And a needless one at that.'

'Not needless if you're Jamie,' said Sofie. 'He wants more land ... more power ...'

'Doesn't he have enough?' said Rose.

'He doesn't think so,' said Sofie. 'Gemma and Elliot are still there, on the West Coast ... are they not?'

Rose gave Sofie a look, then nodded. 'We have no more information than what Ira's already shared.'

'Fucking technology,' said Henrik. 'You can't get away with a single thing these days ... everywhere you go ... fucking cameras ...' He took a gulp of the amber liquid in his glass.

'Oh, don't pretend you don't love it when it helps us,' said Sofie, swatting him on the thigh.

Henrik gave his soulmate a heated look, then took another swig. 'The footage from the attack on the Slayers,' he said, 'now that was good viewing.'

'They drew human attention,' said Rose. 'Jamie used *guns* … it's been a nightmare for the Registerium to cover up.'

'I know, I know,' said Henrik, waving his arm. 'But it was something … wasn't it? Something real …'

Raina had hated the footage … the carnage … the death. She had only ever delighted in such things when there was a reason … when the ends justified the means. But then, for Jamie, wiping out the Slayers probably justified the guns. And the West Coast would defend their actions, because Jamie had attacked them …

'It was something,' Raina agreed.

'They must have lost much of their strength,' said Sofie. 'Such a massacre …'

'Maybe we should attack them!' said Henrik. 'An opportune moment …'

'Keep your voice down,' Rose hissed, with a scowl. 'I know you're joking—even if you're tempted—but the rest of the demons in this room do not, and this is a delicate moment.'

'I can assure you,' said Henrik, 'if Jamie is behind the disappearance of my demons, it will be no joke.'

Rose shrugged. 'I won't argue with that. But in that case, the Registerium would be behind you.'

'If the Registerium still exists,' said Sofie.

'It will,' said Rose. 'It has to, or nations like the Templars and the West Coast can do what they like, with no consequences …'

'And what consequences are there now?' said Henrik, screwing up his face in derision. 'None that I can see …'

The demons gathered by the barn early the following morning, at least, those who were not morally opposed to killing animals …

Zahora joined them and helped herself to a sausage sandwich and a steaming mug of tea. It was surprisingly pleasant, being outside, on a crisp winter's morning, wrapped up against the cold.

'Today, my friends,' said Talli, humming with excitement, 'we celebrate a Yule tradition as old as any … the hunt!'

Sofie and Henrik cheered loudly, and Zahora couldn't help but smile at their exuberance. Talli shared the details of the day, which involved stalking for deer, but a presence behind Zahora made her turn.

'I'm afraid we need you,' Rose said quietly, looking apologetic.

Zahora nodded, despite her pang of disappointment, and followed Rose back to the house, where Ame and Alerac were sitting at the kitchen table.

'As you know,' said Rose, 'we don't have long before the inquiry into the Registerium's conduct begins again. I think it's likely the Registerium will be found guilty of many—if not all—counts against them, but the question that remains is what should happen after they are found guilty.

'Some would like us to disband the Registerium entirely, some want to keep it as it is, and others—like me—want to see reform. My question for you is what is possible … magically speaking? And what will it take to change the Registerium's magic?'

Alerac and Zahora turned their heads to look at Ame, the only one of them who might know the answer.

Ame looked back at Rose with a frown. 'Each nation's magical bonds are pinned to the Registerium … each demon connected to their nation via the Registerium's stone. If you were to disband the Registerium, you would simply take out the middleman, leaving only a demon's connection to their nation … and how easy or difficult that is … who can say?

'If you want to change the magic, you might be better off starting from scratch … But why do you care? The Registerium brings nothing but trouble …'

'Without the Registerium,' said Rose, 'nations … especially the smaller ones … will frequently attack each other. The big nations don't feel the effects so acutely, but the small ones will suffer not only at the hands of each other, but also at the hands of the large. That's why so many nations merged.'

'So you're doing all this for the small nations?' said Ame, skepticism laced through her words.

'And I disagree with nations holding onto demons against their will,' said Rose.

'So it's about getting Callie back?' said Ame. 'If that's all, there are easier ways …'

'No,' said Rose, 'that is not all. I'm doing it for any demon who's been sold by a hunter into effective slavery. Especially young demons, who were found early in their lives and exploited … who have known nothing but abuse and subjugation. And when they do realize there's a better world out there, they can't escape, because they're magically tied.

'The tether to a nation may once have been necessary … for stability … to stop people becoming double, or triple agents, but with modern technology, it's needless, other than as a mechanism for control. The Registerium was supposed to stop the abuse, to treat everyone equally, to ensure some level of transparency when demons register. It was supposed to be a deterrent to needless war through sanctions, but they've deviated from that path … and times have changed so very much.'

Rose's impassioned speech made Zahora realize how little she knew about the past, about other nations, about the shady underbelly of their world …

'The binding magic … the part that means a demon can't leave,' said Ame, 'pre-dated the formation of the Registerium. It rests with each individual nation, so good luck changing that.'

'We have to try,' said Rose.

'You're an idealist,' said Ame, 'and a control freak. You'll never make everyone see things the way you do … and even if you could, why would you want to? You're a hypocrite …'

'How so?' said Rose, who, much to Zahora's admiration, didn't even flinch at the insult.

'Your nation is one of the worst for playing politics … Raina …'

'Oh, for Gods' sake,' said Rose, her composure cracking in spectacular style. 'Not you too? How has Raina become a scapegoat for all the wrongs of our nation? Do you think I had nothing to do with the things she's blamed for? Or Caspar? Talli? Christa? Meredith?'

Ame's whole body stilled. 'None of them had an affair with my son. None of them cast him aside like a plaything, or sold him out to his enemies. None of them are responsible for his death …'

Rose bowed her head and took a breath. 'I'm sorry for your loss,' she said. 'I had no idea …'

'Of course you didn't,' said Ame, 'because you're so focused on Raina's child, you have no room to think about anyone else's. And now you want *me* to turn the Registerium into something of your creation ... I will not help you Paganize the world.'

Ame left, and Rose slumped into a chair. 'I shouldn't have snapped at her,' she said, playing with the biscuit crumbs no one had bothered to clean off the table.

Zahora was at a loss. Rose ... the great and powerful, ancient and glorious, impeachable, a fount of knowledge ... was just as fallible as everyone else. Zahora didn't know whether to laugh or cry.

'Rose,' said Alerac. 'It would be helpful if you could start at the beginning, and explain fully what you are trying to achieve. Then maybe I can help you ...' It was an unusually tender gesture from Alerac.

Rose nodded, collecting herself. 'The Registerium was set up as a response to the warring and stealing of people that used to occur. So many died, because there was no way to resolve the disputes ... no central, impartial record of who belonged to whom, and of which territories belonged to which nation.

'Empire building became so prevalent, the fighting so bad, that many nations had no choice but to band together with others, or face certain death. Eventually, when most of the smaller nations had merged into the nations we know today, the more peaceful among us sought a better, more stable existence.'

'They proposed the Registerium,' said Alerac. 'I remember that day.'

'The Aztecs were not keen to start,' said Rose.

'Until the Wakan—of all people—killed our leader in his bed ...'

'It was a bloody time,' said Rose. 'We lost many good demons ... my soulmate included ...'

Zahora was suddenly filled with the urge to hug Rose, although self-preservation warned her not to go through with it.

'Anyway, the more peaceful nations proposed the Registerium. We offered Pagan land to house it, and then we fought tooth and nail to convince the others. It took over a hundred years, and its eventual formation was one of my proudest moments.'

'Everyone had fought themselves out by then,' said Alerac.

'Even the Vikings,' said Christa from the doorway. 'You called?'

'You worked for the Registerium, back in the beginning ...' said Rose.

'Talli was playing hard to get, so I thought I'd make her miss me ...' said Christa, with a shrug.

Zahora smiled at the image. She could imagine exactly how that would have played out.

'Once the leaders of the member nations agreed on the purpose and structure,' said Rose, 'and selected the first Registrar, we took a step back, so no nation had undue influence. They asked the Nation of Stars to help with the magic ... but, do you know more than that?'

'No one was supposed to know anything, but we were all such terrible gossips ...,' said Christa. 'The Nation of Stars did the magical side, but the political agreements were far more interesting ... that's what we all wanted to work on ... the fines and sanctions ... how we could make nations care enough to adhere to the rules.'

'That stuff isn't magical?' said Rose, with a start.

'No!' said Christa. 'It's contractual. I assumed you knew ...'

'And if the magic tethering demons to their nations is merely funneled through the Registerium ...' said

Alerac, 'changing the Registerium's magic might not be the answer after all.'

'Indeed ...' said Rose, thinking hard.

'I'm still not clear what exactly you want from us,' said Alerac, who, having listened patiently, was now becoming agitated.

'Given magic seems to have a much smaller role than I thought,' said Rose, 'neither am I. But I want to put an end to people being held hostage by their nation, and I want to ensure future leaders of the Registerium can be relied on to do the right thing. It worked well for hundreds of years, until they appointed bad Registrar after bad Registrar, coveting power, accepting bribes, caring about influence and celebrity, wooed by promises from the likes of Jamie. But I do believe, wholeheartedly, that having the Registerium in place is better than the alternative.'

'Anarchy,' said Christa, putting the kettle on.

'Yes,' said Rose. 'But what we have isn't working ... needs improvement.'

'Changing how the Registrar is appointed, and asking nations to alter their ideologies are political problems,' said Christa, 'not magical ones.'

'We wouldn't need any magical input at all?' said Rose.

Zahora thought of all the effort they'd gone to, probing the Registerium's magic, trying to understand it, all the magiks at the compound in Wales. Had it all been for nothing?

'Ame said the Registerium is just a middleman,' said Zahora, 'and that would make sense from what I've seen. Each demon's magic is tied to the Registerium's stone ... part of a colossal spiral ... but there are other lines ... thick and straight ... only a few, that connect to the stone as well. They could be the links from the Registerium back to the nations.'

'That makes sense,' said Alerac, 'as each nation has its own terms for members.'

'But how do nations set those terms?' said Rose. 'When a demon joins our nation, there's no document for them to sign … nothing but a verbal reminder of what it means to be Pagan.'

'Which has been passed down over thousands of years,' said Christa. 'I guess, in the beginning, some long dead Pagan magically infused the terms of membership into the nation bond.'

'But what happened when the nations amalgamated?' said Rose. 'When we did, there was never talk of changing the terms of our magical bonds …'

'I don't know,' said Christa.

'Maybe everyone switched unwittingly to the dominant nation's terms,' said Zahora. 'Maybe the others still exist, but just aren't used …'

'Maybe other nations know more,' said Christa. 'Maybe they kept better records than we did, or were better at passing the knowledge down …'

'We can ask our friends,' said Rose, 'although it's a sensitive topic, and … could anyone use this against us?'

'We should think on it,' said Christa, 'and ask the others to do the same.'

Rose nodded. 'And we must keep an eye on Ame … Raina may not be safe.'

111

The evening's cavorting was in full swing by the time Raina joined the party. Sofie had been the only successful member of the hunt—having single-handedly brought down a deer—and it cooked on a spit, a pig on another beside it.

Sofie was on Henrik's shoulders, being paraded around the dance floor as Queen of the Hunt, and Raina was glad to see someone having a good time. Rose had told her about Ame, which had put her on edge, her eyes darting to Callie at regular intervals, making sure she was still safe.

Meredith had increased security, assigning several guards to discretely watch Callie and Raina, and several more to keep tabs on Ame, but that did little to calm Raina's nerves; Ame was a powerful magik.

Raina had let things slip ... had been so wrapped up in having her family together, she'd ignored the uncertainties around Ame's past, her allegiances, or why she'd been so aggressive towards Raina. Would it ever end? Would they ever be able to just live a peaceful life together?

Probably not ... Raina's past was too messy.

Arms slipped around her waist, and Caspar's soothing tones filled her ear. 'I missed you today,' he said, running his nose down the shell of her ear.

They'd been in different hunting parties, Raina with the Egyptians, and Caspar with the Wakans.

'I missed you too,' she said, leaning back into his warmth. 'It went well with the Egyptians.'

'That's good to hear.'

'Talli said the Holy Star sat today out?'

'Ira's a vegetarian,' said Caspar. 'He stayed with Eka ... they're getting along well ...'

Raina raised an eyebrow. 'How well?'

Caspar chuckled. 'I don't know, but a strong alliance between those two nations is good for us.'

'Do you know how it went with the Animists?'

'No,' said Caspar, 'but Callie seems to be winning them over.'

Raina followed his eyes to where a teenaged boy listened intently to whatever Callie was saying. She stood, then pirouetted, and the boy's face split into a wide smile. He wasn't really a boy, of course … he was well over a thousand, but they'd hit it off. He pulled a deck of cards from his pocket, and Callie made a delighted grab for them.

'I think it's going well,' said Raina. 'Who knows if they'll agree to Rose's proposals, but at least they'll listen.'

'Which is good, given what Rose learned earlier …'

'No magical quick win for us … just to make a change.'

'Hey,' said Caspar, nipping her ear. 'At least we know politics … understand it.'

'True,' said Raina, with a shiver, because she knew firsthand how dangerous magic was. She wondered if anyone could ever really, truly understand it … She spun in his arms and wrapped her hands around his neck just as the music changed to a Scottish jig.

Their faces split into smiles, and Raina followed as Caspar pulled her by the hand to the dance floor. It amazed her that still, after all her many lifetimes, the frantic beat of a drum, the trill of a pipe, the call of a bow on string could be so electrifying. That the simple pleasure of twirling, and jumping, and stamping with friends could give such unabashed joy.

Raina stepped out into the frigid night air. She'd been dancing for three hours straight and was drenched in sweat. She spotted Ame, sitting on a hay bale near the stone circle, wearing too few clothes for the weather, and Raina froze.

She thought about heading back inside, ignoring Ame, keeping the past in the past. But Ame was a grieving mother ... she must have questions ... questions that had been burning for too long. Raina grabbed a cloak from a peg just inside the entrance and wrapped it tightly around herself.

Ame didn't even look up as Raina sat on a hay bale. She just stared towards the altar stone, lit by an enormous candle in a storm lantern.

'I'm sorry,' said Raina, watching the flickering flame. 'Truly ... I ...'

Ame remained still, showing no sign she'd heard Raina's words.

'If there's anything you want to ask ...'

Ame inhaled then, a labored breath, and turned her eyes to Raina. 'What could I ask that I don't already know? You made him fall in love with you, then discarded him, then later, when it suited your purposes, exploited the love he still felt for you, and sold him out to his enemies.'

'No,' said Raina.

Ame shook her head. 'Which part?'

'All of it,' she said, vehemently. 'We first met when we were children ... did you know that? I was in my first reincarnated life … I had no idea what was happening when he found me.'

'He was never a hunter …'

'He was,' said Raina, 'he had the ability, and he refused to join a nation, because you'd warned against it … told him they would use his magical abilities for their own ends, then toss him aside.'

Ame scoffed. 'And I was right.'

'He fascinated me. He was … unusual … people didn't understand him, but to me, he was like a beacon in the darkness. I found his magic mesmerizing, and asked him to teach me.'

'He didn't …?' said Ame, a flutter of unease in her eyes.

'He did, and it was a disaster. I …' She looked away. 'It ended badly …'

Ame sucked in a breath. 'What happened?'

Raina watched the candle's flame as she weighed her words, then looked directly in Ame's eyes, cast in shadow as they were. 'I killed my human parents.' Raina had never told another living soul, not even Caspar …

'His magic was unstable,' said Ame, 'but Willam refused to seek help … I told him not to use it.'

'I became almost obsessed with magic after that. I made him teach me everything he knew, and encouraged him to experiment with his own power. I thought, if I could master the magic, it would be some sort of atonement for what I'd done.'

'That's not how it works,' said Ame, sadly.

'No,' agreed Raina, 'but we tried anyway, and we fell in love, or at least, we became infatuated with each other. I'm sure our magic heightened the sensation. It was linked … impossible to distinguish between what we felt because of the magic, and what was really us. It was a drug … an addiction.

'But we ran out of money, and neither of us was a member of a nation. We'd spent what little my parents had saved. So we decided he would sell me to the Pagans, and live off that money for a while.'

'But then you met Caspar …' Ame said, the words a snarl.

'No. I met Rose and her soulmate, who led our nation back then. I'd never met another demon, aside from your son … didn't appreciate the scope of the world, the nations, what I could be a part of … Rose took me under her wing and trained me. I told her I wanted to do magic, but I was shocked to find the Pagan magic was almost entirely different from what I'd been doing with Willam.'

Ame put her head in her hands, like this wasn't a surprise.

'By then, he ran out of money once more, and he refused to join the Pagans, so they refused to look after him. He went off hunting for demons, and in that time we grew apart. I didn't want that kind of life any longer, where the only thing that consumed us was the magic and each other … I'd found there was more, and I wanted it all …'

Images from the past flashed before Raina's eyes, of the handsome, magnetic, chaotic man who had once been her entire world.

'When he came back, he asked me to leave with him. I said no, and he stuck around for a while, but eventually I ended it. As soon as I did, it was like the spell between us snapped. He told me I'd only ever been a casual fling to him, and I believed him, because … that's what it felt like by the end. I assumed the magic had made it into more … and … Caspar …'

'But Willam was lying,' said Ame. 'He returned to me and told me all about you … how he loved you … how he'd screwed it up.'

Raina hadn't known he'd gone back to his mother. He'd always hated her lack of ambition, and that she wanted him to put his magic aside.

'Then he disappeared,' said Ame, 'for lifetimes … I didn't know what had become of him, until he resurfaced, saying everything in the world was right once more, because the two of you were back together …'

Raina hung her head. 'Caspar and I had a bad patch in the early seventeen hundreds. Our lives went in separate directions for a time, and I craved something different. I dabbled in magic again, found Alerac, and got him to teach me. It felt good … natural to be back doing magic, but the craving continued … worsened. I wanted what I'd had with Willam.

'Then one day he sent for me, magically, and I didn't even hesitate. We had an affair, and it was …'
Brutal, carnal, frenzied …

'Destructive,' said Ame, filling the silence.

'Yes,' said Raina. 'It was bad for both of us, but I thought it was just a bit of fun for him … and—I'm sorry to say—but that's all it was for me … I thought we both knew that, otherwise I never would have …' She faltered, her eyes back on the candle. 'When I ended it, he was upset. He threatened to tell Caspar everything, but I'd already told him … had rubbed it in his face, actually …'

Ame tisked, but said nothing.

'I didn't hear from Willam for a while. A lifetime … maybe two. When he got back in touch, he needed money … threatened me … was vicious and angry … said he'd watched my recent wedding to Caspar from afar. I was working with Rose to try and shore up relations with the Templars at the time, and in his desperation for money, Willam had done a deal with the Templars, then reneged.'

'So you killed two birds with one stone,' said Ame. 'One of them literally.'

'Yes,' said Raina, 'I gave him to the Templars, but they swore they wouldn't true-death him …'

'Did you see the body?' said Ame.

Raina shook her head.

'Have you seen him since that day? Or heard anything of him?'

'No,' said Raina quietly.

'Then he's dead.'

'Maybe he didn't want to come back,' said Raina.

'No,' said Ame, sharply. 'My son would never do that.'

Raina stood. 'Maybe he made his sacrifice to the magic … maybe he'll come back one day … or … ask the Templars; they have no reason to withhold the truth.'

Raina returned to the party to find the mood there as somber as she was. 'What happened?' she asked Caspar, who took her hand.

He nodded to where Henrik stood, a phone to his ear, Sofie statue-still at his side. Henrik hung up. 'Another of our demons is missing,' he said. 'Disappeared with no signs of a struggle, and no note.'

'Have you tried using magic to call them back?' said Heba, the Egyptian leader.

'We don't reserve that right over our people …' said Sofie.

'Try anyway,' said Heba. 'The Wakans have successfully recalled one demon that way.'

Henrik's eyes flicked to the Wakan delegation. 'Is this true?' he said, his voice carrying easily to the other side of the barn.

One of them nodded. 'Yes, but that demon swears they weren't leaving us, so … I don't know.'

'We will try,' said Sofie. 'We must return to our nation.'

'Of course,' said Raina, clasping her friend in a fierce hug. 'If there's any way we can help, you must ask.'

Chapter 8

The treasure hunt Talli had planned for the following day was a muted affair, the result of too much alcohol, too little sleep, and the missing Viking. No other nations had reported additional losses, but everyone was on edge, as though waiting for their own call.

Callie was the only one who didn't seem affected, dashing around excitedly, looking for the priceless hidden objects Talli had planted around the grounds. 'I found a bracelet!' Callie squealed, rushing to Raina for help putting it on.

Raina laughed and hugged her daughter. 'It's beautiful,' she said, and then off Callie dashed again, snagging Zahora's hand and pulling her along too.

Raina squeezed Caspar's arm. 'Zahora's so good with her.'

'She's a saint,' said Caspar, putting his hand over Raina's.

'So full of energy at that age,' said Heba, joining them. Her smile was sad.

'Still no news about your son?' said Raina. He'd been stolen in a joint mission between the Templars and Slayers, and they all feared the worst.

Heba shook her head. 'It's a precious time, when they're so young,' she said. 'I'm glad to see you're making the most of it.'

Raina smiled. 'I never thought I'd have a child of my own.'

'Neither did I,' said Heba. 'A rare privilege for our kind …'

Raina's phone buzzed in her pocket. 'Sofie?' she said, picking up.

'We don't know how to call a demon through their nation bond …' said Sofie. 'We haven't done it in … oh … hundreds of years, and we don't have any magiks left … at least no one who knows anything useful. Do you know?'

'No,' said Raina, 'but we can ask Heba, or the Wakan?'

'We'd rather not, if we can avoid it,' said Sofie. 'Politically … these are sensitive times.'

Raina wasn't sure what, other than pride, made Sofie say that, but she agreed. 'Okay … I'll ask Alerac and Ame,' she said, taking off to look for them.

But Ame wasn't in her room or her workshop. In fact, no one could recall seeing her since the night before. And Alerac was missing too … he hadn't been seen since he'd strengthened the shield that morning.

'Some of Ame's stuff is gone,' said Zahora, coming out of Ame's workshop. 'She left most of it, but a couple of tinctures are missing, and her coat and boots, and some clothes from her room.'

'Shit,' said Raina.

'No luck with Alerac either,' said Caspar.

'We should search the village,' said Raina, and then she realized Meredith was missing too.

'Zahora, I need you to help me through the shield,' said Raina. 'Caspar, watch Callie … don't let her out of your sight.' He nodded, and she took off at a run.

Zahora let Raina through the shield, then put it back in place. 'I'm going to check Meredith's house,' said Raina.

Zahora nodded. 'I'll wait for you.'

Raina ran. Meredith wasn't answering her phone, and dread ate at her guts. Meredith always answered her phone. Had Ame done something? Was Alerac secretly working against them? Were Ame and Alerac working together?

Raina burst into Meredith's house, but was brought up short by what she found … Meredith and Alerac on the sofa … Meredith straddling him, naked. Meredith's head whipped around. 'What do you want?' she said, with murderous eyes.

'Ame's gone, we couldn't find Alerac, and Sofie wants to know how to call their missing demon through their nation bond. They've tried a few things, but nothing's working, and they don't know if they're doing it right …'

'I don't know how to do it using the Vikings' magic,' Alerac ground out. 'Tell them to ask the Registerium.'

'I'll … give you a minute,' said Raina. 'I'll be outside.'

Raina walked back through the pretty garden and sat on the old stone wall by the road, far enough away to be out of earshot. Poor Meredith … she never had a moment off duty. Did she like Alerac, or was he just an enjoyable distraction …?

By the time they all made it back to Maltings, the guests from the other nations were preparing to depart, and Ame was still missing.

'I don't think the Vikings want to ask the Registerium while the inquiry is under way,' said Raina.

'Then we'll have to suck it up and ask Heba,' said Meredith, who was in a punchy mood, presumably because of what Raina had witnessed. 'I'll ask her.' And off she went, marching up to Heba, who was saying goodbye to Rose. Raina followed.

'I can't help,' said Heba, looking genuinely apologetic. 'It's unique for each nation … so even if I told you how we summon demons through the bond, I don't know if it would work for you. The Registerium should be able to help though … assuming their magiks are still capable.'

Raina gave Heba a non-committal smile. 'Thank you,' she said, 'and it's been so nice to see you. Thank you for coming.'

'The pleasure was all mine,' said Heba. 'It was a special pleasure to meet your daughter.'

Raina watched Callie work her way around, giving everyone bear hugs. 'She enjoyed meeting you too.'

Meredith and Raina rejoined the others. 'The Templars don't have any magiks of their own,' said Raina, 'so how are they using magic to summon Callie?'

'They don't have any allies left,' said Meredith.

'Then the Registerium must be helping them,' said Alerac.

Raina nodded. 'And we need to put a stop to it.'

Talli handed out hampers full of homemade treats to their guests as they departed, along with Yule garlands. Callie grabbed a handful of garlands and wrapped them around herself as she skipped here and there, waving and singing and laughing.

A Wakan man about to step through the open hole in the shield hugged Callie warmly, and then, to Zahora's horror, picked her up and pulled her through.

'No!' screamed Raina, trying to go after them, but she was on the wrong side of the shield ... all the Pagans were, and the other Wakans were defending the hole, preventing the Pagans from following ...

Figures appeared in the gardens of the picturesque cottages outside the shield, knives drawn, and then they were rushing the shield, attacking.

Zahora didn't have time to think. She acted, dropping the shield entirely, then running as fast as she could towards Callie. Callie screamed and flailed, making it as difficult as she could for her attacker, but she was small, and the Wakan was prepared.

Zahora heard carnage behind her, the sounds of bodies dropping, of screaming and confusion. She let it wash over her, ignoring everything but Callie. But then, as they neared the end of the street, a man stepped into the road, a knife in hand ... Jamie. Zahora had only seen him in pictures, but there was no mistaking it was him.

The Wakan practically threw Callie at Jamie, then formed up behind him, along with ten or so others. Jamie held his knife to Callie's throat.

'No!' screamed Zahora. 'No ... please don't.'

Callie was terrified, crying, her eyes wild.

What could they do? What could Zahora do? Magic?

Raina came to a halt beside her, eerily calm, and it had a soothing effect on Zahora, quashing the panic, helping her think. Think, think, think. She had to think. How could she immobilize Jamie using magic?

'Jamie,' said Raina, 'what are you doing?'

'Taking back what's mine,' he said, pulling back Callie's head.

Zahora sent a wash of calm at Callie, willing it to have the same impact on her as Raina's presence had had on Zahora. It seemed to work, Callie's tears drying up as Raina kept talking.

'Just give Callie back and walk away,' she said.

Jamie sneered. 'No,' he said, then turned, hauling Callie against him.

He was leaving … No … she couldn't let him take her … and then Callie went limp. She slid through Jamie's grip and hit the floor … Jamie would need two hands to pick her up.

Zahora stood watching in confusion, but Raina didn't. She sprang forward, and at the same moment, Meredith, Caspar, Talli, Christa, and a full team of Pagan guards appeared behind Jamie's line, clashing with his demons.

Zahora saw the moment Jamie realized he was defeated, the instant he changed his intent from picking Callie up to stabbing her with his knife. And Raina wouldn't get there in time … she was too far away. Zahora watched in horror, unable to think of a single thing she could do … but then Callie's leg extended in a lightening kick, and Jamie recoiled, bent double in agony.

It gave Raina the time she needed to grab Callie, haul her to her feet, and drag her away at a run. Oh, thank the Gods … Zahora pelted after them, back towards the shield … the shield they needed … that was currently down. But Alerac was there … had already replaced it … was already creating an opening for them to pass through.

125

Tears pricked Zahora's eyes. Thank the Gods. And Noah was there too, racing towards the shield.

They crossed through the shield, and Alerac closed it behind them, Raina clutching Callie to her. Noah pulled Zahora to his chest.

'Are you okay?' he said, pushing her back to get a good look at her.

Zahora nodded, then turned, desperate to see if they were winning the fight. But it was all over … they'd won.

'Your wife got away,' Meredith said to Noah, throwing her bloody knife on the table as she joined the others in the kitchen at Maltings.

All their guests had departed, the dead bodies had been buried, and everyone but Meredith had showered and changed.

Zahora clutched a mug of hot sweet tea. She'd tried to refuse, but Talli had glared at her and told her she was in shock. She had to admit, it was making her feel better.

Callie was curled up in Raina's lap, and Zahora kept catching herself staring. Feelings of self-loathing ate her from her stomach out. She hadn't done a thing … had frozen … panicked. She'd been worse than useless … and the others had been amazing.

'Wait,' said Zahora, Meredith's words finally making an impact. 'Noah's *wife*?'

'Pixie?' said Noah. 'She was here? She's working with Jamie?'

'Yep,' said Meredith. 'And they both got away.'

'Ira's trying to find them,' said Caspar.

'They've probably already flown out,' said Meredith. 'The coward ran … left his soldiers to die so he could escape. Pathetic piece of shit.'

Zahora got the feeling Meredith had a dose of self-loathing flooding through her veins too.

'But you …' said Meredith, walking over to Callie, crouching before her, taking her hand. 'You were a lion.'

Callie gave Meredith a tentative smile. 'I did what you told me. At first I didn't remember, but then … I did. I played dead, and then I kicked him in the privates, like you told me.'

Meredith beamed at her. 'You're a warrior, just like your mamma.'

Callie gave a little shake of delight, and Raina cuddled her closer.

'What was Jamie trying to do?' said Rose. 'It doesn't make any sense. He's been probing us for so long with small skirmishes, undermining our investments, building alliances … putting himself in a position of strength. But now … he's erratic …'

'He lost Raina and Callie,' said Caspar, 'and his alliance with the Aztecs, and his rule over the Registerium. The tide's turned against him.'

'And if he's listening to Pixie,' said Noah, sending an apologetic look at Zahora, 'he's listening to the wrong council. She's power hungry … it was all she seemed to care about in the brief time I knew her.'

'Her and Jamie both,' said Raina.

'Well, he's screwed now,' said Rose. 'Although, the Wakans working with him was a surprise.'

'It was only some of them,' said Alerac. 'The rest of their delegation were just as surprised as we were.'

'Fragmented nations …' said Rose. 'You can never get them all on side. Regardless, which nations will support him after a display like that?'

'Maybe the Aztecs,' said Alerac, darkly.

'You know something?' said Meredith, rounding on him.

'No,' he said. 'But from what I hear, they've been antagonistic during the inquiry.'

Rose nodded. 'No offense, but that's run-of-the-mill stuff from your nation.'

Alerac shrugged. 'Our leader can be as erratic as Jamie. He's high at least half of the time, and has driven the nation's finances into the ground. He covets wealth, so who knows what he'd do if Jamie made him an offer he found appealing …'

'Why does no one overthrow him?' said Meredith.

'Who?' said Alerac. 'Most of our good demons left lifetimes ago. Only the weak remain … and a few good women—wives our leader bargained for in deals with other nations … they were the final nail in our financial coffin.'

Zahora shuddered. The notion of being sold into marriage was horrific. She couldn't believe nations still did things like that … reminded once more of how little she knew of the real world, of what a sheltered life she'd led.

'The Aztecs should worry about being Jamie's next target if you ask me,' said Meredith. 'Jamie's almost out of options, and he badly needs a victory …'

Gemma stood beside Ares and Aphrodite, dressed as a goddess, with a wreath of golden leaves in her hair. Elliot stood a pace behind them, deferring to her superior status. Gemma's insides churned … was she really going to do this? Elliot had given her his blessing, but … was this who she really was? Who she wanted to be?

Hades approached with his usual confident swagger, and she let her eyes rake over his perfect form. He gave a cocky smile, but visibly faltered when he caught sight of Elliot behind her.

'Goddess,' he murmured, kissing her hand.

'Lucifer,' she said, inclining her head. 'That name suits you better.'

He shrugged. 'I must have misunderstood,' he said. 'I believed I was to accompany you …'

'You are,' she said, cutting across him. 'You may walk next to Elliot.' She nodded her head in Elliot's direction. 'A step behind me.'

'Goddess, I …' He flicked his eyes to Aphrodite, who did nothing, a look of pure amusement on her face.

'Is there a problem?' said Gemma. Ares was smirking now too, and they all watched Hades, waiting to see what he would do.

'Very well, Goddess,' he said. But as he moved past her, he caught her hand, stopping in her space, their faces close. 'But I request we speak privately as soon as this … display … is over.'

Gemma inclined her head. 'Very well, Lucifer,' she said, echoing his words.

Aphrodite strutted alongside Ares as they entered the amphitheater. No signs of the Templar attack remained, everything back to its usual, millimeter perfect state.

The space was filled to the brim with men and women dressed in identical uniforms, lined up in neat rows. An army, Gemma realized, concentrating on keeping her features blank as she eyed the ranks.

Someone called out an order, and the soldiers stood to rigid attention, the sound of boots landing sending a shiver down her spine. Well-trained soldiers.

They reached the front, and the commander saluted them. Ares saluted back, then they sat on the chairs—thrones—that awaited them. Or Gemma, Aphrodite, and Ares did. Elliot and Hades stood behind Gemma, flanking her like guards. She couldn't help the thrill that shot through her … usually she was the guard, the nameless figure in the background. Not any longer … and it made her feel powerful … invincible … less like herself than ever. Or maybe this was who she truly was, never able to find a route to the surface … until now.

They watched as the soldiers put on a display, and then they walked through the ranks, inspecting their uniforms, asking questions, making small talk. Gemma, the dignitary … something about it still didn't fit right, like she wore a coat that belonged to someone with broader shoulders than her own.

'Do our soldiers meet with your exacting standards, my love?' said Ares, loud enough for everyone to hear.

Aphrodite stayed quiet for a moment before leaning into Ares. 'They do,' she said. 'Goddess? What do you think of our army's finest soldiers?'

Gemma inclined her head. 'They're very good,' she said, as the weight of attention shifted to her. 'Excellent, in fact.'

Aphrodite's face split into a broad-yet-calculating smile. 'Then we shall feast to celebrate. After all, it is Yule, is it not?'

The afternoon was a whirlwind from that moment on, demons scurrying around rearranging furniture, bringing food and drinks, playing music, and dancing for the entertainment of a select few. The military commanders were in attendance, as well as a few of Aphrodite's favorite demons—mostly men—with a few voluptuous, scantily clad women too.

Elliot had lost Gemma in the scrum, and Hades was nowhere to be seen. Gemma had agreed to a private meeting with Hades, which made Elliot all the more antsy as he stalked around, trying to find them.

He heard moaning and steeled himself as he rounded the corner leading to Aphrodite's balcony. He shouldn't be looking for her. He should walk away. He should allow her the privacy he'd promised ... but he couldn't. He needed to see ...

But as the moaning woman came into view, he found it wasn't Gemma, but Aphrodite, pressed back against a wall, a man's head between her legs. He was about to retreat, but her eyes flew open, catching him staring. She smiled, issuing a gasp as her eyes locked with his, as she tipped her head back. Elliot couldn't look away. She cocked a finger at him, beckoning him towards her, her other hand opening the front of her dress.

He was off guard and faltered, not quite believing his eyes. He shook his head, saying, 'Gemma is the only woman for me,' then stalked away, which made it all the more difficult when he finally found Gemma and Hades alone in an alcove.

Hades loomed over her, and Elliot had to fight every fiber of his being screaming at him to punch Hades in the face. But Gemma wasn't doing anything he hadn't told her she could, and her flirtatious tones told him she wasn't unhappy about it.

Elliot had to get it together. He had to … to breathe. He ducked into a back corridor, followed it to a secluded balcony, then slumped into a seat, looking out over the crashing waves of the sea.

'We'll have to step things up,' said Ares, his voice floating up from the patio below. Elliot peaked over the edge to see Ares and his general reclining on a sofa, smoking cigars.

'I agree,' said the general. 'The inquiry looks to be wrapping up sooner than expected, and Jamie's behavior is unpredictable … a most unstable moment.'

'Shame he wasn't successful in his attempt to retrieve the girl,' said Ares. 'That would have really shaken things up …'

'The instability is already making it easier to bring others to our cause.'

'Yes,' said Ares, 'and our new facility is coming along well. Once it's functional, we'll be able to do so much more.'

Silence stretched between the two men. Elliot was about to return to the party, when the General said, 'Forgive me if I talk out of turn, but what is it with the Pagan? Why single her out?'

Silence descended again, and Elliot wondered if Ares would answer. But he did, eventually. 'She's Aphrodite's little project.'

'You disapprove?' said the general.

'I'm ambivalent. She means nothing to me.'

Elliot made his way back to the party, his mood even blacker than it had been before. When he returned, he found Gemma sitting next to Hades on a sofa, his hand on her leg as he leaned in to whisper something in her ear.

Elliot wanted to be sick, but he'd told her it was okay, and he couldn't let her see anything but acceptance on his face. Try as he might, he couldn't convince his features to comply, so he left, careful not to let her see him go.

Chapter 9

The Yule break from the inquiry ended all too soon, and Rose returned to the Registerium with more questions than answers, but also with a renewed determination to win the others to her cause. Because her cause was just ... of that, she had no doubt.

They gave evidence for two further days, and then, when all had spoken, the chair, Jamila, stood, removing herself from the circle around the standing stone in which the others sat. 'We have heard all evidence both for and against the charges,' she said. 'We have held a fair, balance, equitable inquiry, and for that I must thank you all. Now, we will vote.'

Rose shifted so she could easily look around the circle, feverishly counting in her head. Who would vote with her, and who would vote against ...?

Janet's skin had taken on a green hue ... did she know something Rose didn't? It made her nervous. Janet had never before shown a single ounce of weakness ...

'On the first count,' said Jamila, '*supporting false, covert, and illegal registrations of demons to the Templar nation.* How do you find the Registerium?'

Rose stood, voting for guilty, as did all the other nations, with the exception of Janet, the Aztecs, and the Persian Zorros. Rose breathed an inward sigh of relief as the vote for the second count: *favoring one nation—the Templars—above all others*, went exactly the same way.

Count three: *allowing the new West Coast nation to grow powerful, with no formal investigation or invitation to join the alliance*, was unanimous. They all found the Registerium guilty, as they did also for count four: *failure to maintain sufficient magical skills*, and five: *failure to appropriately investigate recent demon disappearances.*

Rose slumped back in her chair. The first step towards reform had gone their way ... a welcome moment of respite. But then Janet stood, and Rose's stomach sank.

'I propose a vote on the disbandment of the Registerium,' said Janet. 'We have just voted unanimously, recognizing their many failures. Now is the time to act ... to vote on whether the Registerium should be a part of our future.'

'Will anyone second this motion?' said Jamila, her eyebrows raised in judgmental fashion.

Janet looked to the Aztec representative, who had been distracted by a messenger. Janet's brow furrowed, but the Persians' representative stood. 'I will second this motion,' he said.

'Very well,' said Jamila.

'I propose a recess before we vote,' said Rose, standing too. 'It's been a heavy morning ... I'm sure we would all benefit from taking a breath.'

'I second that motion,' said Janet, surprising everyone.

'Any objections?' said Jamila. No one raised their voice. 'Very well; you have an hour. Then hopefully we can wrap this up and be out of here by lunch ...'

The Aztec hastened away, Rose following him with her eyes. She was making a mental list of who she needed to speak with, and in what order, when Janet grasped her arm. 'May I have a word?' she said. 'In private?'

Rose met Janet's eyes, and—seeing no hostility there—nodded. They walked a short way into the woods, and Rose waited for Janet to spit out whatever she had to say.

'I have a proposition for you,' said Janet, her voice low.

'I'm all ears …' said Rose impatiently. She needed to speak with many others in this precious time.

'I'll side with you, in this vote, if you support my bid to overthrow Jamie.'

Janet had her attention now … 'What kind of support do you require?'

'I have the numbers inside my nation. Jamie's lost our trust with his recent moves, and with his choice of … companion. But afterwards, when the inquiry into our nation comes—which it surely must—I would like you to support my bid for reform, rather than decimation.'

'Jamie's done the decimating already,' said Rose. 'It would be easier to finish the job …'

'Not if the Pagans want to show the world they're peaceful,' said Janet. Her features were neutral. She wasn't goading Rose so much as pointing out a fact.

'You would have to change your rules on the free movement of people,' said Rose, 'and magically transfer Callie to the Pagans immediately. And we'll need to know what happened to Heba's son. If he's alive, he must be returned. In fact, all prisoners of war must be returned—without argument or question—to their destination of choice.'

Janet nodded. 'I agree to all of that.'

136

'And you will support my proposed reforms of the Registerium … assuming it remains after this vote.'

Janet asked about the proposed reforms, and Rose told her. She agreed, they shook hands, and then Rose hurried off to speak with her allies. By the time they came back together, Rose was nervous. From what she could tell, the vote rested on a knife edge …

Jamila brought the group to order, and, when no one requested time to advocate for or against the motion, wasted no time in getting to it. 'All those in favor of the Templar motion to disband the Registerium, please stand now,' she said.

Rose stopped breathing as she watched demon after demon stand. The Egyptians, the Persian Zorros … the Wakan even. When Sofie stood, Rose's heart almost stopped. That would be it, surely. But then the Aztec, who had been teetering on the edge of his seat, chewing his lip, sat back and crossed his arms.

The Aztecs wanted the Registerium to continue? Why the sudden change of heart? If no one moved, they'd won … the Registerium would continue … And then Rose realized that every other face in the circle was watching Janet, waiting for her to stand and claim victory.

Rose's heart pounded. Was this what a heart attack felt like? In all her lives, she didn't think she'd ever actually had one … But Janet didn't stand. She remained resolutely still as Jamila declared that the motion had failed, that the Registerium would continue.

Pandemonium broke as soon as Jamila ended the session. She hightailed it out of the clearing as fast as she could, without even a backward glance.

Leaders peppered Janet with questions, accusations, and insults. The half who'd wanted the motion to succeed called her a coward, the other half were dazed, wondering if what they'd witnessed was really true.

Rose stepped in front of Janet, forcing their attention away from the Templar. 'I know some of you are upset that the Registerium will continue to exist,' she said, her hands outstretched in placating fashion, 'but there is little to be done about that now.'

Angry shouts filled the air, and Rose waited for them to die down before continuing.

'There is common ground here,' she said, turning stern. She would not tolerate petulance in any form. 'We can all agree that the Registerium does not function well today. We must seek reform, put in place a new structure, and improve transparency. The world has moved on considerably since the Registerium was formed, and there is a desperate need to make updates in light of that fact.

'I propose we form a committee to determine the changes required, and that we do so immediately.'

'No,' said the Waken representative. 'What we must do immediately is put the Templar nation on trial. They must face the consequences of their actions—the use of guns, blackmailing the Registerium—it cannot stand.'

Murmurs of agreement rippled through the group.

'I agree,' said Rose. 'Believe me, I have no love for the Templar nation. But we should reform the Registerium first, to ensure we have an appropriate structure to bring the Templars to justice.'

'No,' said Heba, the Egyptian leader. 'If it weren't for the Templars, my son would still be with me.'

'Justice must be the priority,' said a Persian Zorro.

The ripple of agreement became sticky, then set solid like concrete, and when they voted, the majority was overwhelming: the Templar trial would happen first.

As the crowd dispersed, Rose walked with Janet back to the castle. 'I will support you,' said Rose. 'My nation is behind your coup, but there are those it will be hard to convince ... you heard them ... and as soon as you are victorious, you will transfer Callie, or our deal is over.'

Janet nodded, unusually solum. 'Wait,' she said, as Rose made for her waiting car.

Rose turned, cocking her head to one side. She was weary, looking forward to returning to her nation for at least a brief reprieve before the investigation into the Templar nation began.

'You've got experience ... with coups ... I ... haven't. I was wondering ...' She trailed off, and Rose stepped back towards her.

'You want my advice?' Rose smiled at the irony.

Janet met Rose's gaze defiantly, a gesture that gave Rose hope she could actually achieve her aim.

'Plan everything,' said Rose. 'Do not neglect even the smallest detail. Trust only the very few you must. Eliminate Jamie's staunch allies the moment you take power; do not make the mistake of thinking they will ever be truly loyal to you. Isolate anyone with the power to overthrow you and legitimize yourself immediately. Grab the purse strings and do not let go ... and most importantly, give your nation genuine reasons to line up behind you. They must truly believe you will make their lives better. Apart from that, fight like hell, believe you will win, and act like you were born to do it.'

Rose got into the car she was sharing with Sofie to the airport, Sofie already inside.

'What the fuck is Janet up to?' said Sofie.

'I'll tell you on the flip side,' said Rose. If Janet was to win, she would need the element of surprise, and although Rose trusted Sofie with her life, the fewer people who knew, the better.

Sofie gave an intrigued half smile, but let it go. She knew how these things went ...

'More to the point,' said Rose. 'What's going on with the Aztecs? They've been a thorn in our sides for the entire inquiry, and suddenly they're one of the good guys?'

'Ira's looking into it,' said Sofie. 'I already called him ... he said it looks like something big's going on with the Aztec leadership.'

'Someone finally overthrowing their useless leader?' said Rose.

'Maybe,' said Sofie. 'Stability in that region would be a welcome change ...'

'Any news on your missing demon?' said Rose, but she knew what the answer would be ...

Sofie shook her head.

'Where could they be going?' said Rose.

'I thought maybe to the Templars ... but now, I don't know ...'

'Seems too subtle for Jamie,' said Rose.

'Maybe the mysterious West Coast,' said Sofie. 'Or maybe some new cult has sprung up ...'

'Gods, I hope not. The last one was such a nightmare to shut down.'

Sofie laughed. 'You flatter our efforts! We never shut them down … they still exist to this day.'

Rose rolled her eyes. 'Well, at least they're not the rampant threat they used to be …'

'I will give you that much,' said Sofie. 'Any news from Elliot and Gemma?'

Rose shook her head. 'Nothing. I fear we have lost them …'

'Maybe that is where all the missing demons are … it's not like we know anything about the nation …'

Rose shrugged. 'I suppose it's possible, but if they are the culprits, how in the hell are they doing it?'

Sofie's phone buzzed, and she looked at the screen. 'Henrik … on a group call with a number I don't recognize …'

She answered the call, then shrieked with glee. 'Torsten!' she cried. 'By the Gods … my old friend! It is good to see you! What happened to you?'

Torsten beamed through the phone as he pulled a woman into view, his arm wrapped around her. 'I'm with the Aztecs … in fact, I now lead the Aztecs, along with my wife. She is a fearsome warrior, just like you, Sofie. A worthy queen.'

Rose's face split into a broad smile. This was the best—and most unexpected—news she'd had in some time.

'I thought Meredith was my true love, but now I have found Yanah, my soul mate, I see how I was mistaken. She is a marvel … a warrior … a great woman, and we will rule together for many lifetimes.'

'How did you do it?' said Sofie. 'They captured you …'

'Yanah was the leader's most favored blade and sought-after council—a rare light in the Aztec swamp of darkness. She saw in me an opportunity to take control … and it wasn't even hard … we took the place with only ten trusted blades!'

'I am so glad, my friend,' said Sofie, a hand clutched to her chest, 'so very glad to see you … because you are beloved … but also, this is such welcome news for our world.'

Noah lit candle after candle in the small bedroom of the cottage they were borrowing for the night. They needed to be outside the shield, so were staying in the village. Zahora watched him as she undressed, then climbed, naked, onto the table set up in the only free space. She shivered as she lay face down, the cool air assaulting her skin. Noah covered her with a warm towel, the feel of it blissful, her eyes fluttering closed as she waited with anticipation for the first touch of his hands.

The smell of lavender and eucalyptus filled the air, and Zahora breathed deeply, letting the scent soothe her. Noah positioned himself by her head, placed his hot, oiled hands on her skin, and dropped a kiss on her neck. 'Ready whenever you are,' he said.

'Thank you,' she said, twisting to look up at him, stroking his leg.

'I'm glad I can help,' he said, coasting his hands down her back.

'Mmm,' said Zahora, exhaling as she dropped her head back to the table, tension melting from her muscles. She closed her eyes and reached for the Nexus, not using the Pagan wheel, or an anchor stone. She needed the raw, unfettered connection she could only achieve this way, even if it meant forgoing protection. The risk was worth it.

Zahora flew across the Nexus, willing the magic to show her Ame. She had to find her and convince her to come back. The Pagan leaders didn't care that Ame had disappeared—at least past her ability to spill Pagan secrets—but to Zahora, Ame was the only hope of understanding her magic ... her only hope of decent training ...

Zahora had tried using objects Ame had left behind to track her through the standing stone, but none had given the slightest hint of where she was. Zahora had tried using the objects without the stone too, hoping for a vague sense like she'd achieved with Noah. But again, nothing. So this—putting her soul into the Nexus—was the only way ...

Zahora held Ame in her mind, concentrating on her eyes, the color of her hair, her height, mannerisms, expressions ... Something prickled her skin, and she reached for the sensation, following its speeding retreat. Zahora flew across the Atlantic at such breakneck speed she felt faint, the magic luring her ever further, ever faster ... until it stopped with juddering force.

She recovered from the sickening halt, then took in her surroundings. A large, Roman-inspired pool filled the center of an atrium, and outside, Zahora could see figures ... three of them sitting with their backs to her, and one standing ... Ame.

'Why are you here?' said the woman in the middle of the three seated figures.

Zahora longed to move forward, so she could better hear and see them, but it was too dangerous. Ame was orders of magnitude more powerful than

Alerac, and he had sensed her presence in the Nexus and almost killed her. If Ame found Zahora here, she most likely wouldn't make it out alive.

'My nation has disbanded,' said Ame, 'and I've heard intriguing things about you.'

'Such as?' said the seated man, shifting impatiently.

'That you're forward thinking … have a different way of seeing the world … don't respect the Registerium, or the other nations … that you're more like the nations of old.'

'What does that mean?' said the third seated figure.

Wait … was that … it couldn't be … Gemma?

'It means,' said the other seated woman, 'that we make hard choices when we need to, and we protect our own, my Goddess.'

Ame looked up, and Zahora let out a panicked gasp. She threw herself backwards, willing her soul back into her body, but Ame held out a hand, grasping her, choking her.

'No …' said Zahora, her voice no more than a whisper.

'What are you doing?' said the man, his words betraying his alarm. He jumped to his feet and grabbed Ame's shoulders, the action severing the hold Ame had on Zahora.

A sudden force yanked Zahora around the middle, and seconds later, she was back in her body, Noah's hands kneading her skin, his voice crooning soothing sounds in her ear.

Zahora pushed herself up, gasping for air, and Noah took hold of her face, relief washing over his features. 'Thank God,' he said. 'I thought you were having a seizure … I didn't know what to do …'

Zahora closed her eyes and concentrated on breathing. She told herself she was fine … alive … still in possession of her soul. But it had been close.

'Whatever you did, it worked,' she said finally, her pulse still hammering. 'Ame had me …'

'Oh my God,' said Noah, wrapping her in a towel and pulling her to his chest. 'Please never do that again. I …'

'It's okay,' she said, as much to herself as to him. 'I'm fine. I need clothes … we have to find Rose … right away.'

Rose, Caspar, and Raina sat in the sitting room at Maltings, drinking red wine in front of the crackling fire.

'Do you trust Janet?' said Raina. 'I mean, she was the most levelheaded Templar I met, but she's also cutthroat and ambitious.'

'She's trying to take over the Templar nation … of course she's ambitious … but I trust her more than I trust Jamie, which is … something.'

'Or it's all a ploy,' said Caspar, 'to get us to help save the Templars from destruction.'

'Maybe,' said Rose, 'but you can't deny Jamie's really fucked everything up … he took a strong, powerful nation, and squandered every advantage they had.'

'And they've lost any hope of Aztec support now Torsten's taken over,' said Caspar.

Raina smiled. 'It makes me want to dance every time I think about it.'

'You and me both,' said Rose. 'Worst case, we support the Templars during their trial, and they stab us in the back afterwards. In which case, we're well within our rights to finish them off.'

'If we can get our friends to support us ...' said Caspar.

'It comes down to whether we can trust Janet ...' said Raina, before taking a long sip of her wine. She rolled the liquid around her mouth, turning the question over in her mind. 'I think we can.'

'I do too,' said Rose.

The door to the sitting room crashed open, and an icy draft sucked at the warm air.

'Close the door!' said Raina, as Noah and Zahora scampered in.

'It's Ame ...' said Zahora, as Noah swung the door closed.

Rose circled her hand in an impatient gesture that implied Zahora should continue.

'I tracked Ame using magic, and ... she's with the West Coast nation. She'd just got there ... and Gemma was there—with their leaders—sitting like she was one of them ... and ... they called her *Goddess*!'

'And then Ame attacked Zahora,' said Noah, reaching for her hand.

'But Noah pulled me back.'

'I thought we agreed it was too dangerous to spy magically on the West Coast ... or on Ame ... or pretty much anyone!' said Rose.

Zahora bowed her head. 'I know, and I'm sorry. I was only trying to get a sense of where Ame was. My plan was to find her rough location and then leave. But ... I was so shocked ... and if I'm honest, intrigued ... I was sucked into the conversation ...'

Caspar pulled out his phone and called Ira. 'Ame's with the West Coast nation,' he said. 'Great, thanks.' He hung up. 'Ira's going to search the surveillance footage around their headquarters to see if he can find anything more.'

'Why would they call Gemma a goddess?' said Zahora. She looked around at each of the older demons' faces, as though expecting one of them to know.

'Your guess is as good as ours,' said Rose. 'Maybe it's part of how they convinced Gemma and Elliot to stay.'

'Gemma was never one for flattery though ...' said Raina, frowning.

'Maybe their ranks include the title *Goddess*?' suggested Caspar, half-heartedly.

'Maybe,' said Rose, 'but goddesses are generally superior to mortal ranks ...'

'And if that is the case,' said Raina, 'then we're dealing with extreme narcissists.'

'Gemma's never been that way,' said Rose.

'No,' Raina agreed, 'but at this stage, we can't rule anything out.'

'Explain yourself,' said Ares, holding Ame's arm behind her back.

'You are unprotected ... magically speaking,' said Ame. 'I sensed a threat, was preparing to deal with it, and then you stopped me.'

'You're lying,' said Aphrodite. 'You came to kill us.'

Ame went very still. She looked Aphrodite directly in the eye, not a bit intimidated. 'If I had come to kill you,' said Ame, 'you would already be dead. You would be wise not to underestimate me.'

Gemma believed the magik; she'd conducted enough interrogations to know when someone was telling the truth, and Ame was.

'Where have you been?' said Gemma.

Ame gave her a perplexed look. Now the look … that was a lie.

'You said your nation no longer exists,' said Gemma, 'and yet you've had time to learn about our existence … so … where have you been?'

'I've been with the Pagan nation,' said Ame, watching Gemma closely.

Ares and Aphrodite turned their heads, doing the same.

'Why did you leave?' said Gemma.

'Let's just say I didn't get along with Raina.'

Gemma laughed. 'You wouldn't be the first.'

'You may stay,' said Aphrodite, 'but you will be watched, and you will tell us everything you learned from the Pagans.'

Ame inclined her head. 'As you wish.'

The rest of the day passed in a blur of training, handshaking, and preparation for the evening's activities. Aphrodite insisted on a grueling schedule of nightly entertainment, and Gemma was both expected to attend—it was her duty to those who worshiped her—and to look the part.

This was no easy feat, and involved endless sessions with beauticians and trainers. She enjoyed the workouts—at least they were familiar—but could live without the beautification. Although, she had to admit, at the start it had been nice to be pampered, and for those pampering her to consider it an honor … she had never, in all her lifetimes, experienced that glow.

She'd allowed Hades to accompany her to the night's festivities, although she had no clue what they were. Elliot had barely batted an eye when she'd told him, and that had stirred something in her … something ugly, like irritation.

As she entered the dining hall with Hades, she wondered if Elliot cared about what might happen … about what would inevitably happen if she kept spending time alone with him.

They donned masks as they entered, and as Gemma slipped hers on, she felt immediately emboldened. It was a shield … a veil of shadow … an invitation to indulge in the illicit.

Hades handed her a blood red Kir Royale. She raised her glass to him, meeting his smoldering eyes, then took a sip, bubbles popping sensually on her tongue. The music, the cocktail, the dim lighting, her dress, the mask … together they made her drunk, excitable, brazen …

'Dance with me,' she said, and he complied without hesitation. He placed their glasses on a low table, then slipped a hand around her waist, his fingers gliding across the satin silk to sit low on her back. Prickles of desire sang in her blood, making her loose … lightheaded.

Gemma lost track of time as they danced, and drank, and danced some more. She had no idea who else was at the party, or if there was entertainment on offer besides the music, and she didn't care. She knew the room watched on with interest, speculating if tonight would finally be the night. Gemma reveled in the knowledge that they were talking about her. No longer in the background. No longer expendable. No longer given the jobs no one else wanted.

Something in the back of her mind told her that was unfair … that the Pagans valued her, and she had never once complained about the jobs they'd assigned. Even so, they didn't appreciate her like this … like Aphrodite and Ares … like Hades …

Gemma wasn't sure how they ended up in Hades' room … if that's where they were. She remembered stumbling along a corridor, remembered the feel of his hand in hers … big and smooth … so unlike Elliot's. But not the opening of the door, or walking to the balcony.

Hades looked out to sea, his face illuminated by the full moon, and Gemma was struck once more by his beauty. Tall, dark, lean, handsome, with the confidence of someone who always got their way in the end. She wondered if anyone had ever said no to him, but wasn't sure she could form the sentence to ask.

He turned back towards her. 'Don't you agree?' he said.

Had he been talking? She'd been mesmerized by his face, but hadn't realized he'd been saying words.

'Huh?' she said.

He cocked his head to one side, studying her, then smiled a dimpled smile. Had he always had dimples? Or had she never really seen him smile?

'It'll be better to show you, anyway,' he said, stepping into her space. He put his hands on her waist and pushed her back a step, so her back was flat against a cold stone pillar. He crowded her, the musky, enticing smell of him enveloping her.

She tipped her head back as he slid a hand to her neck, the caress of his fingers making her melt. 'Kiss me,' she murmured, her eyes fluttering closed, her lips tingling in anticipation.

Firm lips pressed against hers, and she gasped at the feel of it … so different to kissing Elliot … strange, but … she liked it. His kisses were confident, self-assured, dominant, and she surrendered to them.

Hades pushed deeper, probing her mouth with his tongue. He tasted like smoke … a taste she hadn't experienced since … she pushed the thought aside as Hades skirted a hand up from her hip, across her waist, to her breast.

But the same assertiveness she'd considered a welcome change only seconds before became something altogether different in her mind. Forceful, pushy, hurried. The kiss hadn't changed … but it had.

She turned her head, freeing her lips, and panted for air. Hades didn't seem to notice anything was amiss as he buried his face in her neck. He pressed his hips against her, his erection hard and uncomfortable against her belly, and a wave from the past washed over her … panic … terror.

She didn't want this … didn't want him … She pushed him back, no shred of lust remaining, but he moved back into her space, pressing against her once more. 'You like it rough, Goddess?'

'No,' she said, pushing him away with more force than she'd intended. He stumbled, and she fled, fumbling with the door handle in her drunken state. Her pulse pounded in her ears as she listened for footsteps, worried he would chase her.

The chill of the stone floor against her bare feet helped her focus … when had she taken off her shoes? She reached the end of the corridor, and found, to her surprise, Elliot walking past. Was he a mirage?

She sobbed at the sight of him, and he threw up his arms in surrender. 'I wasn't spying on you … I just … wanted to make sure you were okay … just in case …'

Gemma flung herself into his arms and clung to him as tears poured down her cheeks. Everything about him was right … the smell, the feel, the way he touched her … treasured her. How had she not seen it before? How could she have been so foolish as to take him for granted?

He picked her up, making soothing sounds in her ear. 'It's okay,' he said. 'It's all okay.'

'I love you,' she said, again and again, her face pressed into his neck. 'I'm so sorry.'

'Sussh,' he said. 'You don't have anything to be sorry for.'

'I should never …'

'Gemma,' he said, as he placed her on their bed. How were they here already? 'You've done nothing wrong.'

He made to get up, and she clutched at him. 'Don't leave me.'

He stroked her hair. 'I'm getting you some water. I'll be right back.'

She nodded and closed her eyes, but her head spun, making her nauseous. More tears spilled from her eyes … how could she have been so stupid?

Chapter 10

Rose felt like a Yo-Yo, with so much travelling backwards and forwards to the Registerium. She'd had enough of it, but at least today some good would result; a new demon registering to their nation.

The Pagans had neglected to compete for new blood for many lifetimes … it had been remiss of her as their leader, but she'd been focusing on other things … namely, preventing war with the Templars. But soon, a lack of fresh blood would impact their nation, and Rose couldn't let that happen.

Noah stepped up beside her, placing his hand on the Registerium's standing stone. Zahora was at Maltings, much to her displeasure, but they couldn't risk the shield coming down … not at a time like this, when no one knew where Jamie and Pixie had gone.

Pablo had returned to the Registerium when the inquiry had concluded, and he stood next to them, ready to document the registration.

'Ready?' said Rose.

'Yes,' said Noah. He looked nervous … was fidgety … and Rose remembered her own first registration. It had been different back then—before the Registerium had been formed—but it had been nerve-wracking all the same.

'Then say the words,' said Rose, not unkindly, although a hint of impatience crept in.

'I pledge my allegiance to the Pagan nation, from now until the end of this life,' said Noah. He waited a beat, then looked round at Rose and Pablo.

'You felt it?' said Rose, her brow furrowed at his expression.

'I felt nothing,' said Noah. 'Did I do it wrong?'

'You did it fine …' said Pablo, his forehead also creased. 'You're sure … you felt nothing at all?'

'Not a thing,' said Noah.

'Have you had any other registrations since the inquiry?' said Rose.

Pablo shook his head. 'No, but I don't see how that could have done anything …'

'Try it again,' said Rose.

Noah took a deep breath, then put his hand firmly on the stone and repeated the words.

'Well?' said Rose, praying it had worked … because otherwise, this was another thing to add to her never-ending to do list.

Noah shook his head. 'Maybe I'm not a demon after all …' he said, his voice small.

'You're a demon alright,' said Pablo. 'I'll have to get the magiks to investigate …'

'Can you wait?' said Rose. 'At least until you've tried to register someone else? I don't want rumors about trouble with Pagan registrations …'

'I have another scheduled for tomorrow,' said Pablo. 'I can wait until then.'

'Which nation?' said Rose, without thinking. 'Sorry … I know you can't tell me that.'

'I will tell you the outcome,' said Pablo.

Rose nodded. 'Thank you, old friend.'

Pablo left them, and Rose shook her head in frustration. This was supposed to be a simple task to accomplish … a celebratory item to tick off her list. Instead, her life was nothing but problem on top of problem.

'You can't stay here,' said Rose. 'If a hostile nation discovers you're here, and that you're unregistered, they may try to steal you.'

'Steal me?' said Noah, recoiling at her words.

'It doesn't happen often, but the way things are going, I'd rather not risk it.'

'Where should I go?'

'Back to Maltings. I'll send for you when the problem has been rectified.'

Zahora hung up the phone and headed immediately for the stone circle. Finally, she could do something. Ame had helped her see the bonds as they swirled into the Registerium's stone. If there was a problem with the magic, maybe she could see that too …

She sat on the altar stone. Talli would probably tell her off if she saw, but Zahora didn't care, and the ground was wet and muddy. She felt for the Nexus, connected, then located her own bond, following it at breakneck speed, although without employing the Triskelion … she'd finally learnt her lesson on that front.

155

But to her surprise, the journey was shorter this time, and her bond, instead of leading her to Scotland, took her to Wales, to the standing stone in the Pagans' magic compound. Zahora halted just before hitting the stone and gaped at her surroundings.

'Fuck,' she said, then pulled herself back. She tried to travel across the Nexus to Scotland, but something prevented her from moving away from her bond … the shield. 'Bugger.'

She put her soul back into her body, then jumped to her feet, shouting for Meredith. She found her in the barn, which was filled with sweaty, pissed-off looking demons, Meredith perching on the back of a bench at the front, instructing them. Zahora didn't let the scowls deter her.

'Meredith,' said Zahora, rushing towards the fearsome woman. 'I need your help.'

Meredith didn't look at her. 'Hold the squat,' she shouted at the others, who, Zahora now noticed, were squatting on one leg. It looked painful … she would scowl too if she were them. 'What's happened?'

Zahora continued to watch the poor, squatting souls, then realized Meredith was talking to her. 'I think the bond between our nation and the Registerium's stone has broken,' she hissed, hoping her voice was low enough that the others didn't hear.

Meredith stood, towering over Zahora. 'Fuck,' she said.

'I need to check, but I can't do that inside the shield …'

'Let's go,' said Meredith, selecting five others to join them. 'Higgins, take over.' A scary looking male demon in the front row nodded, but Meredith was already on her way out. Zahora hurried to catch up.

'Do you know where …' said Zahora.

'… in the kitchen,' said Meredith, cutting her off.

They took off at a run towards the house, finding Alerac at the kitchen table, preparing tinctures.

'We need you,' said Meredith.

Alerac threw down his pestle and jumped to his feet. They explained on the way, grabbing warm coats and boots before heading out into the cold winter air.

They ran for the shield, Alerac letting them through, and Zahora sank to the ground as soon as she was on the other side, no longer caring about the water seeping through her clothes.

She connected to the Nexus, and flew for Scotland, sorely tempted by the Triskelion. She didn't use it … she would learn from her mistakes.

She searched for the magical bonds, finding it harder to see them now she wasn't following her own. As she neared the Registerium, there was no spiral stretching out as far as the eye could see. In fact, there were no bonds at all …

What had happened? But as she drew back towards her body, creeping dread wrapped around her guts. Had she done this when she'd crashed into the Registerium's stone? Had Ame set her up? Zahora had blacked out when she'd hit it and hadn't been back since … had she severed every nation's connection with the Registerium's standing stone?

As Zahora landed back in her body, Meredith's phone buzzed. 'Yes,' she said. 'Oh my God. Okay … will do.' She hung up and looked at Alerac and Zahora's expectant faces with an expression of glee. 'Ira's found a way into the West Coast nation … finally, a break.'

'That's good,' said Zahora, 'because in other news, the Registerium's stone is completely fucked.'

Caspar put his phone on speaker so the others could hear. Someone inside the West Coast had downloaded a black-market messaging app, created by Ira. The app had spread quickly across the nation's lower ranks, which meant Ira had eyes and ears across pretty much everything. Everything except from whatever the leaders were up to. None of them seemed to carry phones at all.

'Their leaders—Ares and Aphrodite—have called them together for an announcement,' said Ira.

They couldn't see anything, as the phone they were listening to was in someone's pocket, and they had to strain to hear the words, but Raina sat on the edge of her seat, bristling with hope.

'Some of you asked when we would be ready,' said a deep, male voice, 'and I can tell you, that time is now.'

A cheer went up, and if the man kept speaking, they couldn't hear it. The crowd quietened, and a woman took over. 'Our Pentalpha has assembled, and we are ready to take back what is ours by right ... what has always been ours, but was stolen from us ... Mount Olym-' The crowd cheered again, drowning out the woman's words.

'Did she just say Mount Olympus?' said Zahora.

'I think so,' said Meredith.

'That's in our territory, right?' said Zahora.

'Yes,' said Raina.

'What did they mean about their Pentalpha assembling?' said Caspar.

Everyone drew a blank. 'The Pentalpha is a magical symbol, of course,' said Alerac, 'a five-pointed star …'

'Does he mean five people have assembled?' said Zahora. 'Or five types of magic? Are there five different types of magic?'

Alerac shrugged. 'Depends what you call a different type of magic …'

'We're searching the other devices now,' said Ira, 'seeing if we can get a visual … wait … hang on, I'm sending one now.'

Raina pulled out her phone and showed the blurry picture to the others. They crowded round, straining to see, but it was on an angle, and mostly obscured by a pillar.

'Here's another,' said Ira, and a new picture appeared on Raina's phone.

'Five people,' said Caspar, counting the figures standing on a raised platform.

'Oh my Gods,' said Meredith. 'One of them is Gemma!'

Gemma could barely believe what she was hearing. Take back Mount Olympus? A Pentalpha—whatever that was—that she was supposedly part of? Aphrodite had told her to smile and wave before pushing her out onto the platform, standing alongside Hades, Ares, Aphrodite, and a man she didn't know, but who had a distinctly Viking look about him: tall, long plated blond hair, copious facial hair.

159

She was ushered back off the stage and into a private room, and Aphrodite introduced Gemma to the man. 'Hephaestus, this is the Goddess of Spring, although she prefers Gemma. Goddess, this is Hephaestus, God of Fire, and my ex-husband,' she said with a laugh.

'Call me Hefi,' he said, holding out his hand. 'Hephaestus is such a mouthful.'

Gemma's head swam. Aphrodite's ex-husband? She didn't know what to say …

'She had an affair with Ares,' Hefi said in a low, conspiratorial voice. 'I miss my Aphrodite … I mean, look at her … who wouldn't? But I am no longer angry, and we are part of something bigger than ourselves.'

'To take back Mount Olympus?' said Gemma, recovering some of her wits.

'The mountain, and everything else that's ours,' he said. 'Just think of it … ruling again … living as true gods, with no equal.'

Gemma did think of it, and the thought did little to warm her. She forced a coy smile to her lips. 'Indeed,' she said. 'What do you remember, of when we ruled before?'

Hefi blinked several times in quick succession. 'I have only impressions,' he said, after a long pause. 'But I know I shall like it when we recreate our old lives, hey?'

He didn't seem entirely sure of himself, but she said, 'Of course,' with complete vehemence. 'How long have you been here? Not long, I think?'

He shook his head. 'No, not long. But long enough to know this is my true nation … my true home.'

'You were Viking?'

'I was. And you a Pagan?'

Gemma inclined her head, wondering what in the world was going on.

160

The Templar trial began the day after Noah's failed registration, and Rose could barely focus, waiting impatiently to hear from Pablo if the other registration had also failed. She fully expected it to, after Zahora's discovery, but she held onto a tiny shred of hope that it might not be so bad.

The Registrar—a man everyone knew was not long for his position—strode to the front of the light-filled room. They were upstairs in the castle, the room set up like a court, and packed with demons from all nations.

'Demons,' said the Registrar, 'I shall not preside over this court, given the obvious conflict of interest. My deputy will do so.' The Registrar looked pale and shifty, his eyes frequently flicking to the Templars in the room.

A woman in the front row stood and made her way to a desk by the windows. She sat facing the room, the Registrar leaving without another word.

'Something's going on,' Rose said into Malcolm's ear. 'I can feel it. See what you can find out.'

Malcolm nodded, then made for the exit as the Deputy Registrar began her preamble. Gemma occupied Rose's thoughts … and the Registerium's broken stone …

'… call my first witness, Jamie Vanderveld, leader of the Templar nation.'

Rose couldn't help but join the collective gasp that filled the room. Sure, Jamie had been called, but nobody had really entertained the notion he would come ...

Jamie took the stand. First, the Deputy would ask all she wanted, and then the nations would get a chance. It was a long, tedious, and invariably repetitive process. Nations were not permitted to repeat a question already asked, but that rarely stopped anyone from asking something only microscopically different ...

The Deputy's questions were not overly interesting. Even if she'd had no part to play in the Registerium's corruption—and that was a big if—she was still most likely loyal to the Registrar. He had, after all, hand selected her for this role. One of the many things that needed to change ...

The Deputy finished with little information gained, and Rose was up next. She stood and walked to the front.

'I bring before the court evidence of the Templar nation using guns to overthrow the Slayers—a prohibited activity for Registerium members—and the documents drawn up to support Raina Halabi's enforced—and fake—transfer from the Pagan to the Templar nation,' Rose said, then paused. 'Why is it that you believe yourself to be above the rules?'

'That's funny coming from you,' said Jamie.

'Neither I, nor my nation, are on trial here,' said Rose, 'and deflection will not work on a room full of demons, most of whom are older and doubtless wiser than you. Please answer the question.'

'No comment,' said Jamie.

A titter of laughter rippled across the air. 'You know why they laugh?' said Rose.

Jamie sat still, saying nothing.

'They laugh, because they remember a time when you could be strung up for such insolence in front of an audience as mighty as this. But you wouldn't know that, because no one ever taught you better, and you never thought to teach yourself.'

Jamie scowled.

'Still no answer?' said Rose. 'You agree then, that you believe yourself to be above the rules? Rules which have kept us in a state of peace for many years … that have created a fair playing field for all …'

Jamie smirked. 'No comment,' he said again.

Rose took a breath. 'Here is evidence proving that you were blackmailing and bribing the Registrar, in return for access to records and favors. What …' But before she could complete her question, the door at the back of the room thundered open.

A young, agitated male demon appeared. 'The Registrar … he's dead!'

And then a second demon came rushing in, this one going to Jamie, whispering in his ear. Jamie jumped to his feet. 'I must request a recess,' he said.

'Granted,' said the Deputy. 'We meet again in one hour.'

As the Deputy hurried from the room, Rose caught sight of Malcolm pushing against the tide of exiting demons.

He finally reached her, out of breath. 'Looks like the Registrar truly killed himself, and,' he gasped for air, 'Janet's coup has begun.'

'Then I doubt Jamie will be back in an hour …'

'And today's registration failed too,' said Malcolm, his voice so low that Rose could barely hear him.

Rose inhaled deeply, held it, then exhaled. 'When will it end?'

The Registerium was in total chaos, no one quite sure whether the Registrar had killed himself, or if he'd been the victim of a brutal attack. Rose cared not at all, and his eyes were intact, so either way, he would most likely be back in another life to tell the tale.

Avoiding the commotion as best she could, she sought out Pablo, to discuss the much bigger and more concerning issue of the failed registrations. She found him in the room at the end of the corridor along from the courtroom, in his usual place of work.

'I informed the Registrar,' said Pablo, 'but he barely seemed to hear me.'

'You know he's dead?'

'Oh … no … I didn't …' said Pablo, collapsing into a seat. 'I hope I didn't push him over the edge … he seemed … preoccupied. Maybe I shouldn't have left him alone …'

'You couldn't have known what he was about to do …'

Pablo raised his eyebrows. 'Another inquiry, no doubt.'

Rose grunted in frustration. 'Malcolm told me today's registration failed too?'

Pablo nodded.

'Zahora says the magic bonds are no longer connected to the stone here. She said her own bond travels straight to the Pagan stone. No middleman.'

'Well, then the magic's broken ... my job is defunct, and registrations must take place within each nation, as they did before.'

'Unless we find a way to fix it,' said Rose, prickling with annoyance. Was he going to give up so easily?

'Why?' he said.

'So demons can't be stolen, or forced into nation transfers they don't want.'

Pablo waved a hand. 'That still goes on. Look at what happened to Raina.'

'Nowhere near as much as it did before the Registerium, and if we can push through reforms, force each nation to allow the free movement of people ... then we can stop it altogether. But only if registrations take place in a central location. Otherwise, free movement will make it worse.'

'Indeed,' said Pablo. 'It would be in everyone's interests to restrict free movement if the Registerium ceases to exist ... that way, at least demons can't be stolen, and forced to switch nations without their home nation's permission.'

'We can't allow that to happen,' said Rose. 'We just can't.'

'Then what do you propose we do about it?' said Pablo. 'It's my duty to inform the leaders of the Registerium about the failed registrations, and I must also report what you've told me about the bonds.'

'Do you think they'll make it public?'

Pablo shrugged. 'Depends who's selected as the next leader ... a decision that will distract them for a few days at least.'

'I could suggest we discuss reforms immediately,' said Rose, 'before a new leader's selected.'

'It would be wrong to do that without telling everyone about the bonds ...'

'Unless we find a way to reinstate them first ...'

'How?' said Pablo. 'No one has magiks anymore. Who would do it?'

'We have Zahora.'

'You would trust her with something of such great consequence? She's impulsive and inexperienced ... it would be a disaster.'

'She learns fast,' said Rose. Although she knew Pablo was right. And maybe Zahora had caused the bonds to break in the first place ... she'd smashed into the Registerium's stone after all. A dark thought trickled through Rose's mind, like sand sinking through a newly opened hole. Ame had been there ... teaching Zahora ... she'd encouraged Zahora to follow her bond. Had Ame planned to break the Registerium's magic all along?

'Push for access to the Registerium's records,' said Pablo. 'Maybe there's something in those that could help.'

Rose nodded. He was right ... maybe the answer was sitting beneath their feet, just waiting to be discovered.

Janet sat at Jamie's desk and put her feet up on the glass surface. Her hands were bloodied, and she was exhausted, but she'd taken the nation. She'd taken the mother fucking nation. She tried to make it sink in, but she felt ... exactly as she had before, only with a side helping of relief. And now she had a new source of apprehension ... running a nation. A big one. She put her feet back on the floor … this felt nothing like she wanted it to.

Her three generals trooped in, their usual dower expressions on their faces.

'Pixie escaped,' said one. 'I'm sorry … someone must have tipped her off.'

'And Jamie's plane landed, but he wasn't on it,' said the second. 'We're not sure if he's still in Scotland, or elsewhere.'

'But we have rounded up all those loyal to Jamie, and given them the true death,' said the third general—a petite woman with shiny blond hair. She looked like an acrobat, not a cold-blooded killer.

Janet's stomach roiled. She was a diplomat, not a warrior … but the actions had been necessary. 'Very good,' she said. 'Thank you all for your loyal service. Keep looking for Pixie and Jamie. He has a … facility in Mexico experimenting with genetics. Please ensure it's destroyed.'

The generals nodded.

'And close down the Slayers' building. I want their organization dismantled … and … do any of you know what happened to the Egyptian Leader's son? He was captured …'

The generals shook their heads. 'We'll find out,' said the first.

Janet nodded. 'Thank you. Please keep me informed, and send in the accountant on your way out.'

Rose was deep in thought, looking out across the loch, when her phone buzzed. 'Janet!' she said. 'You were successful?'

'I was,' said Janet, who sounded like the burden of leadership already weighed on her shoulders.

'Heavy losses?' said Rose.

'No,' said Janet, 'but Jamie and Pixie got away. We're looking for them.'

'He's like a rat, that one,' said Rose. 'Not a moment's hesitation before fleeing the sinking ship.'

'I'd feel better if I knew he was dead … but those loyal to him are.'

'Congratulations,' said Rose. 'What now?'

'Change,' said Janet. 'I'm looking for Heba's son, and I've instructed the Registerium to stop the recall on Callie, and to transfer her from my nation to yours.'

'The Registerium was causing the pain then?' said Rose. They'd suspected, but hadn't known for sure.

'Yes,' said Janet. 'We don't have magiks of our own. I found out they could do it in the Registerium's records, and their magik followed the instructions … although it took many tries.'

'Then you don't know how to transfer a demon to another nation without going through the Registerium?'

Janet laughed. 'I can't think of a single example of anyone being allowed to transfer out of the Templar nation. And no, we have neglected to use magic for a long time. We have no magiks of our own … certainly none with any power or experience.' Silence filled the line. 'Why?'

Rose sighed. 'The Registerium's in chaos … did they say when they would do the transfer?'

'No,' said Janet, 'but I'm flying in tomorrow; we can do it then.'

'Good,' said Rose, then hung up. But in fact, it wasn't good at all.

The following day, Zahora took down the shield, and every demon at Maltings packed their bags. Janet had publicly announced her intent to release Callie from the Templar nation, and Callie's pain was gone. Although, maybe it had been gone for a while, since the Registerium's magic was broken …

They flew to Scotland, Zahora and Callie overjoyed to have escaped their cage, but everyone else seemed nervous. Zahora supposed they were worried about a double cross from Janet. Maybe she hadn't overthrown Jamie at all, and this was all some big ploy …

She was just happy to be out in the big wide world, and not be tied to the shield any longer. She hadn't felt so refreshed in weeks.

They joined Rose in the large house the Registerium had allocated to the Pagans for the duration of the Templar inquiry. Zahora was glad to find lunch spread out on a rustic wooden table, in a room with sweeping ceilings, circular lighting fixtures hanging on chains, and antlers on the walls.

'Janet arrived this morning,' said Rose. 'She admitted to almost all the crimes the Templars are accused of. The Registerium is keen to wrap up the trial quickly, given the other challenges they face, so have found them guilty, and told them to reform.'

Most of the demons sitting round the table laughed, incredulous.

'They're to determine their own punishment?' said Raina.

'What if Janet's lying?' said Talli.

'These are strange times,' said Rose. 'The Registerium's magic is broken, and they're leaderless ... if they'd decreed anything else, how would they have enforced it?'

'The magic's really broken then?' said Talli.

Rose nodded. 'And there's no one left with the skill to fix it. I'm not even sure the nations will want to fix it when they find out the magic's gone. The vote to disband the Registerium was so close ... but regardless, we will search the records for a way to reinstate the magic. All of us. That's why you're here.'

'And we will transfer Callie to our nation,' said Marla, from the entrance.

'Marla!' said Rose. 'I am glad to see you.'

'Likewise,' said Marla. 'I've been stuck training all of those damn magiks you sent. None of them shows any promise ... Has Janet agreed to the transfer?'

'She has,' said Rose.

'Then we must find another stone,' said Marla. 'Until we know the extent of the damage, it would be foolish to trust the one here.'

They located another stone half an hour's drive from the castle, and met Janet there. She came alone to face almost the whole Pagan leadership.

'You're brave,' said Raina, as Janet approached.

'Or stupid,' said Meredith, her hand on her knife.

'I come in peace,' said Janet.

'So you say ...' said Raina.

'And if you kill me, Heba will never get her son back.'

'He's alive?' said Rose, turning sharply.

'He is,' said Janet, 'although he's in a bad way. The Slayers had him ... were torturing him. We're fixing him up and will return him as soon as it's possible. But if you kill me, you kill him too ...'

Rose nodded. 'No one's killing anyone. We're here to transfer Callie, nothing more.'

Janet nodded. 'How do we do that?'

'Place your hand on the stone,' Marla said to Janet.

Janet tramped down the brambles as she stepped up to the listing, lichen-covered stone, and did as she was told.

'Now, Callie, you touch the stone too.'

Callie stepped forward, shy under their collective scrutiny. She touched the stone, looking back at Raina for reassurance. Raina smiled and nodded encouragingly.

'Callie,' said Marla, 'please confirm the nation you would like to be a part of.'

'I want to be a Pagan,' she said, absolutely resolute.

'Janet,' said Marla, 'please release Callie.'

'I release this demon, Callie, from the bond tying her to the Templar nation.'

'Thank you,' said Marla. 'Callie, did you feel anything?'

Callie shook her head.

Marla frowned, but continued. 'Please pledge your allegiance to the Pagan nation.'

Callie nodded. 'I pledge my allegiance to the Pagan nation?' she said, sounding unsure and tripping over the words.

'Say it firmly,' said Marla.

'I pledge my allegiance to the Pagan nation!' Callie shouted.

'Did you feel anything that time?' said Marla.

Callie shook her head again, looking worried.

'Hmm,' said Marla. 'That's all it usually takes … unless …' She looked suspiciously at Janet. 'You are in charge of the nation, yes?'

'Yes,' said Janet. 'The nation answers to me … unless Jamie has to be dead for the magic to recognize my leadership?'

'I don't think so,' said Marla. 'At least, it hasn't been that way in the past.'

'I could look at their bonds?' said Zahora, stepping forward. 'If that helps?'

Marla frowned. 'I don't see how that would help … unless Callie isn't really a member of the Templar nation …'

'She's a member,' said Janet. 'I was there when she registered.'

'Then …' said Marla.

'Oh, for goodness' sake,' said Zahora. 'I'm doing it; it can't hurt.'

Marla looked put out, but stepped back from the stone. Zahora stepped forward, rubbing off a piece of lichen as she connected with the Nexus. She concentrated on her own bond, bringing it to the fore, making it shine. Then, when all their bonds became visible, Zahora concentrated on those attached to Callie and Janet, which hovered side by side in the air.

Zahora followed them, once again temped to use the Triskelion to speed her trip across the Atlantic, but once again fighting the temptation. She would not screw this up by being rash.

After what seemed like an age, the bonds of other demons littering the air became more concentrated, collecting together as they approached the Templars' primary stone.

The stone was atop a mountain, and both Callie's and Janet's bonds terminated there. Zahora wondered what would happen if she reached out and pulled on Callie's bond. Could separating her from the Templar nation be so easy? She should probably ask the others first …

Having confirmed Callie was indeed a Templar, she turned to head back, but a bond protruding from the top of the stone caught her eye. It looked a little different to the others; darker, thicker … and it *pulsed*. Not to mention, it headed straight up into the sky …

Zahora turned her eyes across the world, looking for others that did the same. She saw one … no … two … maybe even more, although she was too far away to be certain. But the Pagan stone didn't have a line that reached into the sky … did it?

Zahora watched closely as she returned to the stone in Scotland, but as she neared the Pagan's stone, she could see no strand reaching skyward.

She returned to her body to find Noah by her side, holding her hand that wasn't pressed against the stone. She squeezed his fingers as she told the others what she'd seen.

'I can't see bonds,' said Marla.

'Neither can I,' said Alerac.

'But why would some nations have a connection to the sky, and others not?' said Zahora. 'Don't we all use the same magic?'

Marla and Alerac looked at each other, drawing a blank.

'Wait,' said Raina. 'No … we don't …' Raina gave Caspar an apologetic look. 'Many years ago, I had an affair.'

'Oh, we know …' said Talli.

173

Meredith chuckled, but Raina continued without a glance in their direction. 'It turns out the man was Ame's son.'

'What?' said Talli.

Christa raised her eyebrows. 'When did you discover this?'

'At Yule,' said Raina.

'Are you the reason she left?' said Christa.

'Maybe,' said Raina. 'I think she wanted to meet me, and tell me she held me responsible for his death …'

'Great,' said Talli, 'another enemy to worry about.'

'Were you?' said Christa.

'Yes,' said Raina, without hesitation. 'It's … a long story, but he taught me magic … magic he'd learned from his mother—Ame—and the Nation of Stars. He was the reason I sought out Alerac.'

'Hang on,' said Alerac. 'The man who summoned you … that was Ame's son?'

'Yes,' said Raina, 'but he went off the rails … honestly might always have been … He told me many things that turned out to be false, or exaggerations, but he also told me there was more than one Sphere: one below us, one above us, and probably more besides. What if that's true, and the Templar stone is connected to the magic of a different Sphere?'

'I don't know,' said Marla. 'I've devoted hundreds of years to magic, and I've never heard of this.'

'Me neither,' said Alerac.

'Yes,' said Raina, 'but you're insular … Pagan magiks hang out with other Pagan magiks. When was the last time you saw anyone from another nation? And do you remember,' she turned to Caspar, 'that story you told me, about magic sometimes doing more harm than good? Where trying to control arrows on a battlefield could lead to accidents?'

Caspar nodded. 'A Buddhist told me that when I was part of their nation.'

'Have you two ever worked with a magik who could control flying objects?'

'Well …' said Marla. 'I mean … I've heard stories … but they're just stories …'

'What if they're not?' said Raina. 'What if magiks can do those things by calling on a different Sphere?'

'Sky magic …' said Zahora. 'I could try to access it …'

Marla scowled. 'If your past performance is anything to go by, that's a terrible idea.'

'I could follow one of the bonds and see where it goes,' said Zahora, bristling at Marla's tone.

'No,' said Rose, 'at least, not yet. It could be dangerous …'

'Rose is right … we have to focus on transferring Callie,' said Raina. 'Before the connection was broken, nation transfers worked for all nations through the Registerium's stone. If we can find out how it was done, we might be able to replicate it.'

'The records,' said Janet. 'I've been combing them for months; I know where to look.'

Gemma felt like such a fool. She could barely look Elliot in the eye … ever since she'd kissed Hades. And even though Elliot had told her she could … had encouraged her … had put not one single barrier in her way … it didn't make Gemma any less of an idiot.

She watched him pad back from the bathroom, his joggers slung low on his hips. How could she have thought she needed something else? Why would she want anyone but him?

'Hey,' he said, lying behind her, pulling her hair back so he could see her face. 'I know you're not asleep.'

Gemma opened her eyes, her cheeks going red. 'I'm sorry,' she said, still unable to look at him. She buried her head in the pillow.

Elliot's face was a sea of confusion. 'Why?'

'No. I mean … about … about Hades. Please forgive me.'

He spooned her, holding her hand in his against her chest. 'I know,' he said, 'but there's nothing to forgive.'

'But I … I don't know why I even wanted to … explore …' Tears filled her eyes … she'd lost count of how many times she'd cried since the kiss.

'Hey,' he said, kissing her shoulder. 'What you went through … in your past … I've never been through anything like that … not even close. If you want to experience something other than what I can give you, who am I to stop you?'

'Do you want to?' she said. 'To … explore other options?'

'No,' he said gently, 'but I've had other relationships … have done my exploring. I know you're all I want.'

Gemma sobbed. Sometimes she wished he'd shout and throw things, because that was what she deserved … and it would be easier that way.

'Gemma … what happened? Did he …'

'No,' she said. 'We kissed. He got pushy. I ran away. We've only exchanged small talk since.'

She felt the tension melt out of Elliot's arms.

176

'But I still feel dirty ... and guilty ... about leading him on, as well as what I did to you.'

'You did nothing to me,' he said. 'I won't deny I was jealous—wildly jealous—but you needed space. And you didn't lead him on. He threw himself at you, and after you kissed, you decided you didn't want to go any further. And, might I add, he should have waited until you weren't blind drunk ...'

A sob wracked through her.

'I'd love nothing more than to punch him for that, if you'd be so kind as to let me.'

Gemma laughed through her tears. 'I don't think that would help.'

'It would make me feel better,' he said, kissing her neck.

'It brought back memories,' she said, holding his hand to her chest with both of hers.

'I'm sorry,' he said soothingly.

'They were the first flashbacks I've had in this lifetime ... I thought they were over ...'

He stroked her hair. 'What you went through is unimaginable for most ... you suffered for not only one lifetime, but for many ... it's going to take a long time.'

Silent tears flowed down her cheeks as she tried to push away the memories. Memories of being beaten, raped, starved ... the plaything of a repulsive group of demons, with no way out. She clutched his hand harder, rolling herself into a ball.

'It's never going to happen again,' said Elliot. 'You're a Pagan now. You have a family who cares about you ... and you have me.'

'I'm so sorry,' said Gemma. 'This place ... it got under my skin. Everyone's been so nice to me ... called me Goddess. In our nation, no one thinks of me like that ...'

'They do,' said Elliot. 'They just don't show it the same way ... don't realize you'd appreciate it if they did. Honestly, it surprised me ... I thought you preferred it in the background ... I thought you were happy for the likes of Talli to steal the limelight.'

'Being in the background wasn't so much a conscious choice as something I fell into,' said Gemma, trying to find the right words. 'I was the center of attention in the worst possible way for so long ... I guess, in the background, it was easier to hide ... felt more comfortable ... safer. This is the first time I've been the center of attention in a good way ... the first time someone's made me feel so important.'

'I'm sorry,' said Elliot. 'We should have done more to ...'

'No,' said Gemma. 'I don't mean that. I'm not sure I ever could have done this with the Pagans. They know my history ... have opinions about who I am, what I want, how I'll behave ... When I think about casting aside the expectations they have of me, it feels like walking uphill in the dark, alone, dragging bags of sand behind me. I don't have the energy for it.'

'And when we came here, Aphrodite did the heavy lifting for you,' said Elliot.

'Yes,' said Gemma, rolling over. 'Exactly. It was such a relief, and exciting to live a different life ... to be someone else. More than that, Aphrodite told me I was already someone else underneath. All I had to do was believe her. And then she told me Hades and I were meant to be together ... fated ... but that's not true.'

'Aphrodite says a lot of things that aren't true.'

'But why? What does she gain if Hades and I ...' She didn't want to say the words ... didn't want to think about being with anyone but Elliot.

'She enjoys fucking with people ... the puppet master pulling strings. I don't know exactly what they're planning—her and Ares—but nothing about this place is what it seems ...'

'Elliot ...' she said, skeptically. But the earnest expression on his face made her stop. 'Sorry, go on.'

'This complex is chock full of demons who believe they're serving a higher power.'

'Isn't that the case for most nations?' She prickled with discomfort, but made herself listen.

'Some nations worship a God, or Gods, but none of those Gods walk the earth alongside us ...'

Gemma was going to refute his words ... say he was being ridiculous, but then she remembered what Aphrodite claimed to be ... what she claimed Gemma was ... *Goddess.*

'Fuck,' she said. 'They're made to worship us ... me ... the Pentalpha?'

Elliot nodded. 'Believe me when I say you're a goddess in my eyes. I will happily worship you until the end of my days, but I don't believe you're truly a Greek goddess reincarnated. And I don't think you really believe it either.'

Gemma's face went hot, and she rolled away again, embarrassed. Had she really been that stupid? Was everyone else here so stupid?

'How?' But an unwelcome word invaded her brain, small at first, but growing in insistence. It fanned the flames of her humiliation, setting her cheeks on fire. *Cult.*

No, no, no. Not again.

'Gem, Aphrodite's been brainwashing you and everyone else here. She barely tried with me, and that was her mistake, because if she'd done that, instead of trying to drive me away, it probably would have worked.'

'Don't lie.'

'Gemma, look at me.'

He waited, but she was back to not being able to look him in the eye.

'I'm not lying. Gemma ...' he said, gently taking her chin and tipping her eyes up towards his. 'This place seems like a dream come true. Nothing but love, and entertainment, and houses on the beach, but it's not like that for most of the demons here.'

'They told me they wanted to worship me ...'

'Yes, because they genuinely believe you're a goddess. Ares and Aphrodite have brainwashed them. They came from other nations, convinced over the internet. The West Coast found susceptible demons ... those who never quite fitted in, or had grown restless for a different kind of life, or wanted to be someone other than who their nation wanted them to be ... They found their buttons, and they pressed them, eventually helping the demons leave their nations quietly, with no fuss ... helping them come here.'

'It's really a cult?'

Elliot nodded. 'I think so.'

'But what's their higher purpose? What do they ... Mount Olympus ...?'

'The web they've spun is to legitimize war. For who could truly own Mount Olympus but the Greek Gods?'

'Fuck,' said Gemma. 'I should have seen it ... I'm so sorry ... I've helped them. Mount Olympus is in Pagan territory ... they're using me as further justification.'

'None of that matters. All that matters is that you see it now ... and that we figure out a way to stop them.'

'Still nothing?' Noah asked Zahora.

Callie turned her head at the intrusion.

'Hold still, or you'll ruin your plait,' said Zahora.

Callie had given very strict instructions about exactly how her hair should be done, but she kept moving around, and it was infuriating.

'Nothing yet,' said Zahora, 'but we've only just scratched the surface. I'm heading over as soon as Raina gets back.'

They weren't taking any chances with Callie's safety. Jamie could still be in Scotland for all anyone knew, so they guarded Callie round the clock, much to her irritation. She kept trying to lose her chaperones, which kept everyone on their toes.

'Hey,' said Raina.

Callie jumped up with joy, pulling her hair from Zahora's grasp. The plait disintegrated before her eyes … 'Callie!' said Zahora.

'Oops,' said Callie.

'I'll see you later,' said Zahora.

'But my hair!' Callie whined.

'Ask your mum.'

Zahora and Raina shared a long-suffering look as Zahora headed for the door.

'I'll keep you company,' said Noah, following her out.

Zahora took his hand as they stepped into the crisp winter air. They walked in silence down the grand drive, then veered off onto a path through ancient woods that led to the Registerium's castle. The trees creaked in the wind, and Zahora sucked in a deep breath, nature's restorative balm soothing her soul.

'It's so peaceful here,' said Zahora, breaking the comfortable silence.

Noah smiled, but said nothing.

'What's up?' she said, halting him with a hand on his arm.

'It's just the registration stuff. I guess I still feel like an outsider ... and now who knows when I'll be able to register ...'

'No one else thinks of you that way,' said Zahora. 'You're a Pagan.'

'Just not quite as much of a Pagan as everyone else ... and I feel useless ... I'm just hanging around here, waiting for something to happen.'

'Help me search the records.'

'Rose didn't seem keen ...'

'Don't worry about Rose,' said Zahora, waving a dismissive hand. 'She's got so much on her plate, she doesn't seem keen about anything.'

'I don't think ...'

'You're coming with me, and that's the end of it,' said Zahora.

Noah shrugged, and Zahora tugged him forward. 'What is it exactly we're looking for?'

'Anything that references magic, or the Registerium's formation,' said Zahora. 'There has to be a way to reconnect each nation to the Registerium's stone. And even if we can't do that, maybe we can find something to help us understand the bonds that go up into the sky ...'

'Did you notice if any of them belonged to our allies?' said Noah. 'If so, we could ask them for help?'

Zahora stopped in her tracks. 'That's a great idea.' She found a fallen tree and sat on the trunk.

'What are you doing?' said Noah, sitting beside her.

'I'm going to see which nations have bonds that point to the sky.'

Noah rolled his eyes affectionately. 'You're …'

'Amazing … I know.'

Noah leaned into her space. 'Not what I was thinking, but it'll do.' He kissed her, then took her hand. 'Don't do anything stupid.'

'Bring me back if I get into trouble.' She pecked him on the lips, then closed her eyes.

Noah and Zahora found Rose poring over a table full of scrolls in the castle's underground record room.

'Noah had an idea,' said Zahora, without preamble.

Rose looked up, and her eyes flicked from Zahora to Noah and back again. 'Oh?'

'We could ask our allies for help … the ones whose stones have a bond to the sky,' said Zahora.

'If they still have magiks,' said Noah, 'they might know how to do the transfers.'

Rose nodded. 'Make a list, and I'll see if we can trust them …'

'Already done,' said Zahora, handing over a crumpled scrap of paper.

Rose scanned the list of five names: Templars, Animists, Persians, the West Coast, and Buddhists.

'Obviously the Templars can't help,' said Zahora, 'but what about the Buddhists? We're friends with them … right?'

Rose nodded slowly. 'From this list, they would be our first port of call. I'll contact their leader, Tsering, although, you'll have to be patient, the Buddhists don't comply with western timelines.'

'Keep us posted,' said Zahora, excitedly.

Rose nodded, then put her head back down, but Noah lingered.

'Was there something else?' said Rose.

'I want to register as a Pagan,' said Noah.

'Yes, I am aware …'

'No, I mean right away. If we can't use the stone here, then why can't we use the stone in Wales? It should be as simple as me putting my hands on the stone and saying the words, right?'

'Yes,' said Rose, 'but if we do it that way, the Registerium will have no official record. Your allegiance to our nation could be disputed …'

'His bond would be to us,' said Zahora. 'I'd be able to see it.'

'But most wouldn't,' said Rose, 'and what people can't see, they tend not to trust … not to mention, if we stop using the Registerium for our own registrations, and word gets out …'

'It won't,' said Noah.

'It always does, eventually,' said Rose. 'The better course of action is to wait.'

'But …' said Noah.

Rose put her hands flat on the table. 'Look,' she said, obviously trying to keep her irritation in check, 'I appreciate the sentiment, really I do. I'm glad you want to join us … we will be glad to call you a Pagan, but we find ourselves in a tricky political predicament. I understand your impatience—part of me applauds it—but I implore you not to do anything stupid.'

Rose's eyes flicked to Zahora, and she scowled.

Rose laughed. 'Zahora, my dear, you can hardly pretend to be a calm, measured influence.'

Zahora huffed.

'If we find the solution in this pile of paper, it will speed things up immeasurably,' said Rose.

'Fine,' said Zahora, then pulled Noah towards a desk at the back of the room.

Chapter 11

'I call this meeting to order,' said the newly appointed Registrar. It was a man Rose didn't recognize, not the deputy the old Registrar had lined up for the task, and Rose was yet to decide if she liked him.

'I won't beat around the bush,' said the reedy man with red hair and horn-rimmed glasses, 'the first order of business—I dare say the only order of business for a time—is the reformation of this great institution.'

Rose was pro-reformation, of course, but there was a pompous edge to the way the man talked that smacked of self-importance. The last thing they needed was an egomaniac.

'I will start as I mean to go on, and be frank with you all. It has come to our attention that the magical link between the Registerium and each of our member nations has been severed.'

The demons in the room fidgeted at the news, and a couple of the younger ones let out an audible gasp. This wasn't the approach Rose had been expecting, but she wasn't against it, per se. Honesty was often the best policy …

'For the time being, we are unable to register demons or perform nation transfers. It is unknown what caused the problem, or how we can fix it … it is regrettable that my predecessors allowed the magical skills of the Registerium to deteriorate to such a degree. We are scouring our records for a solution, and are actively recruiting new magiks. If any of you have magiks who can help, either by sharing knowledge, or by giving practical assistance, that will speed our progress.'

'How should we register demons in the meantime?' said a demon from the back of the room—the same room that had been used for the Templar trial. Rose sorely wished she could turn her head to see who'd spoken, but she wouldn't crane her neck with all the others … she'd ask Malcolm later, given he was hovering at the back of the room.

'You have two options,' said the Registrar. 'You can either wait until this mess is sorted out, or complete registrations at your own standing stones.'

'Will you recognize those registrations?' said an Animist a few seats down from Rose.

'I cannot say for certain at this stage, however, so long as the registrations are undisputed, I am hopeful we can find a way.'

'When did this happen?' asked a demon from the Shindu Council.

'I don't know for certain,' said the Registrar. 'The last successful registration was two weeks ago …'

'What about the other magical services the Registerium provides?' asked an Aboriginal.

The Registrar took a fortifying breath. 'I will state this as clearly as I can,' he said. 'The Registerium has no magic. We have only the political power conveyed to us by the nations sitting in this room. While we find a way to reinstate our magic, I intend to agree reforms to ensure we are never in this position again. With that in mind, I ask that each nation outlines their proposals for change.'

The following day, every nation sent representatives to the record room, scouring every last scrap of paper. With the increased manpower, they made short work of the task, and, assuming no one had withheld information, finished a week later, knowing little more than when they'd started.

They found only one thing of interest: a document implying records relating to the magic were held by the Nation of Stars.

Rose wanted to curse loudly, but she had an audience, so kept it in her head. 'We found a powerful magik—Ame—the daughter of a member of the Star Nation. Unfortunately, she left us, and has joined the West Coast.'

'Free movement strikes again,' sniped a Persian.

'She was never registered to our nation,' said Rose, with a scowl.

'I'll look her up,' said Pablo, immediately jumping to action. 'Maybe I can find something of use.'

As everyone dispersed, making Pablo promise to share his findings without delay, Zahora took Rose aside.

'No, I have not yet heard from Tsering,' said Rose, before Zahora could open her mouth.

'But … have you …' said Zahora

'No, I have not sent another message. The more messages I send, the longer he will take to reply. He thinks he's teaching us patience or some such nonsense, and fighting his strange ways is not in our interests.'

'I hate this,' said Zahora.

'You and me both,' said Rose, testily.

'I want to register at the Pagan stone,' said Noah. 'Now everyone knows about the magical issues, there's no reason not to.'

Rose didn't want to think about it … another item to add to the list. 'Fine,' she said, because she had no good reason to refuse.

The following day, Tsering finally responded to Rose's request with a simple message: *We send envoy.* It was anyone's guess when he would send an envoy, and he'd probably neglected to write a full sentence just to wind her up … she would not let him succeed.

'Pablo found something,' said Zahora, rushing up the stairs as Rose was coming down for breakfast.

'What?' said Rose, distracted by the reform proposals she would put forward that afternoon.

'A location for the Nation of Stars,' said Zahora. 'Or at least, a location where two of their members once lived.'

'Tenuous,' said Rose, 'but a lead's a lead. Where?'

'Azerbaijan,' said Zahora. 'Near the Caspian Sea.'

'Then to Azerbaijan Talli and Christa shall go,' said Rose.

Zahora glowered.

'I would remind you that you and Noah have plans to visit Wales … unless you've changed your mind on that score?'

Zahora's features smoothed, and she shook her head.

'Good.' *Young fucking demons.*

Rose continued down the stairs and joined Raina and Caspar in the breakfast room, which, like the sitting room, had a glorious view of the loch. The sun was rising, and it gave the whole place a beautiful golden glow.

She sat and helped herself to a buttery—a Scottish cross between a croissant and a bread roll—wondering how many years eating these things every day would take off her life.

Casper picked up his phone, answering an incoming call. 'Heba, Janet,' he said, 'good morning.'

'Middle of the night for me,' said Janet.

'What is this about, Caspar?' said Heba. 'I have no desire to speak with that woman's nation.'

'You might when you hear what she has to say,' said Caspar. Rose moved to stand behind him, so she could see the screen.

'I doubt that,' said Heba, but her expression turned expectant.

'I've found your son,' said Janet, who looked exhausted, with red eyes and pale skin.

'What?' said Heba. 'Is he …'

'Alive?' said Janet. 'Yes. The Slayers had him. I will warn you, they were not kind, but we have healed him sufficiently to move him. He's on a plane to Egypt as we speak.'

'Oh my,' Heba clapped a hand over her mouth, tears pooling in her eyes. 'I thought I'd never see him again …'

'Just don't blame me for his state. It had nothing to do with me.'

'I … thank you,' said Heba.

Banging sounded from the phone, Rose uncertain whether it was coming from Janet or Heba, but then Janet looked over her shoulder, just as the door behind her flew open. Four demons entered, and Janet put up her hands, and then the screen went dead.

'Shit,' said Caspar.

Raina pulled out her phone and dialed Ira. He picked up straight away. 'On it,' he said. 'Looks like a demon attack.'

'Other Templars?' said Heba, who Rose had all but forgotten was still on the line.

'No,' said Ira, 'I think it's the West Coast … they're wearing uniforms …'

'Uniforms?' said Caspar. 'That's … unusual.'

'It's like they're trying to draw attention to our race,' said Raina.

Caspar shrugged. 'Who knows what the fuck they're up to.'

Gemma held her dagger low, stalking through the corridors of Jamie's warehouse—the Templar nation's headquarters. The West Coast had taken control, but they were yet to find Jamie, so Ares had sent them back in for a last look. Maybe there was an underground bunker, or tunnels, or a hidden safe room behind his office. But as Gemma continued through the warehouse, she saw not a soul, the place deserted.

Gemma made her way back to the huge open plan living space where the West Coast demons were holding the captured Templars, finding Ares and Aphrodite just outside the door, speaking in hushed tones. 'Ame …' said Ares.

'Gemma, darling,' said Aphrodite, cutting Ares off. 'Wonderful work.' She ushered Gemma into the living space, where a row of prisoners were on their knees.

'We no longer serve Jamie,' said one of the prisoners. 'The coup … we want to work with you …'

The soldier behind the prisoner slit his throat, and he collapsed to the floor. The other prisoners looked at each other nervously and kept their mouths firmly shut.

'Put them in the transports for questioning,' Ares said to the soldiers, 'and have everyone formed up back here in twenty minutes.'

The Pentalpha gathered as the room emptied. Elliot had requested to join them, but Aphrodite had refused, saying he lacked the required training. Gemma wondered if it was really because Aphrodite still harbored hopes of Hades and Gemma getting together … or maybe they were worried Elliot would snatch Gemma and make a run for the Pagans …

'Is that true?' said Gemma, sheathing her knife. 'That Jamie is no longer their leader … that there's been a coup?'

Aphrodite shrugged. 'That man is a prisoner of war … he'll say anything.'

He had seemed genuine to Gemma, but she held her tongue.

'Clean up,' said Ares. 'We must look presentable when we congratulate our troops.'

The twenty minutes flew by, then Gemma found herself once again in front of a room full of demons, in the full glare of their watchful gazes. The shine was coming off her new role … she wished she was at the back of the crowd, watching the watchers.

The five of them—the Pentalpha—looked mighty as they stood, victorious, in front of their soldiers. Or, more accurately, Ares and Aphrodite's soldiers.

Ares addressed the assembled men and women with little preamble. 'Rarely are battles so clean,' he said. 'Rarely are soldiers so immaculate in their execution. Rarely have I been prouder of an army.'

The soldiers cheered, and Gemma couldn't help but smile at their enthusiasm.

'This is the first of many steps,' said Ares, 'to take back what is rightfully ours, and I look forward to standing by your side in the battles to come.'

Another cheer, and this time Gemma saw wonder shine in the soldiers' eyes. They believed deeply, fervently in Ares' and Aphrodite's claims … that Mount Olympus was theirs by right … that they were serving literal gods … that Gemma was a god too.

Gemma felt sick. She wanted to go home to the Pagans. Aphrodite had been wise to keep Elliot on the West Coast, or by now they would be long gone.

'And to the magnificent gods of the Pentalpha,' said Ares, 'thank you. Your leadership is legendary, and your might will ensure our victory in the battles ahead.'

The crowd roared at this, and Gemma had to admit, they cut a pleasing silhouette, the five of them on stage. But then, that was doubtless a key part of the reason for their selection. Pride swelled inside her alongside the sick feeling … a strange combination.

'Look at this,' said Caspar, showing Rose and Raina a picture on his phone.

'Gemma,' said Raina, 'wearing one of their uniforms.'

'Ira's confirmed she's one of five leaders they call the Pentalpha,' said Caspar, taking back his phone. 'Here are the other four.'

'Oh my Gods … that's the missing Viking,' said Raina. 'Do Henrik and Sofie know?'

'Ira sent them the same photos,' said Caspar.

'Then the West Coast is where the demons have been going?' said Raina.

'And it looks like Gemma is one of them now,' said Caspar.

'I refuse to believe it,' said Rose. 'Gemma is loyal … has been since the day I pulled her out of the hellhole she'd been trapped in. She wouldn't turn her back on us so easily.'

'And yet …' said Caspar.

'These pictures prove nothing,' snapped Rose.

'They don't *imply* nothing though,' said Raina, leaning back in her tartan seat.

'Ira's calling,' said Caspar, 'and … Janet.' He answered the call, their two faces filling the screen.

'You made it out then?' said Caspar, taking in Janet's drawn, scared features.

'I'm in Canada,' said Janet, 'waiting for a flight.'

'What happened?' said Raina.

'The West Coast attacked us,' said Janet, 'but the soldiers barely knew who I was … they said they were looking for Jamie … asked me to take them to him. I said I would, and that gave me a chance to escape. I killed one of them, stole a uniform, and walked out the back door.'

'They must have known Jamie was gone,' said Caspar.

'I'm sure the leaders did,' said Ira, 'but their soldiers didn't.'

'Maybe Gemma didn't know,' said Raina.

'That's unclear,' said Ira. 'What is clear is that the West Coast believe they're the rightful owners of Mount Olympus.'

'In Greece?' said Janet.

'Yes,' said Ira. 'They believe the leadership are Gods reincarnated—Greek Gods—and their mission is to take back what they think is theirs.'

'Wonderful,' said Rose. 'Just what we need at a time like this.'

'Who are these supposed gods?' said Raina, with a chuckle.

'Ares and Aphrodite,' said Ira, 'a man called Hades, whose background I am looking into, the missing Viking, now known as Hephaestus, and I'm afraid to say, Gemma.'

'And who is she supposed to be?' said Raina.

'The Goddess of Spring,' said Ira.

'Doesn't the Goddess of Spring get it on with Hades?' said Raina. 'Who's her uncle, by the way …'

'A little thing like incest can't deter a God,' said Rose.

'You don't think Gemma and … whoever this guy is …' said Caspar.

'Unclear,' said Ira.

'We can't rule anything out,' said Rose.

'It's a cult,' said Raina, 'plain and simple.'

'The question is,' said Caspar, 'have they got inside Gemma and Elliot's heads …?'

Gemma returned, and Elliot breathed a sigh of relief as they embraced. 'Thank the Gods,' he said.

'It was a walk in the park,' said Gemma. 'The West Coast's soldiers are well trained, and the Templars were in disarray after their recent losses.'

'Did they get Jamie?' said Elliot. At least that would be something good to have come out of all this.

Gemma shook her head. 'He wasn't there,' she said, 'and a prisoner said he was no longer in charge … that there had been a coup …'

'What did Aphrodite and Ares say to that?'

'A solider killed the prisoner, and that put an end to it. Nobody asked any further questions.'

'You think the prisoner was telling the truth?' said Elliot.

'Why would he lie? His claims could be easily validated … and he said the Templars wanted to work with the West Coast.'

'But the West Coast wouldn't want that,' said Elliot. 'They want justifications for war, and nothing else.'

'They told me we were going after Jamie,' said Gemma, sitting on the bed. 'That's the only reason I went … to help bring him down. Jamie attacked the

West Coast … they were well within their rights to fight back.'

'But not if there really was a coup,' said Elliot. 'If the Templars are under new leadership …'

'Did anything happen here while we were gone?' said Gemma.

'Not much,' said Elliot, 'but they were watching me, so I didn't have a chance to snoop around.'

'Something's going on with Ame,' said Gemma. 'I overheard Aphrodite say her name, but then she saw me, and stopped.'

'Have Ares and Aphrodite recruited any other magiks?' said Elliot.

Gemma shrugged. 'You probably know more than I do.'

'Then unfortunately,' said Elliot, 'we don't know much.'

Chapter 12

The morning Zahora and Noah planned to travel to Wales, Tsering's magik arrived in Scotland, derailing their plans. The monk was short, bald, and dressed in nothing but maroon robes, despite the cold. He was the happiest soul Zahora had ever met, nothing seeming to deter him.

'The magic broken,' he said, smiling away to himself.

Zahora explained they wanted to find out about the bonds that travelled to the sky, like the Buddhist nation's did.

'Ah,' said the monk, nodding. 'Sphere in the sky.'

'Yes,' said Zahora. 'How do we transfer Callie from the Templars, who use the Sphere in the sky, to the Pagans, who use …'

'Sphere in the ground,' said the monk.

'The Sphere in the ground,' repeated Zahora.

The monk screwed up his face. 'It tricky.'

'Do you know how to do it?' said Zahora.

'Yes,' he said, nodding fervently.

'Can you do the transfer for us?'

'No.'

'Or teach us how?'

'No.'

'Um … why not?' said Zahora, trying to keep her voice light … diplomatic.

'Need Templar.'

Zahora's heart sank. The Templars had no magiks … at least, none that practiced in the open. She nodded. 'We'll ask Janet when she gets here.'

The monk nodded. 'No worry,' he said, taking Zahora's hand. 'We find way.'

'And what about the Registerium?' said Zahora. 'Do you know how to reinstate the bond to the Registerium's stone?'

The monk smiled broadly and nodded. 'No,' he said.

Zahora furrowed her brow. 'Do you mean you can, or you can't?'

'No,' he said again. 'I can't. No need.'

'Why do you say that?' said Zahora.

'We do without them.'

'You think we should disband the Registerium?'

The monk nodded enthusiastically.

Great. 'Do you know how the Registerium's magic was set up?'

'Of course! But Star Nation not nice people.'

'How did they do it?'

'They pin it, but refuse to say how, so no one control but them.'

'Can we try?' said Zahora. 'Experiment?'

The monk beamed and nodded. 'Yes. We try.'

Given the West Coast's attack on the Templars, the discussions about Registerium reform had been delayed. Rose wasn't sure why ... it wasn't like the new Registrar could do anything—the West Coast weren't members of the Registerium, and the Templars were as good as done after the attack. It turned out that not only had their headquarters been taken, but almost every other one of their strongholds too.

Rose walked into the meeting, the room set up in conference style—unusual for demons to be so modern—and her eyes landed on Janet, who was conversing quietly with the Registrar. Rose's hackles rose ... what was Janet saying that the others couldn't hear? Was she back to her old tricks so soon? But to what end? Her nation was finished ...

'Janet,' said Rose, striding towards her. 'I'm glad you made it.'

'Thanks,' said Janet, her features drawn. 'It wasn't easy.'

'I was so sorry to hear about the extent of your losses,' said Rose.

'I doubt you were *that* sorry,' said Janet, 'but I appreciate the words. It will be hard to rebuild, but we must take back what is ours.'

'Rebuild?' said Rose. 'How?'

Janet gave Rose a curious look. 'We still have extensive resources, loyal members, and friends ...'

'Yes, but the West Coast currently occupies all of your territory ...'

'Which is regrettable,' said Janet, 'and we will call upon our friends to house us, until we take back our lands.'

Rose raised an eyebrow. 'I see,' she said. 'You must visit me later … there is much for us to discuss.'

Janet inclined her head.

The Registrar called the meeting to order, then handed the floor to Rose—the first to lay out her proposals for reform.

'I'm sure we have all had our fill of meetings like this one,' said Rose, 'so I shall keep it brief. My proposals are as follows:

One: no nation should lock demons in for an entire lifetime. In order to be a member of the Registerium, a nation must allow their demons to come and go freely. This is to put an end to the use of demons as a weapon, and to hinder the slavery and trafficking that, to my dismay, still continues to this day.

Two: the Registerium must be more transparent about which nation is getting what. We have recently heard how the Templar nation was granted access to information kept from others. This is unfair, and we should put measures in place to stop it from happening again.

Three: the process to elect a Registrar should be more democratic, with shorter terms in office. Nations should elect the Registrar, and terms should be no longer than ten years.

Four: the Registerium must keep skilled magiks on staff. Only a few short weeks ago, it would have been unthinkable for the Registerium's magic to collapse … and yet, here we are. The situation must be rectified, and cannot be allowed to happen again.'

Rose returned to her seat at the conclusion of her proposals.

'Will the rule of transparency apply to the nations also?' said the Registrar.

'No,' said Rose. 'The Registerium serves the nations—that was why it was established—not the other way around. The fact you asked that question shows how far out of balance things have become. Not only is the Registerium guilty of breaking the rules to which it should adhere, it has also forgotten its place.'

A cheer of support went up around the table, and Rose nodded in recognition. On the issue of slapping down the Registerium, it seemed the nations were united ... on how much else, it remained to be seen.

Zahora sat on the floor in the large sitting room overlooking the loch. The monk—who refused to tell them his name—had declared the spot to have good energy, and sat in front of the window, Zahora left with no choice but to do the same.

The monk told Zahora to access the Nexus, wanting to test her abilities. She did, but had barely even brushed against it when something hit her arm with a crack. Her eyes flew open, taking in the monk and the switch in his hand. Where had that come from?

The blow wasn't so hard as to leave lasting damage, but was certainly hard enough for Zahora not to want it to happen again.

'You can't hit me,' said Zahora, indignantly.

'Why?' said the monk, with his trademark smile.

'Because that's not the way we do things here.'

'You want my help?'

Zahora nodded with a, *What the hell?* expression.

'Then my rules,' he said, cracking the switch on a chair. 'Again, but lighter.'

Zahora scowled. 'Lighter?'

He nodded exuberantly. 'Lighter.'

Zahora felt for the Nexus, trying her best to keep it light, although wasn't at all sure what that meant. When no smack came, she assumed she must be doing something right.

She connected with the Nexus, then pulled back, opening her eyes to see what she should do next. Half a moment later, the switch connected with her arm once more.

'Hey!' she said, angrily. 'I did what you said!'

'I say connect. Not come back.'

Zahora let out a frustrated, 'Urgh.'

'You want my help?'

'Yes!' she said. 'But you don't need to hit me. That achieves nothing ...'

'It make me happy,' he said, as though that excused his behavior.

How could this jolly monk be such a freaking masochist? 'Well, it makes me sad ... and angry ...'

Footsteps approached the room, and they both looked towards the entrance. Rose and Janet appeared, and Zahora breathed a sigh of relief. Thank the Gods ... 'He keeps hitting me!' she said to Rose.

Rose looked from Zahora to the monk and back again. 'So?' she said.

'It hurts!'

'Has he drawn blood?'

'No.'

'Sexually assaulted you?'

'No.'

'Done anything that will leave marks?'

'Well … I don't know …'

'He's helping us, so we have to give him leeway with the methods … also, Janet's here.'

Zahora wanted to throw something. 'Great,' she said. 'Maybe he can hit her for a while instead.'

'No one's hitting me,' said Janet.

The monk bowed in greeting. Janet bowed back.

'Do you have any magiks at all in the Templar nation?' said Zahora.

Janet sank into an armchair. 'No. Not officially anyway, Jamie wouldn't allow it … however, seeing as he was always off chasing anything in a skirt, I did some exploration behind his back. He was more lenient after I found a way to use magic to summon Callie back to us.'

'By torturing her,' said Zahora.

Janet shrugged. 'All's fair in love and war … and Callie fitted both categories.'

'You're all crazy,' said Zahora.

'We're just old,' said Janet. 'You only know the modern way …'

The monk laughed. 'You are baby,' he said to Janet.

Color stained Janet's cheeks. 'I'm older than Zahora,' she said, 'by a long way.'

'Alright,' said Rose, 'we don't have all day. Can you teach Janet how to do a nation transfer?'

The monk nodded two or three times. 'Yes.'

Gemma and Elliot strolled towards the front gate, Gemma two paces in front.

The gate guard stepped out of his booth to greet them.

'Ah ...' he said. 'Can I help, Goddess?'

'Yes,' said Gemma. 'Please open the gate.'

'I ... ah ... have received no instructions to open the gate today ...'

'I'm going shopping,' said Gemma. 'You do not need to receive instructions for that.'

'But ... the thing is ...'

'You would deny a direct request from the Goddess?' said Elliot.

'No!' said the guard. 'I would never ...'

'Then open the gate,' said Elliot. 'Or I will be forced to tell Aphrodite of this ...'

The guard hesitated, then turned back to his booth. He pressed the button to open the smaller gate meant for pedestrians.

'Good,' said Gemma. 'We will be back soon. I hope we don't have the same issues then.'

'Of course ... Goddess ... I will look for you ...' The guard bowed as they stepped through the gate, then quickly closed it behind them.

Gemma and Elliot walked casually away, ignoring the impulse to run.

'He's probably already on the phone,' said Elliot, in a low voice.

'Aphrodite and Ares are having a joint massage ... few are brave enough to interrupt that ...'

But even so, as they rounded the corner of the nearest building, slipping out of sight of the guard, they ran.

Chapter 13

Christa and Talli lay on a sun lounger by an aqua-colored pool. 'Gods, this is nice,' said Talli, luxuriating in the beating heat of the sun.

'It really is,' said Christa, taking a sip of her cocktail.

'Everything's been so … tense …'

'Let's hope Ira doesn't have a satellite on us as we speak,' said Christa, 'or things will get even more so.'

'Oh, stop worrying,' said Talli, pressing Christa's hand to her lips, 'they've got bigger fish to fry. And Rose wouldn't deny us half an hour off … hell, if she were here, she'd be out here with us …'

'No, she wouldn't.'

'Okay, she wouldn't, but she should be … everyone needs a break now and again,' said Talli.

'And those massages were glorious,' said Christa.

'Mmm, that guy really got into the knots … his hands …'

Christa shot her a warning look.

'Jealous?' said Talli.

Christa rolled her eyes. 'We both know I'm not the jealous one.'

Talli rolled over and kissed her. 'Don't you forget it,' she said.

Christa gave a mock salute, then looked out over the Caspian Sea. 'It used to be so beautiful here ... until they ruined it with all this ... ugliness.' She swept out a hand, gesturing towards the oil rigs that dominated the skyline.

'Maybe one day the humans will stop destroying the place,' said Talli.

'They're too selfish,' said Christa. 'They care only for status and money, and it will be their downfall.'

'Ours too,' said Talli. 'Maybe we should stop fighting each other and start building nuclear power plants ...'

'Demons are selfish too,' said Christa, 'and we're not supposed to get involved with human affairs, remember?'

Talli laughed. 'Which has stopped us when, exactly?'

Christa shrugged in agreement. 'But before we make it our mission to save the world, we have a date with a mud volcano.'

'You could kill her,' said the monk, with a beaming smile.

Zahora wondered if he was a sociopath. In what world was it okay to say those words with a smile?

'Or lose her bond,' he continued, 'so it float off across Nexus, for anyone to pick up.'

'If that happens, can I follow her bond and pick up the loose end?' said Zahora.

The monk shrugged. 'Maybe. Depend. Not if someone else get it first …'

'What else could go wrong?' said Raina.

They jumped as she entered the clearing. How had she snuck up on them without breaking a single twig? Or maybe they'd been so caught up in their predicament, they just hadn't noticed.

The monk had insisted they go out into the woods, despite Zahora's mild protests. He'd allowed a fire, thank goodness, and she'd brought a flask of hot tea. Even so, she felt the cold in her bones.

'Not much,' said the monk. 'It simple magic. Release bond from Templar stone, then Callie swear allegiance to Pagans. Simple.'

'But you said I might kill her …' said Janet, her face pale.

'If yank too hard. Must be gentle.' He pushed his hands out in a slow, steady motion, then pressed his thumb and first finger together. 'Hold gently, feel magic, pull, and let go.' He opened his fingers and chuckled. 'Very easy, yes?'

'Easy …' Janet repeated skeptically.

'Easy peasy,' said the monk, with a big, round smile.

'Why do you pretend you can't speak English properly?' said Raina.

The monk laughed so hard he bent double. 'Most demons are too scared to call me out on it,' said the monk. 'I like to see if anyone will.'

'What?' said Zahora, scowling.

Raina turned to Zahora. 'A demon with so much magical experience is likely to be ancient. It's hard not to learn languages when you've been around for so long. Pretty much everyone knows English. So if someone pretends otherwise, they're invariably fucking with you.'

Zahora shook her head. 'Demons can be such twats.'

'There's little to keep life interesting after so long,' said the monk. 'When you reach my great age, you might find you do the same.'

'The energy is fluctuating,' said Raina. 'Do you feel that too?'

The monk nodded. 'Yes, but we do not know the cause. Our magic still works … we have seen no changes to speak of … but I can't deny it is odd, and worrying.'

Raina let his words settle, holding his gaze. 'It we try this method of transferring Callie,' said Raina, 'with Janet doing the transfer, when will she be ready?'

'Ha!' laughed the monk. 'I can't say if she'll ever be ready. We will do some basic drills … try to improve her skills, and then, we will see …'

'Is there any other way?' said Raina.

The monk shook his head.

'How about reattaching the nations' bonds to the Registerium's stone?' said Raina. 'Any progress?'

'We haven't had time to even try,' said Zahora, 'and honestly, we're not sure where to start. Have Talli and Christa found anything?'

Raina shook her head. 'Nothing yet.'

Talli and Christa edged around a mud volcano—a hole in the ground that spewed mud into the air at unpredictable intervals—to a cave in a sheer rock face beyond. Ancient petroglyphs of dancing figures covered the face, and it gave Talli a warm fuzzy feeling to look upon them.

'Ah,' she sighed, 'I remember when it was normal to create art like this ... when the world was a simpler place.'

'Oh, to be so old ...' said Christa, shoulder bumping her.

'You may mock, but older means wiser, remember?'

'Does it though?'

Talli shoved Christa into the path of a mud eruption. It splattered her from head to foot.

'You'll regret that when I exact my revenge,' said Christa, wiping the mud as best she could.

Talli laughed. 'Mud is so very good for your skin. I did you a favor, really.'

Christa threw a handful of the offending substance at Talli, who turned and ducked just a little too late. It hit the back of her head, and she squealed.

'Truce!' said Talli. 'Or we won't get any work done.'

'Truce,' Christa agreed. 'For now ...'

Talli linked her arm through Christa's as they moved to the cave's entrance. 'I guess we should just rootle around a bit ...'

'I guess,' said Christa, pulling out a flashlight. She illuminated the deep cave, revealing endless inscriptions and petroglyphs on the walls and floor.

'Wow,' said Talli. 'This could take a while ...'

They moved slowly around the edge of the cave, examining each and every mark. Pablo had been able to identify records for only one member of the Nation of Stars at the Registerium, and he had once been a member of a tiny—now defunct—nation, which had been headquartered in this cave.

'It's going to destroy my soul if there's nothing here,' said Talli, running a hand over the image of a bird.

'Or if there's something here, and we miss it …' said Christa, her eyes wide.

'At least if that happens, we'll probably never know …'

'Our lives are long … there's a good chance we'll find out at some stage.'

Talli moved on, but when Christa didn't follow, she turned back. 'What are you looking at?' said Talli, walking back to her side.

'That's a star,' said Christa, pointing to a spot where a star with four crude points adorned the wall.

'It is,' said Talli, scanning the walls, 'and here's another.'

'And another,' said Christa, pointing to the floor.

'Should we follow them?'

'Or map them?'

'They could be nothing at all,' said Talli.

'Or they could be something,' said Christa.

They spent hours following the stars around the cave, mapping them as they went. There were so many, Talli's brain hurt, not to mention the marks which looked almost like stars, but which could have been something else entirely, worn away over time.

They finally reached the very back of the cave, where the roof curved down to the floor, the ceiling height gradually lowering, and found the number of stars increased.

'Look at this,' said Talli excitedly, pointing to a swirl of stars on the floor next to the back wall.

Loose boulders of all shapes and sizes were strewn along the wall, some of which contained petroglyphs.

Something about them made Talli's skin prickle. 'Do they look … odd to you?' she said, pointing at a cluster of five or six stones.

'How do you mean?' said Christa.

'Why are there loose stones back here? There aren't any down the sides … what are they here for?'

Christa cast around, searching for other loose stones, but found none.

'And the images look different from the others somehow.'

'Maybe a tourist made them,' said Christa. 'Or locals …'

'Maybe,' said Talli, crouching beside one of the biggest boulders, on which a star had been drawn. 'Or maybe not. Help me move this.'

Christa gave her a skeptical look, but crouched on the other side of the stone, helping Talli heave it to the side.

'Nothing,' said Christa.

Talli moved on to another stone, not in the least bit deterred. She moved the smaller ones … the ones she could move alone, but found nothing useful.

'Help me with this one,' she said. It had a moon on it … anything celestial counted in Talli's book.

Christa did as she was told. She'd learned to go along with Talli's eccentric impulses.

They moved every loose boulder in the cave, but found nothing. Talli slumped to the ground, her back to the wall. 'I guess I was wrong,' she said, surveying the carnage they'd caused, 'and now we have to put them all back.'

Christa sat next to her, linking her arm through Talli's.

'I was sure we were onto something,' said Talli.

Christa shrugged. 'Maybe we are and just haven't cracked it yet … or maybe we're not.'

They put the rocks back, the sun close to setting by the time they were done, and sat once more with their backs to the wall.

'It's been a long time since I slept in a cave,' said Christa.

'You can't be serious?' said Talli. 'We have a delicious, soft, comfortable bed waiting for us.'

'We'll maximize our time if we stay here.'

'We don't have any food …'

'I brought some.'

'You planned this!' said Talli, hitting Christa playfully on the arm. She grabbed the stuffed grape leaves, cheese, and Lavash flatbread all the same. It turned out she was hungry, as she ate it all, then looked hopefully at Christa for more.

'Feijoa?' said Christa, handing Talli the green fruit she'd already sliced open with a knife. Talli took it along with the spoon Christa offered her, then scooped out the flesh.

'When did you pack all this stuff?' said Talli. 'You're so prepared.'

'You sound surprised …'

'I know, you always are, but …'

'I did it this morning, while you were taking an unreasonably long shower.'

'When you went out to get breakfast?' said Talli, scraping out the last of the sweet fruit.

Christa nodded.

'I hope you packed blankets in that Mary Poppins bag,' said Talli, eyeing Christa's modestly sized backpack.

'I did, in fact,' said Christa.

The sun was heading for the horizon, and something at the back of the cave caught Talli's eye. 'Wait … is that …'

'Oh my gods,' said Christa. 'Those are rays of sunlight.'

Talli jumped to her feet and rushed to the back of the cave. Three rays of orange light streamed in through holes in the cave's wall, and each hit a petroglyph on the floor ... petroglyphs that were unmistakably stars.

Caspar and Raina sat curled up together by a firepit down by the loch, sipping mulled wine and talking quietly. A cough announced the monk's arrival, and they didn't hesitate to invite him to join them.

'Your daughter is asleep already?' said the monk.

Raina laughed. 'No. Zahora very kindly offered to entertain her for a couple of hours. I have no idea what they're doing, but they're out of earshot, so I can't bring myself to care.'

'Ah, parenthood ... I hear it's mainly trials and tribulations ...'

'Occasionally they do something cute,' said Raina, 'which somehow makes up for all the irrational temper tantrums. You never had any?'

The monk gave her a long look. 'I have always been a Buddhist ... and I've always been a monk ...'

'I'm assuming that means you don't want mulled wine?' asked Raina, refilling her own insulated mug from a flask.

The monk smiled and shook his head. 'No, thank you.'

'Is this a social call?' said Caspar.

The monk shook his head. 'You asked me earlier if there's another way to transfer Callie, and I implied there was not,' he said, perching on a seat across from theirs. Unlike theirs, his had no cushions, and it made Raina cold just looking at him. 'I lied; there is another way.'

Raina sat up straighter in her seat and clutched Caspar's hand. He squeezed back. 'What is it?' she asked.

'I only tell you because I feel like I lied earlier, and that is against what I believe. However, I must tell you this course of action is not one I advise. In fact, I would strongly dissuade you from it ... it would most certainly be immoral, unethical, and an act of war.'

Raina wanted to snap at him to spit it out, but then he might change his mind, and say it was for her own good or some such bullshit.

'Of course ... we completely understand,' said Caspar. 'We appreciate your transparency.'

The monk nodded, then looked down at his hands, only the ghost of his usual smile on his lips. 'There are, in fact, two additional ways. The first would be to convince an accomplished magik to register as a Templar, so they can complete the nation transfer. If I am honest, I would not trust Janet to transfer me without a few lifetimes of training at least.'

Raina nodded, her stomach sinking. It had sounded so easy ... just pluck a strand from the Templar stone, then let it go ... but the moment he'd mentioned Callie's potential death, she'd known deep down it was a no-go. Especially when they couldn't fully trust Janet and her intentions ... and it wasn't like she was operating from a position of strength within her nation.

'And the other way?' said Caspar. They both knew the chances of finding a capable and willing magik were next to zero.

The monk looked at them, not even a trace of a smile remaining on his features. He looked like a different person … a dangerous person, and Raina grasped Caspar's hand harder.

'If a nation ceases to exist,' said the monk, 'all demons registered to that nation become free.'

Raina stopped breathing. Of course … it was so obvious. The way to free her daughter was to end the Templar nation once and for all. They were weak … dead in the water … and maybe Janet could reinstate it after Callie was free …

'I will repeat,' said the monk, 'this is not a good course of action to pursue.'

'Can't another magik just pull Callie's bond free?' said Caspar. 'Zahora can see the bonds … she's stronger than any other magik we've ever known …'

'If she does, Callie will die,' said the monk.

Raina's pulse spiked. 'Thank you for telling us,' said Caspar. 'We can at least look for a willing magik … as much of a long shot as that is.'

'Will you join us for a drink?' said Raina. 'I'm sure we can find something non-alcoholic …'

The monk's smile was back at full wattage, and the change was alarming. Was it an act? Was he a cold-blooded killer underneath? Most demons were, so it wouldn't be so much of a surprise … or was he genuinely ludicrously happy whenever he wasn't discussing the potential downfall of a nation?

'Thank you, but I will retire,' said the monk. 'I feel lighter having told you the whole truth.'

They said good night, and he headed back to the house. Raina looked Caspar in the eye as the monk retreated, thoughts racing at a million miles an hour through her mind.

Caspar laughed. 'We can't do it,' he said, kissing her hand.

'I know,' said Raina. She waited a beat, telling herself to let it go. 'But the Templars are weak …'

'And we're trying to convince the world you're not a power-hungry maniac, even if that's a lie …'

Raina swiped his arm and rolled her eyes.

'The Buddhists could be trying to set us up …' said Caspar. 'Tsering has always wanted to show the world your true colors. What if this is his plan to paint you in a terrible light?'

'But it's the only way we'll get her back in this lifetime.'

'Then we'll wait until the next life—that's not long in the grand scheme of our existence—and we already have her; we should count our blessings, not try to end a nation.'

'But this is the first proper life she's had … I don't want her to be forced to live under a rock. Janet's in charge now, but what if Jamie comes back?'

'He doesn't have any magiks, and the Registerium won't help him anymore.'

'He's realized how important magic is though …' said Raina, balling her hands into fists, 'he's probably already found a magik to help him …'

'He's gone to ground … I doubt it.'

'He's a cockroach, and he always comes back fighting. We shouldn't underestimate him … but if he had no nation to fight for …'

'Raina!' said Caspar, turning his shoulders to face her. 'I want our daughter to be Pagan—to be safe—just as much as you do, but attempting to end the Templar nation will make her less safe, not more. How will our allies see us?'

'The Vikings would be pleased …'

'You're using that as an argument in your favor?' said Caspar.

Raina threw up her hands. 'I just want to *do* something, and we'll never find a magik willing to join the Templar nation just to help us move Callie.'

Caspar pulled Raina into his side. 'Janet's here with us,' he said, stroking her hair. 'The Templars are all but dead … Callie is in no immediate danger. We shouldn't do anything that could inadvertently hurt her.'

'I know,' said Raina, melting into him. Caspar was right; it would be foolish to act against the Templars now.

Caspar kissed her, his lips hot and sweet from the wine. She kissed him back, luxuriating in the unhurried movements. Raina still felt lucky that they were back together, her mind not yet taking his proximity for granted. She knew it would, most likely in only a very short while, as was the way of things, but for now, her body filled with endorphins every time she remembered she could touch him.

She climbed onto his lap, straddling him, and held his face in her hands. He wrapped a blanket behind her, then leaned back into the cushions, watching her watch him.

'Sometimes I worry this is all a dream,' she said quietly, tracing the line of his collarbone.

His fingers slipped under her layers of clothes, caressing the dip of her waist. 'Me too,' he said.

His other hand went to her cheek, and she pressed into his touch, closing her eyes. She breathed him in as he stroked her bottom lip. He pulled it down, and she took his thumb between her teeth, biting gently.

He shuddered, and she released him, then buried her face in his neck, sucking, licking, nipping in slow, controlled movements. Because she *could* take her time, enjoy every touch, feel every tiny sensation.

Caspar did nothing to hurry her. He pulled her face back to his, kissed her lazily, then gently bit her bottom lip, letting it run through his teeth until it sprang free. She hummed with pleasure.

He lifted her and lay her back on the sofa, then settled between her legs, resting his head on her stomach. She buried her hands in his hair, gently tugging and scratching. He pushed up her clothes, and the cold rushed in to make her shiver, but then he kissed her, vanquishing the cold in an instant, his stubbly skin scratchy against her soft flesh.

He explored every inch he could reach, and she tipped her head back, appreciative noises escaping her lips.

He lifted his head and replaced her many layers, then prowled up her body until he lay atop her, his lips finding hers once more. She relinquished all control to him, trusting him, following his lead. He teased her lips as he settled between her thighs, Raina exhaling as he weighed her down. They rocked against each other as they kissed, their bodies falling into a slow, familiar rhythm.

Caspar rolled them, pulling Raina's back to his chest, then created a warm cocoon with the blanket. His fingers explored under her clothes, and she sighed, her hand going to his neck, caressing his skin. He unzipped her jeans and slid his fingers inside, and her back arched, using his neck as leverage.

He growled against her ear, pressing his hips against her in time with his fingers. She moaned softly, not needing to tell him what to do ... lifetimes together had made him an expert.

He rolled half on top of her when she neared the end, caging her ... with anyone else, she would have hated it, but she trusted him ... had only ever fully trusted him. The thought intensified her pleasure when it hit, as he held her down, eking out the spasms with deft fingers.

She hummed with contentment when he finally pulled back, making sure her skin was protected from drafts of cold air before settling around her and nuzzling his lips against her hair.

The shrill ring of a phone jerked Raina awake, and for a moment she was confused about where she was. She checked her watch as Caspar answered the phone, finding they'd been asleep for less than an hour. She tried to blink away the fog in her mind, the sound of Talli and Christa's voices helping her focus.

'You are *never* going to guess what we found!' said Talli, her usual excitable self.

'What?' said Caspar, wrapping an arm around Raina as she sat.

'We've found tablets,' said Talli, 'with inscriptions. They're about the magic ...'

'In all honesty,' said Christa, cutting across Talli's exuberance, 'we're not sure what we've found. But maybe Marla or Alerac can help us.'

'Or Zahora, or the Buddhist,' said Raina.

'Send us pictures,' said Caspar, 'and we'll rally the troops for your arrival.'

'We're already on our way,' said Talli.

'We're here!' Talli called, waltzing into the dining room with their treasure—three carved stone tablets—held aloft.

Callie rushed over to them, hugging them tightly, and the others cheered and heckled in equal measure.

Talli placed the stones on the end of the table that wasn't covered in the remnants of breakfast. 'I'd kill for a decent coffee,' she said, looking pointedly around the room.

'Then you're in luck,' said Rose, entering with a freshly brewed mocha pot.

'Thank the Gods,' said Talli, holding out a mug.

'What did everyone think of the pictures?' said Christa, also accepting coffee from Rose.

'Couldn't make head nor tail of them,' said Rose. 'We were hoping they'd look different in the flesh.'

'Well, here they are,' said Talli, waving her hand with a flourish.

'Did you decipher any more on the journey?' said Raina, studying the stone tablets carefully.

Each was no bigger than a piece of copy paper, maybe three centimeters thick, and made of limestone. Inscriptions adorned one tablet, while the other two contained images, although it wasn't immediately clear of what.

'How did you find them?' said Raina. 'You said there were holes in the wall, and light came in at sunset?'

'Yes,' said Christa. 'The light hit three stars on the floor.'

'And when we investigated,' said Talli, 'we found three small holes, one at the center of each star.'

'The holes were filled with dust,' said Christa, 'but we cleaned them out, and used them to lift a section of the floor.'

'The tablets were inside,' said Talli.

'Was anything else hidden with them?' said Zahora, who'd been so quiet, Raina had almost forgotten she was there.

'No,' said Christa. 'I guess it's possible there's more stuff hidden in the cave, but this is all we could find.'

'What kind of writing is that?' said Raina. It was strange to come across a language she didn't recognize at all. 'It looks almost modern …'

'No idea,' said Talli. 'We couldn't work it out either.'

'Maybe Alerac will know,' said Raina. 'He's travelling up with Meredith now.'

'Gods,' said a voice from the entrance, taking them all by surprise. 'What have you been eating in my absence?' Elliot walked to the dining table, and picked up a buttery. 'These things will kill you … you know this …'

Gemma stood behind him in the doorway, smiling nervously.

'Oh my Gods!' squealed Talli, leaping up from her seat and careering towards them. She squeezed Elliot's arm as she passed, but launched herself at Gemma, pulling her into a bear hug. 'I have missed you so much! Have you got any idea how irritating this lot are to train with? And don't get me started on Meredith …'

Gemma smiled, tears pooling in her eyes as Raina shoved Talli out of the way, pulling Gemma into a bear hug of her own.

'We've missed you both so much,' said Raina, pulling back, moving to hug Elliot.

'We were so worried about you,' said Christa.

'Tell us *everything*,' said Talli.

'We thought you were lost,' said Rose, 'but I knew in my heart it couldn't be true.' She pulled Gemma into the most affectionate hug Raina had ever seen her give.

Gemma clutched her tightly, her tears flowing freely now. 'It was closer than you'll ever know,' she said on a sob.

Elliot took Gemma's hand. 'We'll tell you everything,' he said, 'but first we need a shower, and a change of clothes, and then someone needs to show me the way to the kitchen, because it has been an age since I've been in one, and I *really* need to bake.'

Chapter 14

They all gathered in the kitchen as Elliot rolled up his sleeves and set about creating many culinary masterpieces. Gemma felt complete again for the first time since she'd left the Pagans. She hadn't recognized the absence of the feeling during their time with the West Coast, had only—greedily—pursued the new, shiny role dangled in front of her. But now she was back, she noticed, and it made her heart swell.

As did Elliot's beaming smile as he whisked eggs in a bowl. His shoulders were lower than she'd seen them in weeks, his easy-going nature returned, and a pang of love for him clamped around her chest. He looked up at her, checking in to see if she was still okay, and the feeling intensified.

'Oh Gods,' said Talli. 'I am excited for this! What's cooking?'

'You'll have to wait and see,' said Elliot, but he placed a plate of biscuits in front of her.

'Oh my Gods!' said Talli. 'You whipped these up in what ... like ... two and a half minutes?' She took a bite. 'I'm never leaving your side. These are ... divinity incarnate.'

Gemma tensed at the words, and Elliot stopped whisking, throwing a scowl at Talli.

'What …? Oh … sorry … I got caught up in the moment … I didn't think amid the buttery, chocolaty, citrus perfection.'

'It's okay,' said Gemma, selecting a biscuit of her own. She'd have to get used to them mocking her sooner or later …

'I honestly didn't mean to do that …' said Talli, swiping a second biscuit. 'I'm sorry.'

'What did you do this time?' said a voice from the door.

Gemma whirled to find Meredith in the entryway. She froze. What must Meredith think of her? Her commander … mentor … friend … her insides crumpled, and she lost the ability to speak. 'I …' She shook her head, her movements small.

Meredith pulled her into a hug. 'I'm so glad you're back,' she said. 'I've missed you, my friend.' She pulled back, looking Gemma in the eye. 'This lot are a poor substitute for your company … you have no idea what I've been through in your absence. Inanity … that's the only word I have for it.'

'I can only imagine,' said Gemma, her voice cracking with emotion.

'Please don't leave me again … I'm not sure what I'll do,' said Meredith.

Gemma nodded, a grateful smile on her lips. A movement caught her eye, and she turned her head to the doorway once more.

'Alerac,' said Elliot, 'good to see you.'

Alerac, Zahora, and Noah entered the kitchen.

'Can we eat those?' said Zahora.

Elliot nodded.

Zahora and Noah raced to the kitchen island, taking two each from the fast-disappearing stack.

'Hey, leave some for us,' said Meredith, barging them out of the way.

'Tea,' said Rose, moving to the stove, but Raina got there first.

'You should sit, old lady,' Raina said with a smile. 'You look like you might be on your last legs …'

'It's been a busy few weeks,' said Rose, 'and this body is feeling the strain … I'm not sure how much longer it has left.'

'Christ,' said Talli, 'you can't die yet. You don't want any of us in charge of reform negotiations …'

Apprehension coursed through Gemma. She'd only just come back … Rose couldn't die now … there were so many things she had to say … to atone for.

Rose cast her eyes around the room. 'You're not wrong,' she said, with an evil smile. 'Imagine if Raina turned up in my place …'

Talli cackled.

'Or you,' Raina said to Talli, pulling the boiling kettle from the stove.

'Hey,' said Christa, 'she'd have them singing Kumbaya in no time …'

Talli swiped Christa on the arm. 'Bringing people together is a gift, I'll have you know.'

Raina placed two large teapots on the table, adding them to the mugs, milk and sugar Caspar had already put there. Meredith brought over the cookies as Elliot pulled another delicious smelling tray from the oven.

'Seriously?' said Talli. 'How do you do it?'

'Oh wow,' said Noah, 'are those peanut cookies?'

'They certainly are,' said Elliot, sliding them onto a cooling rack. 'Although we call them biscuits over here …'

Noah picked one, blew on it, then took an enormous bite. 'Whatever you call them,' he said around his mouthful, 'that's the best thing I've ever tasted.'

'Oh, just you wait …' said Caspar. 'And don't think I haven't noticed your thieving hands …' He turned his head to where Callie sat with the dogs—Charlie and Delta—on the floor. She smiled guiltily, chocolate smeared around her mouth. The others laughed, and Callie buried her face in Delta's fur.

'Where's Jon?' said Elliot. 'Is he here?'

Rose shook her head. 'It's a long story, but he's with Raina's human cousin … keeping her safe and out of the way until all the nastiness blows over.'

'Hasn't the nastiness blown over?' said Zahora. 'Now Jamie's gone, and the Templars are on life support?'

Gemma held her breath. Bringing the Templars to the brink of collapse had been partly her doing … although she'd thought their goal had simply been to bring down Jamie … just one of Aphrodite's many lies.

'No,' said Rose. 'Jamie is still at large, and my sense is that things will get uglier before they get better, given the West Coast's goal …'

'They want Mount Olympus,' Gemma blurted.

'We know,' said Rose.

'You do?' said Gemma.

'Ira—from the Holy Star—got their lower ranks to use a messaging app he created,' said Caspar.

'Oh,' said Gemma … then they knew already … had probably seen …

'What happened?' said Rose, gently.

Gemma blinked back tears, and Rose saw, so kept talking, telling her all they knew—of the Pentalpha, their goals, and the belief that their leadership were Greek Gods reincarnated.

'Which makes *no* sense,' said Talli, 'given that gods are immortal. So how could they die and reincarnate?'

'Cults rarely make sense,' said Gemma.

Silence settled over the room.

'What else?' said Raina. 'What don't we know?'

That I believed them … thought I was a god reincarnated too. I loved their adoration and attention and wanted to be special for once in my life.

Elliot cleared his throat. 'Aphrodite and Ares are dangerous. They've created an entire nation—one with land, money, connections—all while flying under the radar. Their people are loyal to the so-called gods, and will defend them to the end. The adoration is … well, it's a cult, so you know what it's like.

'The whole place is geared up towards serving the gods, and access to them is the highest reward. The lower ranks fight for the opportunity to serve them … to be in their presence. From what I could tell, the lower ranks believe they too will live like gods—in a world of abundance—once they take Mount Olympus. But they kept me sidelined most of the time, and had me watched, so I couldn't find out much.'

'They tried to force us apart,' said Gemma, her voice small, and the attention of the room swung to her.

Elliot put a batch of flapjack in the oven, then took the seat next to Gemma, pressing his leg to hers and holding her hand.

'They brainwashed you,' said Elliot. 'Manipulated you.'

'They …' Gemma faltered. Yes, they had done those things … but she'd wanted to believe them. 'They played to my insecurities … told me lies … dangled carrots … made me a celebrity … gave me experiences I've never had before. They made me feel special, and important, and powerful … but it wasn't real. It was tightly controlled, and all so they had a Pagan on their Pentalpha.'

'Someone with a legitimate claim to Mount Olympus?' said Talli.

Gemma shrugged. 'Maybe. Or maybe they just wanted demons from old, respected nations who were stupid enough to listen to their poisoned words.'

Elliot squeezed her hand. He'd consoled her endlessly since their escape, telling her she wasn't stupid … but saying the words didn't make it so.

'How did you get out?' said Raina. Thank the Gods for Raina—rarely one to dwell on feelings at a moment like this.

'We walked out,' said Gemma.

'We waited until the most easily persuaded gate guard was on duty, then intimidated him into letting us leave the headquarters for a shopping trip,' said Elliot.

'He almost had enough backbone to stop us,' said Gemma.

'I dread to think what Aphrodite did to him when she found out,' said Elliot.

'Poor man's probably dead,' said Gemma, shaking her head.

'And how did you get back here?' said Caspar. 'You had no money or passports …'

'Ira,' said Elliot. 'We borrowed a stranger's phone, called him, and he organized everything: passports, money, transport … the works. He swore us to secrecy, to limit the risk of failure.'

'Whatever we're doing to keep the Holy Star sweet,' said Meredith, 'we should keep that up.'

'What are we doing?' said Raina, looking at Rose.

'That's a conversation for another time,' said Rose. 'Is there anything else you can tell us about the West Coast's intentions? When they're planning to attack? Or where? Did you learn anything as part of the Pentalpha?'

'They told me nothing,' said Gemma. 'I didn't even know Janet had overthrown Jamie when we attacked the Templars. They told us he was still in command, even though they must have known otherwise. And in terms of their plan to take Mount Olympus … I have no idea. Although, they can't head straight for Greece … even if they took Olympus, they'd have no hope of holding it.'

'No,' said Meredith, 'you're right … they'll need to weaken us first, to such a degree we can't fight back …'

'They're nasty,' said Elliot. 'Make no mistake, their goal will be to destroy us entirely.'

Several hours and four bakes later, the questioning of Gemma and Elliot came to an end. Callie had long since lost interest, now playing games on a tablet, and the others were so stuffed with sugary goodness, they could barely move.

'More tea,' said Talli, making for the stove.

'And I'd like to look at the stone tablets,' said Alerac.

Zahora had forgotten all about the mysterious stones, so caught up in being included by the leadership. It was a dream come true to sit round a table with them, to banter, to be valued. It was what she'd always wanted, and having Noah there too … it was more than she'd ever hoped.

Christa retrieved the tablets and placed them in front of Alerac. He picked them up one by one and turned them over in his hands, angling them this way and that to catch every detail.

'Hmmm,' he said, several times, the others watching him carefully. No one interrupted, letting him process without distraction.

'Nothing about them seems familiar,' he finally said, placing the tablets on the table and sitting back in his seat, 'and I have no idea how to decipher them.'

Disappointment bloomed in Zahora's chest. If only they had a concrete understanding of how to reinstate the Registerium's magic, she could be useful again. She hated sitting around, waiting like a spare part. And the monk had refused to teach her any good stuff, saying it would be a betrayal of his nation. It was infuriating to have all that knowledge so close and yet so far. Lessons with him reminded her of lessons with Ame …

'What happened to Ame?' Zahora blurted. 'I saw her requesting to join the West Coast, but we've heard nothing through the messaging app …'

'You saw that?' said Gemma.

Zahora nodded. 'I followed Ame across the Nexus.'

'Phones are shunned by the West Coast's leadership,' said Elliot. 'They're used mostly by the lower ranks, and I'm guessing, whatever Ame's up to, it's not something Aphrodite and Ares would share widely. You'd be better off spying magically.'

'Ame will kill me if I try that again,' said Zahora. 'She almost killed me last time, but luckily Ares interrupted her.'

Callie snuck up beside Zahora and wrapped her arms around her. 'I don't want her to kill you,' she whispered.

Zahora hefted Callie onto her lap. 'Me neither,' she said, 'so we're not going to give her the chance, are we?'

Callie shook her head. 'Are those puzzle pieces?' she said, pointing to the stone tablets.

'No,' said Zahora, but then she looked again at the stones … from this angle, they did look like they might fit together … 'Can you pass them here?'

Alerac slid the stones to her, and Zahora pushed them together, but no matter what configuration she tried, they didn't match.

'What about standing up?' said Callie. 'My tablet has games like that.'

Zahora smiled and tried again. 'Oh my Gods,' she said, placing two of the stones on end, then sliding them together. 'That matches … look!'

The others crowded round. 'It does!' said Talli. 'Well done Calls!'

'But, I can't see how this one matches,' said Zahora, trying to fit it every which way.

'What about on top?' said Noah, watching from the open space on the other side of the table.

'Oh shit,' said Elliot, rushing to the oven and pulling out a batch of chocolate brownies. 'Phew—just in time.'

Zahora put Callie down and pushed back her chair, forcing her audience to retreat. Zahora crouched in front of the stones so she could look at the roof of the structure she was building, every eye in the room on her.

'Here,' said Caspar, turning on the flashlight on his phone and holding it to help her see.

'Thanks,' she said, but she couldn't make it fit. She turned it over to try the other side. 'Oh … wow …'

'What?' said Talli, impatiently.

'It's a sphere … and there's … some kind of inscription, spread across the three tablets, and is that image a star?'

'What does it say?' said Caspar.

'No idea,' said Zahora. 'Want to take a look?'

'Yes,' said Raina, taking Zahora's place. 'What if the sphere is the Earth?'

'Then the star is a location we need to find?' said Caspar, peering over her shoulder.

'I'm not sure what the writing says either ...' said Raina. 'Maybe it's a code ...?'

'That seems on brand for the Nation of Stars,' said Talli.

'Maybe I could use the stones to trace who made them ...' said Zahora, 'like I did with Ame's scarf and Noah's t-shirt?'

'You literally just said, when you did it with Ame, she nearly killed you,' said Meredith.

'And the Nation of Stars is more dangerous than she is,' said Christa.

'I'd obviously be more careful than last time,' said Zahora, her cheeks heating.

'I'd rather you didn't do it at all,' said Noah, looking only at her. 'These people are dangerous, and we don't understand their motives.'

'And if they get you in the Nexus,' said Alerac, 'they'll have your soul ... true death.'

'Okay, fine,' said Zahora. 'Any other ideas?'

'We've barely even begun to study the tablets,' said Caspar. 'We should each take turns and see what we can come up with.'

Raina and Caspar went first. The others dispersed, complaining they'd eaten too much sugar.

'I'm so sorry you have to do this,' said Rose, as she and Gemma walked to the Registerium. 'Especially after everything you've been through.'

'Me too,' said Gemma. 'But if it's the only way they'll listen, and if it stops others from having to go through what I went through, then it's a sacrifice worth making.'

'How are you feeling?' said Rose. 'It must have been …'

'Like an idiot,' said Gemma, cutting across her. 'They drew me into a cult for the second time … how much more stupid could I be?'

'Gemma … this isn't the same as before …'

'No … this time, I should have known better.'

'They ran a campaign to seduce you,' said Rose. She stopped in her tracks and made Gemma look at her. 'You obviously needed something we weren't giving you. That's on us …'

'It wasn't that, so much. They offered me something I never thought to want, and the opportunity to try being someone else for a while … and they made it so easy. All I had to do is whatever Aphrodite told me to … it was a relief, honestly. And they all acted like Aphrodite was every inch the Goddess she says she is. They kept making me feel like a fool for questioning her words … turns out I was a fool for believing her.'

Rose took hold of her arm. 'You're not a fool. Some people are masters at manipulating others, of finding weaknesses, or needs, or deeply buried wants and exploiting them. And she had you captive, with no other influences, surrounded by demons already under her spell. Honestly, it could have happened to any of us.'

Gemma laughed. 'You know that's not true … Raina would never get sucked in by a cult, or Meredith, or you …'

'Who can say for sure?' said Rose. 'Caspar's not immune to flattery and tempting ideology … and Talli would be a cult leader like a shot if we let her … and don't get me started on Zahora and Noah … they'd be sucked straight in.'

'They're children,' said Gemma, although she appreciated the sentiment.

'And you've been through a lot … you question yourself, because for lifetimes others undermined you. It would have broken most people, but you survived, and this time, you woke up to the cult and then escaped. You were there for only a few short weeks.'

Gemma nodded, Rose's words easing her embarrassment. 'Let's just get this over with,' she said, and set off towards the castle.

When Rose and Gemma arrived upstairs in the castle, the room was already packed. It quietened down when Rose marched to the front, the other demons watching her with a mix of intrigue and hostility.

Great. Not exactly a supportive audience … Not that Gemma was surprised.

'Good afternoon,' said Rose, 'and thank you for coming. I know there are those among us who do not believe in the free movement of demons. As you know, I have proposed that we make free movement a requirement for all nations affiliated with the Registerium. Some of you don't think this is necessary, and I am here to bring to life why I believe it is. Gemma has agreed—at great personal cost—to share with us her story.'

Gemma stepped up beside Rose, who squeezed her arm, then sat. She looked at the sea of faces and shuddered. It reminded her of the West Coast, the room's eyes on her ... only this time not because they thought she was a goddess, but because she was something else entirely.

'I was a sex slave for many lifetimes,' she said in a rush, the words almost painful. 'When I was a young demon—only in my second life—a man approached me as I was making my way home from the market. I was the youngest of twelve siblings, and my parents barely knew I existed, so when the man told me I was special, I listened.

'The man was young, charismatic, and handsome, and he befriended me. He regularly sought me out, helped me with chores, told me I was beautiful ... I had the romantic notion that he liked me, that he might marry me and take me away from my insignificant life. In the end, he did take me away, but there was nothing romantic about it ...

'One day, he came to my house, and found my brother beating me, my other siblings looking on ... encouraging him. The memories of my previous life had returned, and my siblings thought me possessed. The man fought my brother, then took me with him, like my knight in shining armor ... He reassured me with promises and pretty words. He told me about demons, said he was one too, that we were special, that he could offer me safety as a member of his nation.

'I jumped at the offer. I was a young, impressionable, naïve fool, and knew no other demons.

236

I was terrified of what would happen to me without him.'

'And who among us could say they would have acted differently?' said Rose.

Someone in the middle of the audience laughed, shifting as though about to say something. Rose turned her warning gaze on him, and he shrank back in his chair. To Gemma's surprise, every other demon was listening intently.

'They welcomed me with open arms … were nice to me. I happily swore myself to their nation through their stone. After that, it didn't take long for their kindness to turn into something … else. It happened little by little, so I barely questioned it. First, it was small things like extra chores around the camp, then it was foot or back rubs for the leadership council, and then, one day, one of the leaders took me to their special place …'

Gemma paused and looked out of the window. She took a deep breath, stealing herself before she went on. 'The camp had an area that was off limits to all but a select few. I was intrigued beyond measure, but they said it was a most holy, sacred place, and I would be killed if I went there without permission. As I said, I was naïve, and timid … and I didn't understand the knowing looks the men gave each other, or the looks of pity the older women shared.

'So that day,' said Gemma, blinking back the tears that stabbed like blades in her eyes, 'I was excited when the leader came to get me … thought I was special … that all the extra work had been a test, and that I'd passed. He told me I had to be a good girl, that I had to do what they said, that I would be rewarded … and then he took me into a room with three other men … '

Gemma faltered as the image flashed before her eyes. She could still see it clear as day, as though it were

237

taking place right in front of her. No matter that it had been hundreds of years, no matter that she wanted the image to fade, or better yet, disintegrate entirely.

'The men were naked, and they raped me—all three of them together—while the leader watched. I had no idea what was happening … they'd recruited me for my naivety, after all. It was a common story among the girls they kept in that special group of huts. We believed we were serving a higher purpose, that those men had a right to abuse us in that way … that it was *holy* …'

Tears rolled down her cheeks, but she didn't bother to brush them away … *Let them see.*

'As the years—lifetimes—ticked by, I saw things here and there I wasn't supposed to … overheard conversations … convinced older, wiser women to talk to me. I didn't like what the men did to me—any time of the day or night, as they saw fit—so it wasn't so much of a surprise when an older woman told me it was a cult … explained what that was.

'But the worst thing wasn't the abuse— unspeakable as it was—the worst thing was that after I woke up to the reality, I was trapped, with no way out, because demons of their nation could not move freely. In the lifetimes after that, I reincarnated a little further away every time, some part of me fighting my cage, but I was always too close, and they found me. I had nowhere else to go … knew no one but them, and was scared to death of telling anyone about them. And they knew it … they knew I was powerless.

'Then Rose found me in the market one day. By that time, they'd had me for so many lifetimes, they'd grown bored of me. They still used me as they pleased, but they also put me to work doing chores. I became one of those older women who gave each other heavy looks every time a new recruit appeared.

'Rose befriended me, and over time, told me about other nations. She said she knew others—many others—who could help me. But I was nervous … what if Rose's nation was as bad—or worse—than the one I was in? I had no experience of kindness …

'But eventually she convinced me … she brought other demons to talk to me, and told me how her nation allowed free movement. But even after I'd built the courage to leave, I had to wait for my next reincarnation. I killed myself, wanting to hasten the process, but that made my nation angry, and they paid an army of hunters to find me. They got me before I was awake, and convinced me to swear myself to them, using the same pretty words that had worked before.

'So I had to wait for another lifetime, this time letting nature run its course. Those were the worst years of all … biding my time … enduring abuse even when I'd made up my mind to go. If free movement had been allowed, I could have escaped so much earlier than I did … I could have got others to come with me … could have rescued so many from that life. And it would have been easier for demons like Rose to help.

'I implore you to implement the free movement of demons. I don't dare to think how many are still slaves today …' Silence rippled out across the room, the whole place still for a beat.

'I am sorry for your story,' said a member of the Shindu Council, 'but yours is an extreme case … we can't make rules based on outliers.'

Rose stood from her seat, placing herself next to Gemma. 'It pains me to say that Gemma's is not an extreme case. I am ashamed of our race every time a new story meets my ears. This happens all the time, right under our noses … demons grow bored after many lives, and the mean ones entertain themselves by inflicting pain and suffering on others.'

'It's not only sex slavery,' said a man near the back of the room, 'it's other kinds of slavery too. I know this only too well … The Russian Spirituals will stand with the Pagans on this matter.'

'I too know the violence of which you speak,' said a woman near the front. 'I had to endure it for only a single lifetime, but that was enough.'

Gemma bowed her head. That others in this room—some of the most powerful, influential demons—had also suffered captivity and abuse, spoke to just what a prolific issue it was.

'Allowing free movement will not stop this issue … not by any means,' said a Viking.

'No,' said Rose, 'unfortunately you are right. But it is a step … it will help.'

'We have always insisted on loyalty as a condition of membership to our nation,' said an Egyptian, 'and if we remove it, we leave ourselves open to spies.'

'Many nations—including my own—already allow free movement,' said Rose. 'We do not have a problem with information leakage that is any worse than yours … and just because something has always been thus, does not mean it is right, or that it should continue.

'I ask you to think on the matter … to keep in your minds those you could save. Their suffering is the cost of enforced loyalty. Is it really necessary? For what? Tradition? Are we so old and fusty that we can't change?'

Several of the older demons chuckled.

'Yes, I am aware that I, too, am old and fusty,' said Rose, with a smile. 'But on this matter, I implore you, please, help us make a difference to the lives of those who are suffering.'

'I've got it!' Noah shouted triumphantly. He'd been staring at the three stone tablets for hours, had utilized many webpages and scoured every atlas he could find in the old house—which was four. 'The location's in Crete!'

Noah danced around wildly, catching Zahora up and spinning her with him, then he kissed her. 'Oh my God, it feels *so* good,' he sang.

Zahora laughed. 'How did you work it out?' she said, pulling him back to the table.

He stood behind her, his arms around her waist, chin resting on her shoulder. 'The marks represent landmarks around the world—not all of them current. The inscriptions tell you the direction you should travel from one landmark to the next. The star is the start location—the cave where Talli and Christa found the tablets—not the end location.'

'What does the end location look like?' said Zahora.

'A crescent moon,' he said, 'over Crete.'

'If you're right …'

'I am right,' he said, cockily.

'Then you're very clever,' said Zahora, patting his arm.

'You were going to call me a genius, weren't you? *If you're right, you're a genius*?'

'No,' said Zahora, with an eye roll.

'Come on,' he said, kissing her ear, 'say it.'

'Get. A. Room,' said Meredith, striding in with Alerac, a deep scowl on her face.

Alerac's features were schooled into a blank mask, and Zahora wondered what was going on.

Zahora held onto Noah's arms, holding him in place when he tried to move away ... she wouldn't let Meredith intimidate them.

'Noah found the location,' said Zahora.

'It's in Crete,' said Noah. 'In Chania, I think, although it's hard to tell for sure.'

'Wonderful,' Meredith said sarcastically.

Zahora looked to Alerac with questioning eyes. 'Meredith and I will be the ones to visit the location,' said Alerac.

'Is that a bad thing?' said Zahora, not understanding. The rumor was that Alerac and Meredith had been sleeping together for some time ... a romantic trip away from prying eyes sounded pretty good to her.

'Meredith's been on many similar trips of late,' said Alerac. 'She had hoped to stay put for a while.'

'Don't talk about me like I'm not here,' Meredith snapped. 'How did you work it out?'

Noah walked them through the map, step by step. 'And I think this means it's on the western side, don't you?'

Alerac gave a non-committal nod.

'Then we'd better get packing,' said Meredith, stalking out of the kitchen.

Alerac, Noah, and Zahora exchanged loaded looks before Alerac followed in her wake.

Chapter 15

Meredith and Alerac arrived in the small port of Chania, famous for its military history and towering lighthouse. It was quaint, and Meredith imagined how it would have been in its prime … before legions of tourists descended on the waterfront, and cafes with plastic menus serving plastic food sprung up in their droves.

They checked into their hotel, a couple of streets back from the water, and Meredith was pleased to find her room quiet and serene.

'There's an excellent restaurant on the other side of town,' said Alerac, looking around the room.

'You've been here before?'

He smiled. 'I asked at reception, and the internet agrees,' he said, putting down his bag.

'You're not sleeping in here,' she said. She was happy with her hostile tone, but her heart raced. 'I requested two rooms for a reason …'

Alerac raised his eyebrows but said nothing. Silence descended on them, and Meredith felt suddenly vulnerable, exposed. She turned away, looked out of the window, was about to ask him to leave …

His footsteps approached, and she froze, every muscle in her body tense. He reached her, standing close enough that she could feel his breath on her hair. 'Can I touch you?' he said quietly.

She shivered at the intensity in his voice, then nodded.

He swept her long hair to one side, baring her neck, then lowered his lips to her skin.

'I know what you're doing,' she said, her voice husky.

'Kissing you?' he said, resting his head against hers. The warmth of his skin was soothing, her skin longing for more contact, like her nerve endings were buttons needing to be pressed.

'Wearing down my defenses.'

'I like being near you, that's all. And there's no one here but us.'

'Rose has spies everywhere … Ira's probably listening through our phones.'

'Turn around,' he said.

She obeyed without conscious thought, and he wrapped her in his arms. She delighted in the pressure on her skin.

'It's okay,' he said, rubbing soothing circles on her back. 'No one thinks less of you for this.'

'We'll never hear the end of it … and … I'm married.'

'You mean to Torsten?'

Meredith sniffed. 'Yes.'

Alerac chuckled. 'Hasn't he married the new leader of my nation? I don't think he minds …'

'I made a vow.'

'A fake vow,' said Alerac.

Meredith huffed. Why was this so hard for her? She'd built defenses during her lifetimes of being single … of being alone … it felt so wrong to let him in.

'I'm not expecting a lifelong commitment,' he said, 'but I'd like to kiss you in public, or hold your hand, or to cuddle and not have to jump apart at every sound.'

'I don't know if I can ...' She buried her face harder in Alerac's neck, not able to look at him.

'Why?' he said, stroking her hair with deft hands. 'Because of the others?'

No, her mind shouted what would have been her usual response, but she fought the lie. 'Yes,' she whispered, leaning into his touch. 'Relationships are vulnerabilities, and I don't like those. I have to protect my nation against threats, have to be feared and respected ... I can't run around like a lovesick puppy ... what will my soldiers think?'

'Much as I'd like to flatter myself, no one thinks you're any kind of puppy, let alone a lovesick one ... and no one will think less of you for having a relationship.'

'You're underestimating what judgmental sons of bitches my friends are.'

'They might tease you—I'm not denying that—but they'll also be happy for you.'

'They expect me to be with someone like Torsten ... a warrior.' Alerac was tall, but he didn't have the muscle mass of a warrior. He was strong, but wiry.

'Hey, I'm every bit as dangerous as Torsten ...' he said, his tone like cut glass.

'I know,' said Meredith, 'but you fight with magic ... it's different.'

'What's the worst that could happen?' he said, gently pulling her face out of his neck, forcing her to look at him. 'They make a few jokes? And it's not like we're declaring we've found our soulmates ...'

The wiliness that had drawn her to him glimmered in his eyes, but a wave of nausea flooded her at the word *soulmates*. Alerac wasn't the kind of man who would be her soulmate ... She pulled away.

'I just ...' she said, then trailed off.

'Just take it step by step,' he said. 'This isn't all or nothing ... we're just dating ... there's no pressure.'

Meredith nodded. 'You're right ... I know you're right ... but my gut's telling me something ... toxic ... screaming it at me, and it's hard to ignore.'

Alerac and Meredith walked hand in hand as they made their way to a Lebanese restaurant for dinner. Meredith's shoulders tensed as their fingers entwined, sure that people would look at their joined limbs and judge her ... laugh at her ... wonder why she was with him.

When none of those things came to pass, her shoulders relaxed, the tightness in her chest eased, and she felt like an idiot. What had she been so afraid of? This was fine ... normal ... no one cared.

Alerac threw her a smile, and she smiled in return. He lifted the back of her hand to his lips, and to her surprise, that was fine too.

'I'm sorry ...' she said, trying to find words to convey how deeply she regretted her emotional stuntedness.

'Don't be,' he said. 'Don't apologize for your feelings.'

She faltered. 'Thank you.'

They entered the most beautiful rustic courtyard with four restaurants, two on each side. They sat outside, under a heater, and Alerac played with her fingers across the table.

They over-ordered, the waiter bringing plate after plate of the most delicious babaganoush, hummus, stuffed vine leaves, succulent meats and rice, olives, pitta bread, tabouleh, and falafel. They washed it all down with red wine, the gentle background music and flickering candlelight creating a soft, dreamy ambiance.

'This is my favorite kind of meal,' said Meredith.

'Mine too,' he said. 'I love having lots of bits to pick at.'

Meredith took a sip of wine, rolling the flavors around her mouth. 'Hmmm, red wine always makes me sentimental,' she said.

'Despite the great time we've been on this planet,' said Alerac, 'some things never change.'

'I spent several lives working in a vineyard in the south of France,' she said. 'The smell transports me there every time I crack a bottle. And lavender … there was a lavender farm next door. I love that too … not the fake stuff you get today, but the deep, rich, potent oil.'

'Oils were a big part of my magical training … lots of orchid and rose. It reminds me of having my hands slapped, because I ceaselessly did things wrong …'

Meredith laughed. 'I can't imagine you as a young demon.'

'Good,' said Alerac. 'That's the way I prefer it. I, however, can imagine you, before you became a warrior, carefree and wild.'

Meredith looked away. 'Those days were a long time ago … I've been a warrior for so long, I forget I was ever anything else.'

Silence settled over them as they drank their wine and ate baklava, but then a prickle traveled down Meredith's spine, like someone was watching them. She tensed, casting around for threats, but none was immediately apparent. She raised her glass to her lips, but couldn't relax.

'So,' said Meredith, signaling for the check, her senses on high alert, 'how do we find whatever it is we're here to find?'

'You don't have to,' said a voice from right behind her. She turned with a start to find a short, slight man with grey-streaked hair who looked to be in his sixties. 'It's found you …'

Meredith stared at the back of the magik's head as he led them through narrow streets. He didn't take them far, ushering them through a nondescript door into an airy, open-plan living space.

From the street, the house had looked shabby, but inside, it was jarringly modern, complete with a sunken firepit and enormous television.

Meredith realized her mouth was open as she took it all in. She closed it just as she noticed the star mosaic on the floor. It was a masterpiece, so much so she barely wanted to stand on it.

'Come in, come in,' said the magik, his voice a halting mix of accents. 'Sit.' He picked up a remote control, and suddenly music played, the fire sprang to life, and a panel under the television slid open, revealing a drinks nook.

They sat on the loungers surrounding the fire, Meredith's eyes still darting around, trying to take in every tiny detail. Maybe the mosaic floor contained clues …

'What can I get you?' said the magik. 'I have most things … let me see … grappa? Whiskey? Pisco? Rum? Tequila?'

'I'd take a gin and tonic,' said Meredith.

'Preference on which gin or tonic?' he said.

'Surprise me,' said Meredith.

'I'll take a rum on the rocks,' said Alerac.

The magik nodded and turned his back, making their drinks and pouring a whisky for himself. He handed them cut crystal tumblers, a swirling cloud of pink descending through Meredith's glass.

'Thank you … ah … I'm sorry, I don't know your name,' said Meredith. 'I'm Meredith, of the Pagan nation, and this is Alerac, of the Aztecs.'

The man nodded, then went back for his own crystal tumbler. 'I'm Giorgio, of the Star Nation.' He waggled his eyebrows. 'But I'm assuming you already knew my nation.' He lounged back in his seat, crossing an ankle over his knee as he took a sip of his drink.

'How did you know we were searching for you?' said Meredith.

He gave her a look, one that said the answer was obvious, but he said, 'Magic,' just to hammer the point home.

Meredith would have loved to know specifically what magic … such magic would undoubtedly be a useful defense tool, but she let it go … they had more important topics to discuss.

'Do you know why we're here?' she said.

'I'm assuming you found one of the maps?'

'There's more than one?' said Alerac.

'Ha!' he laughed. 'There are many ... although I think you are the first to find one ... certainly the first to successfully follow it.'

'What are they for?' said Meredith.

'They're a game, of sorts,' said Giorgio. 'We old demons must find something to entertain us, after all. One of our nation—currently under sacrifice, alas—spent years making those damn tablets. It was his hobby.'

Meredith wasn't surprised. The older demons grew, the more eccentric they generally became ... and he was right, demons had to find some way to entertain themselves after spending so long on the planet.

'How long has he been under sacrifice?' said Alerac, shifting in his seat.

'Worried about your own time?' said Giorgio, raising his considerable eyebrows once more.

Alerac didn't respond.

'He's been gone for two hundred years, or thereabouts. But he was an Adept, and used magic heavily every day of his life for many lifetimes. They're all gone ... all the Stars except me ... and I feel the magic's pull ... I shall have to sacrifice soon. I hope at least one of my fellow Stars will have returned by then, but I may not be so lucky.'

'How many members does your nation have?' said Meredith.

'Twelve, at last count,' he said, 'assuming they all come back. So, did you find me to satisfy your curiosity, or is there something more?'

'There's much more,' said Meredith. 'We're hoping you can help us ...'

'Oh?' said Giorgio, raising an eyebrow. 'This should be good.'

'The Registerium's magic is broken, and most nations have not kept themselves magically skilled,' said Meredith. 'We would like to re-tie the nations' bonds to the Registerium's stone, but don't know how to. We know the Nation of Stars set up the magic, so are hoping you can help us.'

Giorgio laughed. 'Ha! That's the most entertaining thing I've heard in fifty years ... maybe seventy-five. But why would I help you? What do you offer in return?'

'The warm fuzzy feeling associated with doing the right thing and helping others?' said Meredith.

'I help at an orphanage ... I have plenty of warm fuzzy feelings already.'

'Looking for sleeping demons?' said Alerac. 'In the orphanage?'

Giorgio shrugged.

'Hardly the purest of motives,' said Alerac.

Giorgio shrugged again, evidently not caring. 'The nations bicker like children, kill each other like fighting cocks, and forget the world is bigger than themselves. They deserve nothing ... especially not help from me.'

'Ame implied as much,' said Meredith.

Giorgio looked at her a little too quickly, the set of his jaw becoming rigid. 'Ame?' he said.

'She said the Nation of Stars never do anything if it's not for themselves ... that you care only about furthering your own selfish aims.'

'Yes, well, not all of us are like that. I for one disagreed with the choices of our leader, but if this Ame is the demon I know, she betrayed both her mother and our nation ... You've seen her recently? She's back from her sacrifice to the magic?'

'She is,' said Meredith, 'and she betrayed us too.'

'No surprise there ... that woman is a snake ...'

'What did she do?' said Alerac.

Giorgio gave him a long look. 'She had an affair with our leader, then ran away with his child. He searched for her ... used every tool at his disposal, but she stayed hidden ... no one knows how, or why. If you ask me, she had a screw loose ... but then, so did our leader.'

'What did you want that was different to him?' said Meredith.

'I was happy to research magic, as was our initial mission, but the more we found, the more knowledge he could sell ... or barter with. The Registerium was one of our later projects ... by then, many of us were tired of being magiks for hire. We wanted to spend our time somewhere quiet, where we could research to our hearts' content.'

'Is that what you do now?' said Meredith. 'Research?'

'It is,' said Giorgio. 'I enjoy the peace and quiet.'

'What if we had something to offer you in exchange for your help?' said Alerac. 'Something unique.'

'I doubt you have anything that would interest me, but by all means, give it a go ...'

'We have a Sage.'

Giorgio laughed. 'There are no Sages ... may never have been. The best we ever had were Adepts. There are myths and legends, to be sure, but that's all they are. Sages—if they ever existed—exist no longer.'

'They do,' said Alerac. 'I don't know what happened in the past, but we have a Sage—Zahora—and she's powerful beyond measure. She touched the Sphere and survived.'

'The Sphere below?' said Giorgio.

'Yes,' said Alerac. 'So it's true there are multiple Spheres?'

'Of course. At least two … we think more … if only others of my nation would awake, we could make progress finding them …'

'Maybe Zahora could help …' said Meredith.

'No one has ever touched the Sphere and survived. I don't know what yarn this Zahora has been spinning, but she's lying.'

'She's not,' said Alerac. 'Remember the magic wave? The anomaly? You must have felt it … must have wondered what caused it?'

'It was her?' said Giorgio.

'It was,' said Alerac.

Giorgio huffed, then put down his glass. 'What proof do you have of this?'

'Zahora is the proof,' said Alerac. 'As you will see for yourself if you agree to meet her.'

Giorgio stood abruptly. 'Well then, I suppose I should get my coat.'

The Pagans left Scotland and headed for the magic compound in Wales. There was little more they could do to persuade the other nations, and Malcolm would represent their interests in Rose's absence. Rose would return for the vote in a few days, after Noah's registration.

Noah and Zahora lay in bed, in the same hut she'd had as a trainee magik … was she still considered a trainee magik? It didn't matter, because Zahora was buzzing. 'Finally,' she said, 'someone who can teach me …'

Noah brushed a strand of hair back off her face. 'Try not to get too excited,' he said. 'This could be another dead end …'

'I know,' said Zahora. 'It's so strange being back here, don't you think?'

'It's surreal,' Noah agreed, 'after everything that's happened. The compound's emptier though … considerably.'

Zahora laughed. 'Apparently, Marla got fed up with all the inexperienced magiks cluttering up the place. She sent most of them away.'

'To be fair, they didn't bring much to the party …'

'No,' said Zahora, 'and it's much more pleasant without them.'

Noah nodded, dropping a kiss on her shoulder. 'And it's nice not to have to sneak around like naughty kids,' he said.

A bell sounded outside, and Zahora and Noah looked at each other in confusion. 'I thought it was a day off …?' she said.

Noah went still as the bell continued to ring. 'We should get dressed,' he said, throwing back the covers. They'd snuck away after lunch, and it was now late afternoon, the sun setting.

Urgent shouts sounded from outside. 'Everyone out! We're under attack!'

Zahora froze, nightmarish images of the previous attack pinning her in place.

'Fuck,' said Noah, throwing Zahora her jeans. The action snapped her out of it, and she quickly put them on, along with a jumper, coat, and boots.

They ran out into the twilight, finding Pagans scurrying this way and that.

'Here,' said Talli, spotting them, 'go with the others, into the caves.'

'What if they know about the tunnels?' said Zahora.

'Marla blocked them up,' said Talli. 'They can't get in that way ... but there's also no way out.'

Noah grabbed Zahora's hand and pulled her towards the caves.

'Thank the Gods,' said Raina, as they reached the entrance. 'Please look after Callie; Caspar and I have to fight.'

Tears filled Zahora's eyes, but she blinked them away ... Callie needed her to be strong. She nodded, then took Callie's hand. 'It's going to be okay,' said Zahora, pulling Callie into the caves. 'Your mum and dad are fearsome warriors.'

They went to the cave with the standing stone, where those who couldn't fight had gathered, and sat down to wait.

Gemma stepped in front of their meagre defense: a handful of soldiers, the Pagan leaders, and a few warrior magiks. It was all they had, and she prayed it would be enough ... and that more of Meredith's soldiers would arrive soon ...

Meredith had installed an early warning system after the last attack, which meant everyone, including their ally nations, would know what was going on. But Meredith was on her way back from Crete, so Gemma was in command. She tried to remember when Meredith's flight landed … where her flight landed … but she wasn't sure she'd ever known …

'Ira searched the footage from the cameras Meredith installed,' said Gemma, looking out over the collection of grim faces. 'It's the West Coast. Aphrodite, Ares, Hades, and Hephaestus are all here.'

Gemma looked at Elliot, who sent her a reassuring nod. He was trying to tell her this wasn't her fault, and she agreed with him. It wasn't her fault, but that made no difference … it wouldn't stop the attack.

'We must hold the gate,' said Gemma. 'With the new fences, it's the only way in. But we must also station guards sparingly around the perimeter, so we know if they breach our defenses there.'

Gemma pointed to specific guards and gave them orders. They nodded, then jogged to their posts.

'The rest of us will form ranks behind the gate,' said Gemma. Meredith had installed a formidable steel structure which would be hard to force, but she'd seen their enemy up close … they were exceptionally well trained.

'We will take it in turns to fend them off,' said Gemma, handing out the spears Meredith had cached near the gate. 'We will switch regularly to keep up our strength. I expect this will be a long, drawn-out engagement. We must keep them at bay until reinforcements arrive.'

'Others are already on their way,' said Rose, her brow furrowed, 'but the closest are over an hour away.'

'When does Meredith land?' said Gemma.

'She should be landing now,' said Rose, 'but it will take at least two hours for her to get here.'

The bell tolled again … the invaders closing in … only a few hundred meters away. 'Helmets,' said Gemma, 'quickly.'

They donned the military helmets and radios, again, curtesy of Meredith's thorough defense upgrades after the last attack, then took up their positions.

Elliot stood next to Gemma and squeezed her hand. 'I love you,' he said in her ear.

'I love you too,' she replied. 'Don't let them catch you …'

'Nor you,' he said, 'and if we should fall, I'll see you in the next life.'

They kissed, a brief, chaste thing, and as they pulled apart, Gemma looked to the others—Raina and Caspar, Talli and Christa, Rose and Marla—finding them saying their goodbyes too.

Then Talli drummed her spear on the ground, and gooseflesh spread across Gemma's skin. The rhythm was menacing, and the others picked it up, adding a deep, terrifying battle chant to the rhythm.

By the time they saw their enemy, cast in a golden glow by the setting sun, the beating, chanting, stamping ritual had banished their fear. They were itching to be the first to draw blood … to kill.

At the front of the attack were five figures—the Pentalpha—and Gemma vaguely wondered who had replaced her … a woman she didn't recognize.

The five of them stopped, but they signaled their soldiers forward, and demons surged towards the gate, screaming battle cries of their own. There must have been hundreds of them.

The narrow trails provided some defense, forcing their enemy to travel slowly, at most two or three abreast as they approached the compound, but the space in front of the gate was wider … wide enough for eight of them at least side by side. The enemy had to be careful though, for if they slipped, the fall down the steep incline would not be pleasant, and could well mean death.

The first wave of soldiers crashed into the gate, and the front rank of Pagans speared them in the chest. They went down, slowing those behind them, who had to pull their dying comrades back before launching their own attack. The Pagans had had the element of surprise with the spears, but the enemy knew the danger now … future kills wouldn't be so easy.

The fighting was tit for tat for a long while, long enough that the Pagans switched ranks four times. The enemy scored a few nicks, the Pagans a few deaths, but neither side made any real progress.

Gemma knew something would change soon. Ares didn't call himself the God of War for nothing, and these tactics wouldn't deliver victory, but the Pentalpha—when she caught glimpses of them— seemed calm … too calm.

And then a buzzing sounded in the sky. Gemma whirled to face it, and her guts churned. 'What the fuck are those?' she said, pointing to the flock of approaching flying machines … and it looked like … demons hanging from the contraptions, ready to … ready to drop.

Gemma sent a stream of urgent orders through the radio. She pulled most of the perimeter troops back, leaving the gate with only one rank, then led the others towards where soldiers dropped from the sky.

Gemma wished they had a way to bring down the flying machines, but unlike the West Coast, they were limited by the Registerium's rules. They couldn't draw human attention, and were only supposed to fight with knives. Firing projectiles of any kind would put them in breach of the rules.

The first of the aerial attackers fell to the ground, and the Pagans were on them in a heartbeat. Marla, Talli, and Christa protected the caves, while the others spread out to wherever their attackers landed. But there were too many of them, and the Pagans couldn't be everywhere at once.

Gemma wielded a short sword in one hand and an axe in the other. She made quick work of two soldiers before they'd even gained their balance after the drop.

But then she saw Rose, only a few paces away, fighting three attackers. Gemma didn't think. She ran, screaming as she went, to draw their attention. Rose felled one, and Gemma took out the second, but the third's blade slid into Rose's chest a fraction of a second before Gemma's axe split his skull.

'No!' screamed Gemma, as she watched the life-force drain out of Rose. 'No … Rose!'

'Fight,' Rose mouthed … and then she was gone.

Gemma had no time to dwell, with more of their enemy dropping every second. She launched to her feet, fighting with renewed vigor, fueled by loss and anger. They would not all die here today. She felled soldier after soldier, her hands and weapons slick with blood, the ground stained red.

'Gemma!' screamed Marla, from the cave entrance.

Gemma ran, jumping dead bodies, but Marla was down by the time she reached her. Gemma couldn't spare a second to see if she was still alive … couldn't help her if she was. If she lost focus for a single second, Gemma would die too.

Talli and Christa fought five of their enemy, and Gemma chased another into the caves. She threw her axe, and the soldier fell to the floor. Gemma collected her weapon, then spun back to the entrance.

Christa clutched at her arm as Gemma emerged into the light, Talli finishing off the last of the immediate threat.

'Go inside,' said Talli. 'Get someone to fix your arm.'

'I'm fine,' said Christa. 'It's just a graze.'

Talli pulled Christa's hand away from her arm. 'That is not a graze.'

'Fine,' said Christa, as blood gushed from the wound. 'But I'll be ...' Christa faltered, then fell forward to the floor, a war axe in her back.

'Christa!' screamed Talli, crouching at her side.

'Talli, I need you,' said Gemma, as seven soldiers raced towards them, grins on their faces. 'Talli ... now!'

Talli came to her feet, and a furious calm spread over her. They fought back-to-back, slaughtering soldier after solider, their enemies' triumphant grins turning uncertain, then to expressions of terror.

But their victory was short-lived, as Raina, Caspar, and Elliot appeared, all of them beaten and battered. 'The gate's about to fall,' said Raina. 'We must defend the caves.'

Gemma nodded and put out a call on the radio for every remaining soldier to fall back to the caves.

They heard the gates crash open, the victorious cheer of their enemy hollowing out Gemma's insides. And then the Pentalpha appeared in front of the cave entrance, flanked by their soldiers, many of whom had, until now, only stood and watched, fresh and eager to draw blood.

'Gemma ... Elliot,' said Aphrodite. 'What a pleasure to see you again. Although, I fear you backed the wrong horse ...' Her smile was sadistic, her true colors shining through.

'Why are you here?' said Gemma, trying to identify the new member of the Pentalpha. She looked familiar, but ... who was the woman behind the war paint?

'I thought that was obvious,' said Aphrodite. 'To destroy the Pagans, so we can take back Mount Olympus ... our home.'

'Yes,' said Gemma, 'but why attack here specifically?'

The new member of the Pentalpha chuckled, and Aphrodite waved a hand in her direction, handing the floor to her.

'It really is baffling how the nations have let magic slide to such a degree,' said a familiar voice.

'Ame?' said Talli.

Ame ... of course. Gemma had only seen her briefly, when she'd sought refuge with the West Coast, but it was obvious now she knew.

Ame smirked. 'You didn't really think you'd seen the last of me, did you?'

'We have no quarrel with you,' said Raina. 'You may hate me for what I did to your son, but that was me and me alone; it had nothing to do with my nation.'

'Your nation is harboring a Sage ... she's a danger to us all and must be stopped. I told you this, and you ignored me ... not a single member of your nation could comprehend the necessity of action.'

'How is she a threat?' said Raina. 'She's little more than a child ... she has no hostile intentions ... all she wants is to be valued ... to have a home.'

'That's what most demons want,' said Ame. 'It doesn't mean she isn't dangerous.'

'Why is she such a threat?' said Raina. 'In times gone by, Adepts like you were hunted, as you are now hunting Zahora. Demons were scared of your powerful magic, just as you fear Zahora's. Should all Adepts be killed?'

'This is different,' said Ame. 'She has the potential to upset the balance ... to break reincarnation as we know it.'

'Sounds a little dramatic ...' said Talli. 'And Raina's right ... I've heard similar claims made about Adepts.'

'You don't understand,' said Ame, through gritted teeth. 'She *took* from the Sphere ... no Adept has ever done that. She wields the power of the Sphere, but doesn't know how to use it safely ... if such a thing is possible. She destroyed the connections between the Registerium and the nations ... she's the cause of so much chaos, and she needs to be stopped.'

'She trusted you,' said Talli, 'and you wielded her as a weapon to serve your own ends. You're the reason the connection was severed, not Zahora. She would never ...'

'Enough,' said Ares. He strode forward, his sword raised. 'You have no hope of holding these caves ... you are few, and we are many. Surrender, or die.'

'We will never surrender,' said Raina, squaring her shoulders, as did her comrades.

'Then ...' But Ares faltered as a messenger approached, murmuring words in Aphrodite's ear.

The Pagans didn't have to wonder what news the messenger had brought, as Ira's voice sounded in their own ears. 'Meredith's arrived, as have two Pagan squadrons. They're fighting their way up to the compound.'

Hope kindled in Gemma's chest, and she stood a little taller as Aphrodite dispatched half of the West Coast's force to meet the new Pagan threat, along with Hades and Hephaestus.

'They're too late,' said Aphrodite, her words a snarl. 'We will be done here long before they make it.'

'Maybe,' said Raina, 'maybe not.' She swung her sword lazily. 'We are warriors ... have beaten the odds in many wars.'

'Have survived fights more terrifying than this,' said Talli, with a smile. 'And you just killed my soulmate ... I'm looking forward to revenge.'

'No more words,' said Ares, losing patience. And then he lunged, with a roar.

Raina barely got her sword up in time to block Ares' bone shattering blow. She twisted to the side, making him move, hearing the others engage as she dodged another savage swing.

'The great Raina ... running away?' Ares mocked.

Raina feigned left, then swung right, slicing his leg just above his battle leathers. Ares went down with a heavy thud, and Raina was on him in a second. Ares rolled, taking Raina's legs out, and she collapsed on top of him, dropping her sword and grabbing his arm as he stabbed with his dagger.

She couldn't match his strength, so she rolled backwards, the change of direction taking him by surprise. She pulled him with her, lifting her feet, then crashed them into his torso, propelling him away. He grabbed at her, but she twisted, escaping his grasp.

She snatched up her sword and crouched, preparing to attack, but before she could, Gemma stepped behind Ares, a dagger in her hand. He sensed her a moment too late, trying to turn, but Gemma's knife was already cutting a path across the exposed skin of his neck. His weight slammed into Gemma, forcing her back, but he went down, clutching his throat. Raina saw in his eyes he knew he was done.

But as Aphrodite roared at the sight of Ares on the floor, the West Coast breached the Pagans' line and flooded into the caves.

'No!' bellowed Raina and Caspar together, pursuing their enemy, who were headed for their daughter.

Aphrodite laughed. 'It's over,' she shouted after them. 'You're done!'

And Raina knew it was true, because they'd barely had the numbers to hold the narrow cave entrance. Now they were inside, unconstrained, there was no way to stop them … they were too many. The only hope was that Raina or Caspar could get to Callie before the West Coast … to kill her rather than let her be taken …

The thought spurred Raina on as she chased after Caspar and their enemy, that, and the sound of more soldiers behind. They pelted towards the standing stone, where Pagans huddling together, terror in their eyes. But as a wave of panic gripped Raina, as they got so close she could see her daughter's face buried in Noah's shirt, the enemy soldiers fell to the ground … every single one.

Raina stopped dead, whirling to look behind her, finding the soldiers there on the floor too. She looked wildly around. 'What the hell happened?' she said.

Caspar shook his head, but then the movement halted. 'Zahora …' he said. 'A shield …?'

'Maybe Ame was right,' said Raina, casting an eye over Callie to make sure she was okay, then rushing back towards the entrance. 'Maybe she is dangerous after all …'

Zahora, Noah, and Callie huddled together, Callie clinging to Zahora like a limpet.

'It's going to be okay,' said Zahora, smoothing her hair. 'They won't get in here … we're all going to be fine.'

But Zahora knew that wasn't necessarily the case, just like last time. There would be deaths … many of them, and Zahora hoped against hope that Raina and Caspar survived.

'It's going to be okay,' Zahora repeated, over and over. But then she heard a buzzing outside, and felt something ripple across the ether … some change that wasn't in their favor. If only she could do something … something magical. If only she'd had proper training …

But then it hit her … there was something she could do … something she'd done before.

'The shield,' Zahora breathed, looking at Noah.

'But you need perimeter markers,' said Noah.

'Let's hope no one thought to remove them,' said Zahora, handing Callie to Noah. 'I have to try something Cals … Noah will look after you.'

Zahora thought Callie was going to argue … hold on and refuse to let go, but Noah pulled a band aid out of his pocket. 'Hey, Callie, I think I have a cut … can you help me?'

Delight shone in her eyes as she momentarily forgot to be scared. She snatched the band aid from Noah's fingers, and set about opening it, instructing Noah to show her the wound.

Zahora didn't hesitate. She stood by the stone and connected to the Nexus. She felt for the perimeter, and found, to her dismay, that many of the markers were gone. She could send a sliver of magic around the circle, but the drain was extraordinary.

Zahora paused, considering that she might not even be able to get the shield up, let alone make it stable. She wracked her brain, trying to think how Ame had reduced the burden, but Ame had never explicitly told Zahora the secret. She had spent time with the woman though … something she'd said must have been a clue …

Then Zahora heard the clash of metal just outside the caves and knew her time had run out. If she was going to do something, it was now or never. Maybe she didn't have enough power to create the shield … but there was only one way to find out.

She delved deep into her reserves, dredging up every ounce of self-belief she possessed, then thought of the Triskelion, holding that in her mind's eye as she pushed her power around the perimeter. But it was no good. Even with the Triskelion, she could barely get the shield an inch off the ground.

Fuck. Fuck. Fuck. Muffled shouts sounded from the cave's entrance … this was it … the enemy was coming, and she'd failed her nation. She looked at Noah, thought of how he hadn't even had a chance to register, to become a proper Pagan, and of Callie, who was still a Templar … It couldn't end like this.

Noah met her gaze, his features grave. He picked up Callie and moved to the stone, to Zahora. They huddled together, Callie clutching Zahora's arm.

It couldn't end like this … it wasn't fair … Zahora put her palms flat against the stone. *It couldn't end like this.* She slapped her palms against the stone in frustration, the sound of footsteps racing from the entrance loud in her ears.

'It will not end like this!' she screamed, lifting her hands, then hammering them down onto the stone once more.

And when her palms connected with the cold, hard rock, the Pagan wheel filled her vision, the Triskelion in its center. The wheel spun. Fast, then faster, until it was nothing but a blur. It spread out from the standing stone, out and out, until it circled the perimeter of the round cave, spinning like a saw blade.

A saw blade …

Cut them down. The words roared inside her head. *Cut them down. Cut them down.*

The spinning wheel of Pagan magic exploded outwards. Zahora's senses came alive as the magic travelled … as she travelled with it across the Nexus.

It felled the soldiers in the tunnel, then the soldiers in the compound outside, and then it raced down the mountain, to where the rest of the West Coast's army battled with the Pagan troops. It felled their enemies, and then it felled Alerac, and a rush of horror hit Zahora hard in the chest.

Stop, she commanded the magic, erasing the Triskelion, pulling back against the weapon she wielded, willing it to cease. It slowed, Meredith rushing forwards, towards where Alerac had fallen. And then it stopped, just in front of Hades, Hephaestus, and a handful of enemy demons who were fleeing towards the road.

And as she flung her soul back towards her body, Zahora watched with horror as Hades spun, as his eyes found Meredith, as he threw his sword …

'No!' Zahora screamed. But it was too late … much too late. *No. No. No. What have I done?*

Raina reached the cave entrance and found a sea of terrible calm. Their enemies lay dead on the ground, all of them except Ame, who stood amid the carnage, casting her eyes around, her expression full of awe.

'I told you she was dangerous,' Ame said, as Raina locked eyes with her.

'How are you still alive, when that ... thing ... did this to everyone else?' said Caspar, casting his eyes across the fallen.

Ame shrugged. 'I don't take chances with my safety when on a battlefield. I have my own shield.'

Raina nodded, then turned her head to assess the damage among her own people. Rose and Christa dead, Elliot down, Gemma standing over him.

'Get a healer!' Gemma shouted, and Talli, clutching her arm, ran into the caves.

'Hades and Hephaestus got away,' Ira said in their ears, 'as did a small number of their soldiers. A man's climbing the path, coming your way. He arrived with Meredith and Alerac ... but ... Meredith and Alerac are down ... they aren't moving.'

'No,' said Gemma, bowing her head over Elliot's lifeless form. 'So many losses.'

The blood in Raina's veins travelled south, the sinking feeling almost choking her. Who was in charge? She couldn't remember who'd agreed to be Rose's second ... had it been Christa?

Talli returned, flanked by five or six healers, and they immediately went to Elliot. 'He has a pulse,' said Gemma. 'He took a blow to the shoulder.'

One stayed with Elliot, and the others spread out, searching for anyone with a pulse. They checked Rose and Christa's lifeless corpses along with the rest, but not even magic could bring them back now.

'We will see them in the next life,' said Talli, tears in her eyes. A healer examined her arm, which had a long, deep gash across it.

'You need stitches,' said the healer. 'Come with me.'

'Mummy!' called Callie, running out of the cave at full tilt, ramming into Raina's legs.

Raina scooped her into her arms, squashing Callie to her chest, not caring that she was covering her daughter in blood. It could have been so much worse … had so nearly been the end of everything.

'I'm assuming we have you to thank?' said Raina, as Zahora appeared at the cave mouth, huddled into Noah's side.

'To blame,' said Zahora.

Her eyes were puffy, and Raina realized she wasn't only leaning against Noah from exhaustion, but also … something else.

Raina handed Callie to Caspar and moved to stand in front of Zahora, giving her no option but to meet her gaze. 'Listen, Zahora, you saved us all. Without you, Callie would be dead. We would all be dead … or maybe captured, awaiting the true death. These people weren't messing around. You're a hero.'

'I'm a killer,' said Zahora. 'The magic killed Alerac … I think it killed every non-Pagan. I used the Pagan wheel … from the stone, and when Meredith saw Alerac go down, she went to him, and Hades … killed her. If I'd let the magic run only a few feet further … or stopped it a few feet sooner …'

'Zahora … this is war,' said Raina. 'There will always be losses … Meredith knew that better than any of us. She would be happier to die, honorably, as she has, than to survive at the expense of our nation.'

'But I could have saved her!' said Zahora, tears streaming down her face.

'You've never used that magic before,' said Raina. 'How could you have known to stop sooner? How could you have known what it would do?'

Zahora shook her head and closed her eyes for several long moments.

'How did Callie and Noah survive?' said Caspar. 'If it killed all non-Pagans …'

'They were in the middle of the weapon with me,' said Zahora. 'I don't think it started killing until it left the cave.'

Zahora's eyes found Ame, who still hadn't moved. 'Ame?' she said. 'What are you doing here?'

'I came with the West Coast,' said Ame.

'You had a shield in place?' said Zahora.

Ame nodded. 'Of course.'

'Ame Sigora,' said a male voice, approaching from the front gate. 'I wish I could say it's a pleasure to see you again, but disaster seems to follow wherever you go.'

'Giorgio?' said Ame. 'What the hell are you doing here?'

'The Pagans found me … they're surprisingly resourceful. Told me they had a Sage, so I had to come and see for myself … can't say I'm disappointed. It's a pleasure to meet you, Miss …'

'Call me Zahora.' They appraised each other for a beat, then Zahora said, 'Can you teach me? So I don't do that again?'

Giorgio raised an eyebrow. 'Most with your power would want me to teach them so they *could* do it again … only better.'

'The only way what I did could have been better, is if it had never happened at all,' said Zahora. 'I killed all of these people.'

'Who came knocking at your door, trying to kill you,' said Giorgio. 'Young demons these days … This is *war*.'

'Well, I don't like it,' said Zahora. 'War is nothing but death and vanity.'

Giorgio laughed. 'You're not wrong there, my girl. But it is ceaseless, so you had better get used to it. It's a part of our nature, I'm afraid … deeply rooted … part of our instinct to survive.'

'Pointing out that we're animals doesn't make it any better,' said Zahora.

'Oh, stop, Giorgio,' said Ame, her voice sharp like a knife. 'She has to give the power back, or die.'

'Now now, Ame, you're hardly able to occupy the moral high ground,' said Giorgio.

'We're not talking about me. She's caused a rift in the magic … can't you feel it? Or are you losing your touch in your old age?'

'Oh, don't worry, I can feel it. But change doesn't scare me as it seems to scare you. Although,' he said, turning back to look at the Pagans, 'if you do want to reinstate the Registerium's magic, as it was before, the fluctuating will have to stop.'

'What do you mean?' said Zahora. 'I thought the Registerium's magic broke because I smashed into it.'

Giorgio chuckled. 'As strong as you are, you're not that strong … nothing ever could be. The magic wouldn't have disintegrated like it did unless it was already weak.'

'The fluctuations weakened it?' said Zahora.

Giorgio nodded. 'I think the constant back and forth rubbed away the bonds … the colossal force of all the magic of at least one of the two known Spheres moving first one way, and then the other … I'm surprised it lasted as long as it did. Your attack may have been the final straw, but the damage was already done.'

'But if I'd never touched the Sphere …' said Zahora.

'Yes yes,' said Giorgio, waving a dismissive hand. 'One day you'll get too old for this indulgent introspection. *What if* this ... *what if* that ... who knows what might have befallen our world if you hadn't touched the Sphere? Maybe we'd all be dead ... The world doesn't revolve around you, you know.'

Zahora shrank back and gave a small nod. 'Can you teach me?' said Zahora. 'Can you help us reinstate the Registerium's magic?'

'I can do those things ...'

'Will you? Please?' said Zahora.

'We shall see,' said Giorgio. 'But first, I image you'll want to tidy the place up, and bury your dead.'

Chapter 16

They wrapped the bodies of the dead in pure white fabric, anointed their feet with oil, and placed snowdrops and daffodils—the first flowers of spring—across their torsos. The bodies rested on wooden wagons, each with four candles, which had been lit for protection and guidance until they were ready for their journey to the next life.

Talli—now their leader as well as their priestess—stood in front of a huge funeral pyre. She'd placed large copper bowls on each of the four sides—one for each element—and woven living plants into the fabric of the structure.

Talli looked to the gathered Pagans as she stepped in front of the bowl of flames. She dropped a handful of herbs into the fire, then raised a knife in her hands, holding it up towards the setting sun. She lowered the knife, cutting it through the smoke from the herbs, then held it aloft once more.

'We call on the Gods and Goddesses of the wild to take our dead into their care, to nurture and protect them, watch over them on their journey from this life to the next, help them find peace as they rest and regrow, then return them to us, safe and well.

'This we ask of you, ancient spirits of the woods, and brooks, and dales, and in return we offer you our service, to live as you wish it, protecting each other and our sacred world.'

Talli pricked her finger with the knife, letting a drop of blood fall into the flames. It hissed and crackled, and Talli's head snapped backwards in a violent motion, her arms fanning out with alarming speed.

She chanted long forgotten words … words Zahora neither knew nor understood, and gooseflesh raced across her skin.

Talli stopped chanting, and a flock of women in white dresses stepped forward, crowns of spring flowers on their heads. They each held a bundle of herbs, which they dipped into the flames, then they held the lit bundles aloft as they moved to stand by the bodies.

They blew out the flames, and smoke poured from their hands, which they smudged across the bodies of the dead. Talli did the same across the funeral pyre, cleansing that too.

A slow, steady beat of drums sounded from a group of demons near the pyre, and deep, melodic singing seeped across the clearing, saturating the space with sound. Talli walked the perimeter, from east to west, and the women followed, each pulling a wagon laden with one of the dead. They circled the perimeter three times, then returned to the pyre, the sun's golden rays warming their backs as they laid the bodies on the prepared wood.

Many had died, and all those present stepped forward to help, lifting with reverence. Zahora helped carry Meredith, telling her she was sorry as she laid her on the wood. She pressed an early wild rose into the fabric they'd wrapped around her, and said a silent prayer, asking the spirits to grant her a safe journey to the next life.

Zahora wasn't even sure she believed in the spirits … not really … but in this moment, it was all she could think to do.

Then, too soon, the pyre was full, and Talli stood before it once more. She plunged a torch into the bowl of flames, then held it aloft. 'Journey well, friends. May we meet again.'

She lowered the flaming torch onto the pyre, lighting the wood under Christa's body. She pressed a hand to Christa's fabric-covered forehead, holding it there until the heat of the rising flames forced her away.

Others stepped up to the flaming bowl, each with their own torch. Raina sent Rose to her next life, Gemma lit Meredith and Alerac, and Caspar placed his torch under Marla's wrapped form. Zahora clung to Noah's hand, tears rolling down her cheeks as the flames devoured them … these people who had become her family.

And then they danced, in slow, circling movements, to the rippling, melodic music, as their loved ones burned. The sun dipped below the horizon, and the flickering firelight cast eerie shadows of the dancers on the earth. A shiver ran down Zahora's spine, because as she watched, she could well believe the spirits had come to collect the dead.

Talli called the leadership together—those who remained. There was still much to do, and two of the Pentalpha had got away …

'Do you think they'll continue to attack now Ares and Aphrodite are dead?' said Talli, her mind's eye replaying the images of Christa falling, and of Gemma slaying Ares and then Aphrodite in return. Gemma had delivered Aphrodite's killing blow moments before Zahora's magic had done its terrible work.

'I don't think so,' said Elliot, who lay on a couch in the hut that had belonged to Marla. The magiks had saved Elliot's life, but he'd sustained many injuries, including the loss of a lung.

Talli looked to Gemma … she'd spent most time with Hades and Hephaestus after all.

'I don't think so either,' said Gemma. 'They're the only remaining leaders, and they have a whole nation of demons conditioned to do their bidding. I think they'll go back to the West Coast and live their lives.'

'How will they convince the other demons to keep serving them?' said Zahora.

'They'll come up with some new story, I'm sure,' said Raina.

'And their followers can't leave unless the nation is disbanded,' said Gemma, bitterly. 'The West Coast does not allow free movement.'

Talli took a breath. 'We'll continue to monitor them,' she said. 'The vote on the proposed reforms is at the Registerium tomorrow … not that they're members …'

'Will you go?' said Raina.

'I think I must,' said Talli, 'but that means I won't have time to plan our Imbolc celebrations.'

'We can do that,' said Raina. She took Caspar's hand.

'And Callie will be delighted to help,' said Caspar, sending Raina a knowing smile.

'Thank you,' said Talli.

'Giorgio's agreed to teach me magic,' said Zahora, 'and we need to register Noah ... he's waited long enough.'

Talli inhaled deeply ... there was no reason to delay. She would have liked to witness it, but it would be selfish to insist they wait. 'Of course,' she said. 'Whenever you would like ... there are plenty of Proficients around who can show you how.'

'Thank you,' said Noah.

'We'll be lucky to have you in our nation,' said Talli.

'What about Ame?' said Zahora.

They'd put Ame in a hut, under guard. All the fight had gone out of her. 'Honestly,' said Talli, 'I don't know. We can't trust her ... not with the way she feels about Raina, and given her past actions ... but I don't favor holding her forevermore.'

'We should ask Giorgio,' said Raina. 'He knows her ...'

Talli nodded. 'I'll leave that with you too,' she said.

Talli cast her eyes over each and every member of their depleted team. How had they lost so many in such a short time, with so little warning? Should she ask the other nations to join with the Pagans on a quest for revenge?

If she let it go ... did nothing ... she would be accused of weakness ... may lose allies like the Vikings. But if she went to the West Coast to fight ... others would call the Pagans warmongers and distance themselves.

This was why Talli hated leadership. She'd never wanted this job ... Christa would have been so much

277

better at it than her. Christa would have excelled, with her level head, quiet authority, and unflappable nature.

Tears welled in Talli's eyes, but she took a breath and shook them away. She had much to do, and she would see Christa again.

Chapter 17

Zahora tentatively took hold of Giorgio's outstretched hand. They sat atop a cliff, away from the magic compound, because Giorgio wanted to evaluate her skills and didn't want to be disturbed.

A part of Zahora wondered if he would try to kill her; Ame hadn't made her desire to kill Zahora a secret, and Giorgio and Ame were from the same world, after all. But Giorgio seemed about as keen on Ame as Zahora was, which was to say, not at all. She wondered about their mutual past as her hand brushed against Giorgio's smooth skin.

Giorgio winced at the contact. 'My word,' he said, then leaned forward, bracing himself. 'Fascinating ... truly extraordinary ... I never would have believed it possible ...'

'What?' said Zahora, snatching back her hand in annoyance.

'I'm sorry?' said Giorgio, as though coming out of a trance. 'Is something wrong?'

'What is so fascinating and extraordinary?'

'Your power ... you're truly a Sage ... Sphere-touched. You could do incredible things with that power.'

'And yet, I can't, because I don't know how to, and I'd rather not destroy everything I hold dear while I experiment ... you saw what happened during the battle ...'

'Indeed I did,' said Giorgio. 'You're an incredible asset to your nation ... but you need to give the power back. The fluctuations you've caused ... no magic will hold against them ... the friction will rub away everything in its path. Maybe the bonds holding demons to nations are already as weak as those you smashed apart at the Registerium ...

'And what else might you have broken already? What might you break next? Maybe a small tap could destroy magic as we know it ... the Sphere below so off kilter it implodes. Maybe reincarnation itself is at stake ... You've upset the balance, created cracks ... who knows when those cracks might become fissures ... when we might all plummet to our deaths ...'

'You're saying we can't reinstate the Registerium's magic until I give back the power?'

'I'd say it's unwise,' said Giorgio, wringing his hands.

'But if I give back what I took—if I *can* even do that—I might not have enough power left to reinstate the Registerium's magic.'

'That is possible,' said Giorgio. 'However, seeing as you were able to take the power in the first place, and lived to tell the tale, I'd say it's unlikely.'

'Can we transfer Callie at least? Before I risk my life going back to the Sphere ...?'

'You need a Templar with the requisite power,' he said, peering at her. 'Do you have one of those?'

'No,' she said through gritted teeth.

'Then there are only two ways to free Callie. One: She dies and reincarnates. Two: The Templar nation ends, freeing all demons bonded to them.'

'You can destroy a nation how, exactly?' said Zahora. 'Not that I ever would ... it's an academic question.'

Giorgio gave her a penetrating look. 'Of course,' he said meaningfully.

'How?' Zahora pressed. 'By smashing into their stone, like I did at the Registerium?'

Giorgio thought on it. 'That might sever every Templar's bond to the nation, but only if every bond is linked to that stone. Although, that wouldn't end the nation. Anyone could put their hands on a stone connected to the Sphere and re-declare their bond to the Templars ... and you might end up accidentally killing them all ...'

'Then how do you end a nation?' said Zahora.

Giorgio huffed. 'It's a long and arduous process ... You must destroy their stones' connections to the Sphere—whichever Sphere they're attached to—and then you true death all the demons, or convert them to other nations.'

'But what about when nations merge?' said Zahora. 'Doesn't that end one of them?'

'Or you merge,' said Giorgio. 'You're right, that's an option. But mergers are significantly easier if everyone is on board, which means both sides invariably make concessions.'

'The Templars are weak, and their leader seems reasonable ... maybe ...'

'Ha!' said Giorgio, clapping his hands together. 'The Templars merge with the Pagans? Hell will freeze over first. Christianity and Paganism? They're oil and water, my dear.'

'They could co-exist,' said Zahora hotly.

'Please, do try. I shall watch from the sidelines with interest. The simplest course of action is for you to give back the power—before you destroy our world as we know it—and then reinstate the Registerium's magic. Once that is done, the Registerium will be able to transfer Callie using a magical shortcut ... a macro, if you will.'

'But they don't have any magiks ...'

'They do,' said Giorgio, 'although they're mostly useless. The Registerium should address that as a matter of priority, but in this matter it will be of little consequence. When we put in place the magic, we made the process so easy, even a Neo could do it. So long as you and I reinstate the magic in the same way, it should be fine.'

'And what if Janet changes her mind, and tries to force Callie back to the Templar nation?'

'Then she's an idiot, and deserves the swift end the Pagans will be justified in delivering to her limping nation.'

Talli ascended the stairs with one hand on the rail, trying to draw strength from the sleek wood. This was the last place she wanted to be ... not least because if they lost the vote today, she would never hear the end of it, regardless that she'd only just got involved.

She entered the room upstairs at the Registerium and headed for her place with the other nations' leaders and representatives. They'd laid the seats out in a circle, with only one member of each nation permitted to sit.

Sofie approached as Talli made for a chair, grasping Talli's arms. 'We—the whole Viking nation—are sorry for your losses. We were shocked and saddened by the news. If you take your revenge, we will stand with you.'

Talli inclined her head. 'It is good to see you, my friend,' she said. 'Especially in this nest of vipers,' she added in a low voice. 'We are monitoring the remaining members of the West Coast's Pentalpha. We have no desire for war … we want peace … but if they give us no choice, you will be the first call we make. It would be an honor to have the Vikings by our side.'

Sofie nodded, then made way for other demons, all the Pagans' allies taking turns to offer their condolences. Talli was finally taking her seat when the doors burst open and Torsten strode in, a tall, formidable-looking woman with close cropped hair by his side.

He made a beeline for Talli, wrapping her in a bear hug. 'I was so sorry to hear,' he said.

'I'm sorry for your loss also,' said Talli. 'Meredith was your wife, even if it was only a ruse …'

'Sush,' said Torsten. 'My new wife doesn't like to be reminded of my previous marriage … she's a jealous sort …'

'It was a means to an end …'

'Believe me when I say she does not distinguish … I have the scars to prove it.' Torsten winked conspiratorially. 'I hear Meredith had the honor of a warrior's death, at least.'

'She did,' said Talli. 'As did Rose, Christa, and the rest.'

'They will be missed,' said Torsten, 'but we will see them again.'

Talli nodded, swallowing the lump in her throat.

The Registrar took to the center of the circle, and the room quietened. He turned slowly as he addressed the group. 'I won't draw this out,' he said. 'We all know why we're here, and you have most likely already decided how you will vote. I will only say this: the vote today is momentous, with long-lasting, far-reaching consequences. I implore you to think about the good of all nations ... of all demons ... both now and in the future.

'We have experienced, in these last few days, the consequences of having a powerful nation outside of this alliance. The West Coast need not account to anyone for their actions, and despite their crippling defeat—their nation's decimation—their remaining demons are trapped ... not able to leave without permission from their leaders. This cannot be applauded, nor held as a desirable state of affairs ...

'I am sure I am not alone in wanting peace among the nations, and in wanting a Registerium that functions in the interests of all. I implore you to take these points into consideration when determining the outcome of the vote today.'

The Registrar had barely finished speaking when the Animist representative spoke up. 'How do we know the Registerium's magic can even be reinstated? Last we heard, you had no magiks to speak of.'

'We have found a member of the Nation of Stars,' said Talli, 'and he has agreed to help us.'

'In return for what?' said the Animist.

'Access to a Pagan magik ...'

'And we're supposed to take that at face value, with no proof?' said the Animist.

'I can vouch for the rarity of the magik in question,' said the Buddhist representative. 'One of our own magiks recently spent time with her … he relayed stories of her considerable abilities.'

Talli nodded. 'She is impressive.'

'But that doesn't prove you've located a member of the Star Nation,' said the Animist.

'True. But I give my word we have,' said Talli. 'I swear it.'

The Animist faltered, deciding how far to push the new Pagan leader in such a public setting. The room held its breath, but the Animist eventually nodded, then sat, backing down from the fight.

'Does any other wish to speak before we begin the vote?' said the Registrar.

No one uttered a word.

'Then I call you to the first vote on reforms, which we have discussed extensively. To summarize, the Registerium will be transparent about the support we provide to each nation, and all nations will have access to all Registerium records. The Registerium will keep magiks of adequate skill on staff, and we shall make the process to elect a Registrar democratic—each nation shall have one nomination and one vote, and a Registrar's term in office will not be longer than ten years.

'Those are the main points of the hundred-page document, of which you all have a copy, and which lays out the exact terms the Registerium shall abide by if this group passes the reforms. Please vote now.'

Almost every demon in the room stood, which came as no surprise, given the content. The next vote was the contentious one, and Talli held her breath.

'The second vote is to make free movement of demons mandatory for Registerium members. This means that no nation may refuse a demon's request to leave, for any reason.'

A ripple of interest spread around the room, and Talli's pulse thundered in her ears. This one was for Rose ... and for Gemma. *Please, please, please let it go our way.*

'Please vote now.'

Talli stood in as commanding a way as she could, willing the others to their feet. Janet stood, as per the agreement she'd made with Rose, as did others. They seemed to come to their feet slowly, as though they weren't quite certain ... as though they might sit again at any moment.

The vote hung on a knife edge, Talli frantically counting the representatives, trying to work out if the reform had passed. And then, the Egyptian leader, Heba, took to her feet, to raised eyebrows. Several more rose after her, and ... oh Gods ... they had a majority! They had a majority!

Call it. Come on, Registrar ... call it already.

'The vote passes,' said the Registrar.

Talli sank back to her seat, her lungs filling with a whoosh. She could barely believe it ... barely heard the remaining votes for reforms other nations had put forward ... only just remembered to stand or remain seated at the relevant moments.

They'd won! Callie was officially free to transfer, regardless of their agreement with Janet. She couldn't wait to tell the others.

'Congratulations,' said Janet, when the voting was done. 'The Registerium stands, reformed, and free movement is mandatory. You got everything you wanted.'

'It doesn't often happen that way,' said Talli.

'More for Pagans than others, I'd say,' said Janet.

Talli appraised Janet for a long moment. Those words could have been hostile, but Janet didn't seem so ...

'I am sure Rose made extensive notes,' said Janet. 'You would do well to read them ...' And then she left, leaving Talli staring after her, wondering what on earth Janet could mean.

Talli spent the train journey to Wales on her laptop, reading everything Rose had written in the weeks before her death. The Pagans all used the same online system to file information, but they rarely bothered to read what the others had been up to unless it was critical.

Talli gasped when she read the final note: *Janet has agreed to merge the Templar nation with the Pagans. Following extensive discussions over many meetings, the terms are as follows:*

One: The Templars shall continue with their traditions without interference from the Pagan nation, and vice versa.

Two: Each nation may attend the celebrations and take part in the traditions of the other, but are not required to do so.

Three: The Templar leadership will have no less than two seats on the new leadership council.

Four: The two nations' assets will remain separate to start, merging over time, as appropriate.

Five: The demon Jamie Vanderveld is not welcome as a member of the newly merged nation. He will be removed from the nation on formation.

Six: Regardless of the outcome of the Registerium's vote, all demons, whether Templar or Pagan in origin, shall be free to come and go as they please.

The terms continued, descending into smaller details, and Talli scanned to the bottom, where it said: *Agreement finalized, but not yet discussed with the Pagan leadership. Agreed with Janet to wait until after the Registerium's vote to discuss with our respective leadership teams, in case of material changes as a result of that vote.*

Talli couldn't believe it. Rose really was a marvel, and the sooner she came back to them, the better.

Chapter 18

Zahora's stomach was in her throat as she looked down at the sea of pulsing lava below. If she fell, she was dead. If she took a misstep or did something wrong, she was dead. Maybe there wasn't even a right way to do it ... maybe she was already dead, just didn't know it yet ... the Sphere, this place, couldn't be trusted.

Open yourself up ... offer no resistance. Let the magic inside you call to the Sphere ... to that which it belongs. Giorgio's words looped through her mind, but that didn't mean she had any idea *how* to do those things.

She tried to clear her mind of everything, including Giorgio, but the more she tried, the more thoughts and ideas and memories wanted to press back in. The dreams she'd had across the Nexus surfaced, and Zahora latched onto them, following them as they scuttled away. The magic she'd stolen had given her the dreams, so it made sense for them to know their way home ...

But the dreams, as it turned out, were evil. They led her to the very edge of the precipice, encouraged her over, wanted her to fall ... She swayed wildly as she dismissed them, grabbing hold of the image of Noah with every ounce of her being.

He stabilized her, as he always did, kept her away from certain death … for now at least.

Zahora sat on the stone—it seemed safer than standing—then called to the magic. She'd navigated through the Nexus to the Sphere in a blink … had barely needed to give her soul the order. Maybe intention was all she needed now …

She willed her soul to release the magic … to return it to the source.

Nothing happened.

'Give it back,' she said aloud, then shouted it.

Nothing.

She appealed to the magic inside her. 'Go,' she said. 'Go back to your home. I don't want you anymore.'

It was a lie. She did want the magic. She loved the possibility it represented, the world it had opened up— her access to the Pagan leadership—that never would have happened without the magic. Would it all go away if she gave the magic back?

When she gave the magic back. She *was* going to do this.

They won't ditch me … they can't … they don't have any other magiks … and I think they like me. They like Noah … everyone likes him … he's so … likeable. But most people don't like me. Marla didn't like me. I'm too abrasive, and reckless … not good traits for leadership.

'Oh, for Gods' sake, shut up!' she shouted across the Sphere. 'Just give the fucking magic back …'

A change below caught her eye, and she watched it, fascinated. Something was moving towards her … something shimmering through the lava. It hit the edge of the stone on which she stood—where the Pagan's standing stone connected to the Sphere—and ricocheted back the way it had come.

The more she watched, the more shimmers she saw—simple now she knew how to spot them. She followed them out as far as she could, the shimmers travelling as far as the eye could see, backwards and forwards.

The fluctuation … our downfall … all because of me.

Zahora leaned forward and reached down with her hand, hovering it just above the lava, somehow managing to reach it, even though she seemed to sit acres above.

She waited until a shimmer approached, then pushed her magic out to meet it. The shimmer came towards her, rising up out of the lava as though alive. But whatever had pushed it towards her now pulled it back, yanking the shimmer away.

She waited for the magic to turn, then reached out with her magic once more. This time, she moved closer, not touching whatever this thing was … should she touch it? What if that was the only way? Maybe if she made contact, the shimmer would pull the stolen magic back to where it belonged.

The thought had barely formed, certainly she'd had no time to consider it, when the shimmer shot forwards and fused with her hand.

'Fuck!' said Zahora. When the magic changed direction, it would pull her into the lava. It would kill her.

Terror filled her, and she scrambled to her feet, ordering her soul to return to her body, regardless of the shimmer anchoring her here. She reached and reached, desperately clawing her way out. The shimmers changed direction, and she felt a pull similar to when she'd stolen the magic in the first place.

If she escaped this time, would she take even more magic? What would happen if she pulled one of those shimmers with her? Is that what she'd done last time? But if she took more, it could be catastrophic. A terrible realization came over her. She should let go … fall into the lava … let it have her and all the magic she'd taken.

She was considering it, even as she resisted the unrelenting pull, as her defenses weakened, and then she heard something from above … music. A feeling of peace flowed through her, as though every nerve in her body unwound, every muscle relaxed.

Noah.

She didn't think as she clawed and fought her way back to him. But as she was at the top of the stone, almost back to Noah, to safety, the pull relented. The shimmers had changed direction, heading back towards her once more. The relief almost made her collapse to the floor, the respite so overwhelming.

But as stillness washed over her, she felt a split within herself, some part of her wanting to return to Noah, some other part calling to the shimmers, desperate to get to them.

The shimmer attached to her hand turned, beginning its tortuous pull once more. It could have the magic … and this time, she meant it. If she had to make a choice between the magic and Noah, it wasn't a contest.

She imagined a knife travelling down the split within her, cutting away that which did not belong. The stolen magic slid out of her, pulled by the shimmer as soon as she cut it free. She kept going, until only a single thread connected her to the Sphere, but the pull increased as her connection reduced, as the shimmer travelled further away. It was unbearable … all consuming … monstrous. It felt as though it would draw her guts out through her skin, spilling them into the lava any moment. And the fatigue ... she didn't know how much longer she could keep it up.

But she only had a single thread to go ... she could do it ... she must do it. She focused on the music above. It changed ... first to a metallic scraping, then to the clear, piercing, hair-raising ring of a sound bowl. Another joined the first, then another in perfect, resonating harmony. The sound fortified her soul, filled her up. She closed her eyes and tipped her head back, letting the melodic tones reverberate through her. And then, she pictured the knife severing the last string connecting her to the Sphere.

The magic pinged away, the shimmer sinking back into the lava, and she breathed a deep, fatigued breath.

Thank the Gods.

She slumped against the stone, willing her soul back to her body. There was no resistance as her magic lifted her, but it was such hard work, most of her energy spent, and she was nowhere near as powerful as she had been moments before.

She let the music guide her, filling her mind with images of Noah, with thoughts of shutting themselves away for days, nothing to disturb them.

She returned to her body to find him hovering over her. 'Thank the Gods,' he breathed, pulling her to his chest. She nuzzled into him as he lifted her into his arms.

'Did it work?' Raina asked Giorgio as they waited in Marla's old hut for Zahora to wake. It had been more than twenty-four hours since Zahora had given back the magic, and Raina was itching for an update.

'It did,' said Giorgio. 'I am anxious to speak with Zahora … to understand how she did it. I was convinced she would die. Have you asked the Registerium if they will accept our assistance to reinstate the magic?'

'I have,' said Talli. 'They agreed, and the free movement clause will also need to be included.'

'It will, will it?'

'If that's something you're able to do,' said Talli. 'Otherwise, we'll have to make that a contractual agreement, rather than a magical one.'

'It always amuses me when I hear of demon contracts,' said Giorgio. 'We don't have a legal system … yet you happily sign contracts.'

'We have a legal system of sorts,' said Raina, defensively. 'Via the Registerium.'

Giorgio tipped his head. 'How's that worked out for you?'

Raina scowled. 'Better than it would have without the Registerium,' she said hotly.

'If you say so.'

'Zahora's awake,' said Noah, entering the hut. 'She's weak though.'

'She's been through an upheaval,' said Giorgio, sympathetically, 'but I'm sure she's strong enough for a conversation …'

He made for the door, but Raina stopped him. 'Giorgio, you know I won't allow you what you want until you agree to help us reinstate the Registerium's magic.'

Giorgio whirled towards her. 'Worth a try,' he said. 'I'll help. When do we leave?'

'As soon as Zahora's ready,' said Raina.

'We'll need a demon with at least an iota of magic from each nation,' said Giorgio.

'Already being arranged,' said Raina.

'Good,' said Giorgio.

Talli nodded, and Noah and Giorgio left the room. Raina headed after them, but Talli caught her arm.

'There's something I haven't told you yet,' said Talli. 'It's been so full on since I got back here … so much to do. I really don't know how Rose made this job look so easy …'

'What is it?' said Raina.

'We're merging with the Templars. Rose and Janet agreed to it before Rose died. They drew up a document and everything.'

'What the fuck?' said Raina. 'Seriously?'

Talli nodded, her features solum.

'Have you spoken to Janet yet?' said Raina.

'No,' said Talli. 'I wanted to speak to you and the others first … discuss our options. I'm sure Rose would have before committing us to a merger.'

Raina wasn't entirely sure that was true. 'It rids us of the Templar threat, I suppose,' she said.

'But … it's the Templars!' said Talli. 'They're Christians … we're Pagan … they've always wanted to annihilate us. Is it even possible for us to come together and function as one?'

'There are hardly any Templars left,' said Raina, her mind racing a mile a minute, working through the implications. 'It's possible that many of those who remain do not wish to be Templars anymore.'

'But do they wish to be Pagan?'

'It doesn't matter,' said Raina. 'With free movement, they can leave at any time.'

'So you think we should do it?' said Talli, her brow furrowed.

Raina considered her response. Is that what she thought? She hated the Templars ... what if Jamie demanded to be allowed into the Pagans' headquarters? What if he plotted to take them down from the inside? But a nation could reject a demon, just as a demon could now reject a nation.

'Did the agreement say anything about Jamie?' said Raina.

Talli pulled it up on her tablet, Raina's heart leaping as she read the sentence about expelling Jamie. Of course Rose would have been on top of it ... but then, Janet probably wanted to keep Jamie away too.

'We're giving up very little,' said Raina, 'and I guess we could add a reversal clause in case it doesn't work out ...'

'We'd have to be careful about asset merging,' said Talli.

'The agreement states that assets will be kept separate to start,' said Raina.

'We should run it past the others, and then talk to Janet,' said Talli. 'But ... do you think we should do it?'

Raina took a moment, then nodded. 'I think Rose is brilliant; this will wipe out the Templars without a war. And Janet's an asset. So long as she doesn't have an ulterior motive, she's a great addition to our team.'

The Pagans decamped en masse to Scotland.

'I will be glad when this back and forth is over,' said Talli. 'I feel like a freaking Yo-Yo.'

But Zahora suspected Talli was really glad for the distraction. None of them had had time to grieve … to come to terms with their losses. Zahora told herself their dead would be back … they would see them soon enough … but she wasn't an ancient demon like the others. Just the rest of this life seemed like an inordinately long time to her. And who knew when Rose and Meredith would reincarnate? There was no rhyme or reason to these things.

'Ready?' said Raina.

Zahora nodded, and they entered the circular meeting room inside one of the Registerium's towers. The Registrar stood in the middle looking up at the ceiling. Zahora cast her eyes up too, following the spiral staircase that hugged the wall to the top.

'So,' said the Registrar, turning his attention to the Pagans, 'how is this done?'

Giorgio stepped forward and took the Registrar's hand. He did it under the pretense of a greeting, but Zahora knew otherwise. The magik—his powers formidable—was using the opportunity to learn as much as he could about the Registrar, getting a sense of his aura … his energy.

Giorgio stepped back. 'You know we created this room to tie each nation's magic to the Registerium?' he said.

Zahora frowned. 'You didn't tie the magic directly to the stone?'

'Oh, we did,' said Giorgio. 'But why use the stone when you can add some pomp … some mystery … somewhere nice and cozy for future meetings? Scotland in the winter is no joke.'

Zahora nodded. 'So you linked the stone to this room?'

'We did,' said Giorgio, crouching by the stone slab in the very center of the floor. He lifted it to a rustle of surprise, everyone stepping forward to get a better look.

'Ha!' he said. 'It glows ... still connected to the stone. That bit was my magic to spin ...'

'Who did the rest?' said Zahora.

Giorgio ignored her. 'You must grab the strands of magic each nation offers you, one by one, and connect them here.'

'I have to reconnect the strands for each individual demon?' said Zahora, a flutter of panic flapping in her chest.

Giorgio chuckled. 'No. We dealt with that complication. You must check they give you their master strand ... the one that connects their nation to the Sphere—either the one above or below. The magic will then pull all of their demons' bonds through the connection.'

'The master strand,' Zahora repeated.

'Yes,' said Giorgio. 'We will teach them how. It shouldn't be hard ... but then, we're not working with the finest magiks to have ever graced the earth, so we mustn't take anything for granted.'

Zahora nodded. 'How do I take hold of them? How do I connect them?'

Giorgio waved a hand. 'All in good time. First, we must make the alteration to ensure free movement.'

'I thought that rule sat within each nation's own magic?' said Zahora.

'It does,' said Giorgio, 'but we can add a condition here to modify their magic ... far easier than changing each nation's set-up one by one ... although, if they ever leave the Registerium, their magic will revert to whatever it was before.'

'If they ever leave the Registerium, they can make whatever decision they want,' said Raina.

'Indeed,' said Giorgio, with a clap of his hands. 'I will get to work modifying. Please gather the magiks … when I'm finished, we have training to do.'

Giorgio shoved his hand into the hole and pulled out a strand of glowing gold. Zahora watched, openmouthed, as he made the strand hover in mid-air, then pulled it apart.

'No … no … no …' he said, working his way through the smaller strands he'd exposed. It reminded Zahora strongly of a rope. 'It is like a rope,' said Giorgio.

Zahora started … she hadn't realized she'd said that out loud …

'It's common practice to twist magic like this, so it can't separate. These stands together make up the whole … if any one comes loose, the whole thing could fall apart.'

Zahora watched, rapt. This was exactly the kind of training she'd wanted. She'd never known magic could be used in this way … she could learn so much from him …

'I must say,' he said, 'it's fun to do this again.' He discarded another few strands. 'We used to have work like this day in, day out. It got very tedious, but since technology all but wiped-out magic use, it's been a lifetime or two since I did anything like this.'

'Can you show me how to do it?' said Zahora, stepping forward.

He looked up from his work, appraising her over the rim of his round glasses. He held her gaze for several long moments, then pulled out a strand of magic. 'Come and hold this.'

Raina and Talli entered the small cottage the Registerium had allocated to Janet for her stay. It was the same cottage Raina had stayed in when she'd reunited with Caspar, after she'd run away from him at the Viking cave. Janet had been Jamie's agent then, helping to force Raina over to the Templars, and Janet's face said she remembered too …

'I …' said Janet.

'It's part of the game,' said Raina, waving a hand.

They sat on the tartan chairs in the living room and immediately got down to business.

'You really want to merge?' said Raina.

Janet stood and walked to the window. She looked out for a moment before saying, 'Rose proposed it. You know what she was like … always shooting for the stars. And of course, I was apprehensive to start. I've only just taken over the Templars … to merge would be to admit defeat without a fight.'

'You've had no shortage of fighting,' said Talli.

'And it's not defeat,' said Raina. 'Your nation is weak … ripe for a takeover … and given the West Coast has unknown intentions, allying with us makes sense … makes you strong.'

'That's what Rose said,' said Janet, 'and I can't say I took much convincing. It's no secret my nation is on its knees. Most of our allies have deserted us, our resources are depleted, and many of our best demons are between lives …'

'Will they accept our merger when they return?' said Talli.

'They won't have much choice,' said Janet, 'and even if they don't like it, I don't think they'll organize against us.'

'Unless Jamie rallies them behind him,' said Raina.

'But even if that were to happen, they'd have no land, no money, no friends …' said Janet.

'Have you found Jamie?' said Talli. 'Are you looking for him?'

'Jamie has a … research compound somewhere in the south. We don't know exactly where—it was a secret he guarded closely—but I assume that's where he and Pixie went. If he resurfaces, I won't hesitate to kill him.'

'You've had a dramatic change of heart …' said Raina, goading Janet just a little.

Janet huffed out a laugh, not rising to the bait. 'I thought we Templars were a team … that we were building something great, and that I was a valued part of the plan. I thought Jamie appreciated me … I thought he liked me … turns out I was wrong on all counts.'

'People like Jamie get easier to spot over time,' said Talli, 'although we all have our weaknesses … our buttons that, when pressed, make us blind …' Gemma was proof enough of that.

Janet shrugged. 'Rose and I hammered out the bones of an agreement, then decided to wait until after the free movement vote to tell everyone. And here we are …'

Raina nodded. She believed Janet had good intentions, and the Templars would only have two seats on their new joint leadership council … there was a limited amount anyone could do with two seats. Of course, if she played a long game … but the Pagans would be watching for that … they'd seen it all before.

'Okay,' said Talli.

'After we transfer Callie,' said Raina.

Talli gave her a questioning look.

'If the merger doesn't work out, and we separate again in this lifetime, Callie will revert to being a Templar.'

'With free movement,' said Janet.

'That's not part of the Templar magic,' said Raina. 'It's being enforced at the Registerium … if you left the Registerium, you would be under no obligation to let Callie go.'

'We have no intention of leaving the Registerium,' said Janet.

'I know,' said Raina, 'and I trust you, but none of us can predict the future, and I've seen some pretty wild things in my time. What if Jamie reappears and challenges you for leadership?'

'He can't … we're going to kick him out,' said Janet.

'That means nothing,' said Raina, 'and there are any number of other ways this merger could go wrong.'

'I'm happy to transfer Callie before we merge,' said Janet, 'but that means we need to wait for the Registerium's magic to be back up and running.'

'It should be soon,' said Talli. 'Giorgio and Zahora have almost finished.'

Janet nodded. 'Then we'll wait to announce the merger until after we've transferred Callie?'

'Yes,' said Raina.

Zahora watched as Giorgio patched the free movement condition into the rope. It was incredible how he grasped a new strand of magic from the air, spelled it until it glowed, then wound it into the rope.

'The new magic will spread through the existing fibers,' said Giorgio. 'In just a second, the rule will reach from end to end.'

'How did you learn all this?' said Zahora. 'In the Nation of Stars?'

Giorgio sneered. 'The Nation of Stars takes ... it does not give.'

'Meaning what?'

'In order to join the Nation of Stars, you must already be an exceptional magik. You are deemed lucky to gain acceptance ... to be a member of such an exulted circle, but membership comes at a price.'

'What?'

'It varies, but sacrifice or betrayal is common. They like to collect knowledge on the other nations ... save it up for a rainy day ... or use it to look more all-powerful than they are.'

'Then why do you stay with them?' said Zahora.

Giorgio smiled a wistful smile. 'Because they are magnificent. Truly extraordinary. The finest minds ... the most revered thinkers and magicists. That group single-handedly discovered ninety-nine percent of the magic we know today ... and will discover more.'

'That's the work you do now? Research?'

Giorgio nodded. 'I will find the other Spheres if it's the last thing I do.'

'That will make your nation respect you?' said Zahora.

'They already respect me,' snapped Giorgio. 'It will make them revere me.'

The magiks from the other nations began to trickle into the circular chamber. Giorgio had trained them on the procedure, had made them practice extensively, and was finally convinced they could do what was required.

'You should join us, you know,' Giorgio said in a low voice.

Zahora twisted her head to look at him, trying to work out if he was being serious. He seemed to be …

'Giorgio, I have a nation, and I'm loyal to it.'

'That doesn't mean you've found your eternal home,' he said.

'We don't even know if I still have interesting powers, now I've given back what I took from the Sphere.'

The corner of Giorgio's mouth twitched into a smile. 'We both know you're an exceptional magik, with or without the boost from the Sphere.'

Zahora knew she was … otherwise she would never have made it back from the Sphere … would never have been stupid enough to blunder recklessly into the realm of magic in the first place. But she had Noah—who was not a magik—and her nation, who finally valued her.

Giorgio put a hand on her shoulder. 'Gods willing, your lives will be long and numerous. You have plenty of time to try many existences. If not now, then in the future. The Star Nation would be lucky to have you … and you them.'

Warmth spread through Zahora's chest. Until these last few months, she'd felt alone, despite belonging to a nation … on the outside clamoring to get in. And now … this.

Talli gripped Zahora's arm as she made her way to the Pagan seat. Zahora smiled and gave a small nod before taking a deep, steadying breath. She could do this. If Giorgio were to be believed, it would be as easy as pie. But Giorgio's interpretation of easy and everyone else's weren't always closely aligned … it would be fine. As Giorgio had said, she had skills.

'Magiks,' said Giorgio. 'If I can truly call you that …'

Zahora swallowed a laugh at the reactions from those sitting around the edge of the room … scowling, smiling, outrage, eye rolls … it was a wonder they'd got everyone to this point … the nations were all so very different.

'You will each grasp your nation's master strand from the Nexus, then walk to Zahora, who will attach it to the Registerium's magic exactly as we practiced. Questions?'

They'd already asked why Zahora was attaching the magic, not Giorgio. Giorgio had replied that he wanted nothing to do with this going forward, so Zahora should be the one linked to it. Giorgio had assured her that if she did it properly, there would be no maintenance, but the notion that she would be tied to this place for the rest of her life made her shiver.

Zahora shrugged the thought away as Talli stood. She'd volunteered the Pagans to go first, both to show her confidence in the plan, and to allay any suspicions that this whole thing was some kind of con. Demons were suspicious beings … had learned the hard way to be like that.

Zahora silently took hold of the blue stand Talli offered her, nodding when she had it securely in her grasp. Zahora blew out the breath she'd been holding, then crouched to the opening in the floor. She picked up the gold rope of magic, shivering as it made contact with her skin, and wrapped the Pagan strand around it. She tied it the way Giorgio had shown her, then placed the golden rope back in the floor. The blue and gold wove together before her eyes until they were firmly merged.

'Good,' said Giorgio. 'One down.'

Janet stood next, grasped the Templar's magic bond, then held it out to Zahora. Zahora tied each nation's strands one by one, breathing a deep sigh of relief when the last one merged with the gold two hours later.

'Very good,' said Giorgio. 'Thank you, everyone. I believe there is a celebratory dinner planned, or some such thing ...'

Zahora sat on the floor as the demons filed out, exhausted from the magical and emotional exertion. She lay back on the uncomfortable stone and looked up at the ceiling, her eyes tracing the spiral staircase again and again.

'It is done?' said Raina from the doorway.

'It is done,' said Giorgio.

'Then we can transfer Callie?' she said, entering the room, Callie following behind.

Callie ran to Zahora's side and lay next to her. 'You did it!' said Callie, squeezing Zahora's fingers.

'We all did it,' said Zahora, squeezing back.

'Here he is,' said Janet, who had retrieved one of the Registerium's few remaining magiks.

Callie sat up and beamed at the man. 'Please transfer me to the Pagan nation,' she said in her most confident voice.

'I ... ah ...' the man faltered, looking first at Janet, then Raina.

'You heard the girl,' said Janet.

'And she no longer needs permission,' said Raina. 'Remember?'

'Uh … yes … of course. If you will just come outside to the stone,' said the magik.

'You don't need the stone!' said Giorgio. 'You can do it right here!'

'I … can?' he said, moving uncertainly towards the still-visible rope that glowed with golden light.

'Don't be scared of it!' said Giorgio, shoving the magik forward. 'It won't hurt you.'

The magik didn't look so sure. 'How … what do I have to do?'

'Christ,' said Giorgio, 'is this really the best the Registerium has to offer?'

Raina shrugged.

Giorgio waved his hand flamboyantly. 'Touch the rope.'

The magik faltered, as though waiting for more.

'Go on … I haven't got all day …'

The magik inched forward, holding out his hand, then pulled it back.

'Oh, for the love of …' Giorgio surged forward, grabbed the magik's hand, and forced it onto the rope.

The magik choked out a cry of surprise, and winced as though bracing himself for pain. When none came, he looked up sheepishly. 'It … doesn't hurt.'

'Of course it doesn't hurt!' said Giorgio. 'What have these people been teaching you?'

'Has anyone been teaching you?' said Raina.

'Not for a few lifetimes,' said the magik. 'I was a Neo when the last Proficient died. It's been tricky since then … none of us know much …'

Giorgio rolled his eyes as Caspar and Noah appeared at the door. Raina visibly relaxed as Caspar came up behind her, wrapping his arms around her waist.

Zahora watched Noah as he leaned against the door jamb, looking suspiciously at the hole with the glowing light.

'Next,' said Giorgio, 'take Callie's hand.'

Giorgio gestured for Callie to get up off the floor, where she still lay with Zahora. Callie went, but Zahora stayed, not caring if she looked foolish. It was oddly relaxing, with her back pressed against the frigid stone.

Callie took the magik's hand. 'Now, Callie,' said Giorgio, 'repeat after me: *I renounce my membership of the Templar nation.*'

Callie knitted her brow, focusing hard. 'I renounce my membership of the Templar nation,' she said.

'Good,' said Giorgio, 'and now, say: *I pledge my allegiance to the Pagan nation.*'

Callie repeated the words, then both Callie and the magik yanked their hands back at the shock of the buzzing against their skin.

Raina and Caspar rushed forward. Raina lifted Callie into a hug, and Caspar wrapped his arms around them both.

Tears gleamed in Raina and Caspar's eyes as they left the hall, and Zahora felt as though a weight had lifted from her too. Callie was safe, meaning one less reason Zahora might be called to action.

'You can feel it, can't you?' said Giorgio.

'Feel what?' said Zahora.

'The magic coiling through the floor. It was a small indulgence … I included it for fun when I built the magic rope … I wonder if anyone else has ever realized it's here …' Giorgio chucked to himself as he left, and Zahora supposed she might get to that stage one day … where she had to do things like coil magic through floors for entertainment.

She closed her eyes, sucking up the strange energy the floor channeled into her. It turned to warmth as it hit her, tension that had filled her for ... she didn't know how long ... melting away. The Registerium's magic was back, Callie was a Pagan ... the only thing left was to merge the Templars with the Pagans, but now the Registerium was functioning, there should be little for Zahora to do.

She opened her eyes and Noah's face filled her vision, hovering above her. Oh, yes ... there was one more thing ...

Noah pulled Zahora to her feet, and she wrapped her arms around him. 'Your work here is done,' he said into her hair. Although part of him was still on edge ... like it might not really be over ... like it might never be over.

'Apart from one thing,' she said, running her hands up and down his back.

Noah tensed; he knew it was too much to hope that he could have her to himself for even a short while.

She pulled back and looked into his eyes, her green irises conveying so many things. She gave a knowing smile. 'Something to do with you,' she said.

'What?' said Noah. 'We're going on a mission?'

She laughed. 'Like Talli and Raina would let us go anywhere by ourselves.'

'Oh, right ... you're a liability.'

'Hey!' she said, then placed a soft, chaste kiss on his lips. 'We're going to the stone outside right now, to register you as a Pagan.'

'Oh,' said Noah, a rush of warmth chasing away the strain. He'd forgotten all about his own registration in the furor around Callie's … which felt like a huge anticlimax now.

'Come on,' said Zahora, slipping her hand into his and intertwining their fingers. His chest pulsed … it was always the little things that got him, reminded him how perfect she was.

'What is it?' she said.

'Nothing.' He dropped a sweet kiss on her lips. 'You're right, we should go before we get dragged into Callie's celebration.'

A mischievous look crossed Zahora's face, but Noah didn't have time to dwell. She pulled him behind her as she left the castle, tugging him towards the Registerium's newly reconnected standing stone.

'Put your hand on the stone, and say: *I pledge my allegiance to the Pagan nation.*'

'That's it?' he said. 'The magik inside held Callie's hand …'

'He didn't need to,' said Zahora with a chuckle. 'I think Giorgio just wanted the magik to freak out when he felt the connection buzz.'

Noah rolled his eyes. 'Will this hurt?'

'No, you big baby … you'll feel a mild tingle.'

'Okay,' he said, blowing out a breath. He pressed both hands flat against the stone. 'I pledge my allegiance to the Pagan nation.'

The buzz of magic hit his skin and made him shudder all over, like when someone scraped a nail down a blackboard.

'Urgh,' he said, trying to physically shake the feeling away. 'That's horrible.'

'I quite like it,' she said, then took his hand and placed it back onto the stone, hers on top of his. 'Close your eyes.'

Desire stirred deep within him at her tone, and her touch, and the fact they were together, members of the same nation. 'Why?' he said, running his nose down hers.

'Because there's something I want to show you.'

'There are a few things I'd like to show you,' he said into her ear, then bit her lobe. 'Just not in public.'

She released his hand and curled in front of him, her back to the stone. He caged her in his arms as she pulled his lips to hers, and he kissed her with deep, passionate, possessive movements. He pressed his body against hers, wedging her between him and the stone, and she moaned into his mouth. The noise lit a fire within him, and he forced himself to pull back before they created a spectacle.

She turned to face the stone, then pulled his back to her chest, this time their hands flat on the cold granite, hers on top of his.

'Push your soul towards the stone,' she said quietly.

Alarm rang through him. 'Zahora … what?'

'It's not dangerous, so long as you go towards the stone, and I'll be right there.'

'I'm not a magik …'

'Everyone's a magik,' she said. 'It's just that some are more powerful than others. You'll be able to do it if you try.'

'Did Giorgio tell you that? Because the monk from the Buddhists, and Ame, and the Pagan magiks all said otherwise.'

'You trust those idiots over Giorgio?' she said, tipping her head back to rub her cheek against his.

He kissed her lips, because they were right there, then said, 'Okay. I trust you.'

Zahora giggled. 'That's not always a wise thing to do, given my track record.'

He huffed out a laugh, then nipped her neck. 'I trust your intentions are good.'

'Then I'll see you in there.'

Noah filled his mind with thoughts of the stone, of entering the stone, of seeing the Nexus for the first time, but nothing happened. His heart sank ... maybe Giorgio was wrong. But he tried again, and again, and again.

Nothing.

He was about to tell Zahora this was stupid ... that he was a demon in his very first life ... maybe he didn't have enough magic yet. But then an idea went off like a lightbulb. Music.

He sang as he thought about the Nexus, as he pushed himself towards it. The stone ... changed. The hard barrier softened, turned into something else under his fingers ... something permeable that his hands could push through, and push through it he did, until he emerged in a strange, distorted place the other side.

'This is the Nexus?' he said, looking around. It was as though the world were small below him ... he could see the whole of the UK and look out across the globe, as though he walked on a map. Zahora sat on the edge of a cliff, her feet dangling over the edge, and she tapped the space next to her.

'This is the Nexus,' she said. 'And this,' she tapped the stone under her hand again, 'is the Registerium's standing stone, which connects to both the Sphere in the sky above, and the one below.'

It was like a surrealist painting, the way the standing stone dominated, the way the world looked so small ... absurd. 'Does it always look like this?' said Noah, still trying to take in every detail.

'No,' said Zahora. 'It varies a little from stone to stone, from what I can tell, at least. It's like each stone—or maybe the nation linked to each stone—has its own personality and outlook on the world. We can zoom in and out if you want, but I like this perspective the best.'

'We're like giants,' said Noah, sitting next to her, 'and what's that?' he asked, pointing to a gentle glow of light around the edge of England, Scotland, and Wales ... around Ireland ... around the edge of every island, Noah realized.

Zahora laughed. 'Islands are prone to magic,' she said. 'I'm not really sure what it means, just that the magic seems to collect wherever the water meets the land.'

'Magic from the Sphere?' said Noah, furrowing his brow. 'The one below?'

Zahora gave him a look he couldn't decipher, then took his hand. As their skin made contact, lines filled the air around them, of every imaginable color, travelling every which way, through the earth, across the water, into the sky ...

'What the hell are they?' said Noah, his pulse racing at the sudden onslaught of color.

'I'm pretty sure they're Spheres,' she said, turning her head to look at him, a childish smile on her face.

'The Spheres Giorgio has been searching for, for lifetimes?'

She laughed. 'Yes! I think so ...'

Noah couldn't help but laugh too. Giorgio, the great and powerful, couldn't find in lifetimes what Zahora had in one ... 'How did you do it?' he said.

'When Giorgio told me he was looking for them, I started looking too. I could already see the connection to the Sphere in the Sky, and I'd already touched the one below, so I started with them, then went outwards. I spotted things I hadn't noticed before and followed them, and then suddenly they all just ... appeared.'

Noah gave her a disbelieving look. '*They just appeared*? Does this mean you're still a Sage?'

Zahora looked back across the landscape. 'I don't know what it means to be a Sage,' she said with a shrug. 'Not really.'

'Are you going to tell Giorgio?'

'No. He'll never take no for an answer about me joining them if I do that … and … I don't know … I think it might be best to leave the magic alone. What good can come from meddling?'

Noah considered her words. She wasn't wrong. People had a disastrous knack of destroying everything good in the world by trying to possess it … pretending they only wanted to understand. Bullshit. People wanted to own. To be supreme. To have what others did not. She was right … the magic was best left alone.

'Have you tried to tap into any of them?' said Noah.

Zahora gave him an incredulous look. 'What, after last time I touched a Sphere went so well?'

Noah snorted. 'Good point.'

'It makes you wonder what they're all for, though, doesn't it? Why do they exist?'

'It does,' said Zahora. 'And how did people discover the Spheres above and below? What makes those two different? And how did they work out how to attach the standing stones …?'

'It's not documented anywhere?' said Noah.

'It would have been if the Pagans had anything to do with it,' said Zahora. 'Have you seen the records they keep?'

Noah smiled. 'But that doesn't mean they've always been that way … the nation's been around since before paper … before it was so easy to document things.'

'Maybe there are cave drawings somewhere,' said Zahora.

314

'I thought you were going to leave it alone?' he said, squeezing her hand.

'I am,' said Zahora, 'but I can't help wondering.'

They returned to their bodies, then meandered back to the large house on the Registerium's estate that the Pagans had once again taken over.

Noah pulled Zahora to a stop outside. 'You're … the most remarkable person I've ever met,' he said, looking deep into her eyes, trying desperately to find the words to convey what he felt.

She gave him a shy, lopsided smile and tipped her head to one side.

'There might be no one else in the universe who can do what you can.'

'That's not true,' she said.

'Who else would leave all that power … untold possibility … unexplored?' said Noah.

'I'm just lazy, really,' she said, moving into his embrace. 'It's too much hassle, and I'd rather just chill out with you … because you're the most incredible person I've ever met.'

He kissed her, but didn't believe her words … not really … she was in a different league to him.

'I'm telling the truth,' she said, somehow sensing his skepticism. 'You gave up leading the Slayers, because you cared less about power than being with me.'

'I mean … turns out it was a sinking ship anyway …'

She swatted him, and he laughed, then pulled back her head so he could press his lips to hers. She hummed into his mouth, and his body turned electric at the sound.

'We can't do this here,' she said, pulling away from their deepening kiss.

'Then let's get inside.'

Her mischievous smile returned as she took him by the hand, leading him up the stairs into the house. As they entered, the Pagans turned as one and rushed towards him, embracing him, calling his name, welcoming him to their nation. As they led him to the towering cake Elliot had lovingly made, Callie pointed to the banner with his name, then put a flower crown on his head. He laughed, overwhelmed, unable to find words.

Noah eventually extracted himself and grabbed Zahora around the waist, crowding her into a corner. 'You planned this?' he said, his heart hammering, emotion almost choking him. He had never felt so loved, so … wanted, for himself, not just as someone's legacy, or as an asset to be wielded.

'No,' said Zahora, shaking her head. 'It was Raina's idea … but if she hadn't suggested it, one of the others would have …' She stroked his face. 'They're as happy you're here as I am.'

'Why?' said Noah. 'Why do they care? I'm not like you … I contribute nothing noteworthy … I mean, aside from my good looks and charm …' He joked, but his chest cratered, years of his father's indoctrination making him vulnerable, making him unable to understand their motives.

Zahora's hand stilled on his face, and she looked into his eyes. 'They just … like you,' she said, shrugging. 'I don't know why, but I have great taste, so maybe they're just following my lead?'

'You do have great taste …'

'And you're kinda hot,' said Zahora, brushing her thumb across his lips.

He pulled her to him, then lowered his lips to hers, kissing her deeply, not caring about the catcalls and whistles from behind.

Chapter 19

Imbolc was typically a frivolous affair full of spring flowers, frolicking around the standing stones, and too much bramble gin. But as they sat around the fire by the stone circle at Maltings, the mood was anything but frolicsome.

Templars sat on one side, casting distrusting glances across the crackling flames at the Pagans. The Pagans weren't much better.

Raina inwardly tutted. How old they all were, and still they hadn't learned to just get on with things? She got up, pulling Caspar with her, moving to sit next to Janet, who was surrounded by the most senior remaining Templars.

The fact they still thought of each other as Pagans and Templars was not a good sign. But then, the agreement had been that the Pagan name would remain, and the Templars' would not, so the friction was no surprise.

The merger had been swift and painless, the hard times yet to come. The mistrust, belittling of each other's celebrations and traditions, digging in on decisions that didn't matter, just to get a win.

317

'Ira says everything's quiet on the Pentalpha front,' Raina said to Janet.

Janet nodded. 'And we haven't heard a peep from Jamie,' she said, doing her bit to show willing in front of the other Templars.

That was good, although Raina couldn't help the uneasy feeling that stirred any time she heard mention of Jamie's name. She wondered how many lifetimes it would be before he was back, causing problems for her family … or would it be sooner even than that?

'Ame's gone?' said Janet. 'I haven't seen her around …'

'She has,' said Caspar. 'Slipped away in the night without a word to anyone.'

'Giorgio's still here though,' said Raina. 'He keeps talking about leaving, but can't seem to tear himself away from Zahora.'

Janet chuckled, and so did one or two of the other Templars, but most remained stoic.

'For fuck's sake,' said Raina, waving her arm as she turned her glare first to the Templars, then to the sullen Pagans. 'Do you think any of us would have chosen this? We all know how it goes … most of us have been part of uncomfortable mergers before. Let's just get drunk and dance around like fools. We don't like you, you don't like us, but who knows, maybe your soul mate is sitting just across the fire … or maybe you'll find some common ground once you *talk* to each other.'

'And maybe we'll start swinging swords!' said Talli, who'd already had a few too many … Raina wondered again how long it would be before Rose returned. She hoped for all their sakes it would be soon.

'Maybe I should come over there with *my* sword,' said a Templar man.

They all laughed.

'Maybe you should,' said Talli, the mood shifting to something darker.

Raina rolled her eyes as the man stood and approached menacingly. 'Dance with me,' she said, taking his hand and pulling him to the edge of the firelight. He snarled, but the musicians noticed them and picked up the tempo and the volume. 'Unless you don't know how to,' she goaded.

The Templar spun her with no warning, and it was all Raina could do to stay upright. A laugh sprang free from her lips as he caught her, the Templar unable to repress his own smile. He did it again as Caspar and Janet joined them, and Raina laughed, a bubble of joy rising through her chest.

'Good,' said a male voice, accompanied by a man stepping into the ring of firelight, 'we haven't missed all the fun.'

'Jon!' said Raina, thrusting her Templar partner into the arms of another.

Leila—Raina's human cousin—stepped into the light beside Jon. They fought their way through endless hugs before joining the dancing. Raina didn't miss their joined hands … the way Jon monitored Leila's every move … the kiss he pressed to her temple.

'I'm glad someone's been having a nice time,' said Caspar, taking Raina's hand.

'Me too,' said Raina, 'but I hope he knows what he's got himself into … the grief when she dies …'

'It's better to have loved and lost …' said Caspar.

'You're a hopeless romantic,' said Raina, wrapping her arms around his neck.

'I am,' he said, lowering his head into her space, 'and I'm proud of it.' He kissed her, and sparks of euphoria fired in her mind. She had everything she wanted …

Caspar broke away. 'That reminds me,' he said, reaching into his pocket and pulling out a gold bangle.

Raina made a choked sound as he put the bangle on her wrist.

'Seems like the right moment for you to be reunited with this,' he said.

Raina smiled at the memory of their first kiss, all those hundreds of years ago, when he'd first given her the bracelet. Tears filled her eyes, and she kissed him again.

'Muuuummm!' said Callie, pulling on her skirt. 'Stop!'

Caspar kissed her one more time before letting her go, then picked Callie up with a roar, twirling her to the music. Callie squealed with glee, and Raina's heart nearly burst with love.

Thanks for reading! Want to read Raina and Caspar's first kiss? Then sign up to my newsletter and the story will wing its way to your inbox! Sign up here: https://www.subscribepage.com/ancient-souls

I hope you enjoyed *Nation of the Stars* and, if you did, I would really appreciate a rating or review wherever you buy books, or on Goodreads, Instagram, TikTok, or any other social media! Just a rating, a few words, or a line or two would be absolute perfection, and will help others find my stories. Thank you for your support.

CONNECT WITH HR MOORE

Check out HR Moore's website, where you can also sign up to her newsletter:
http://www.hrmoore.com/

Find HR Moore on Instagram and Twitter: @HR_Moore

Follow HR Moore on BookBub:
https://www.bookbub.com/authors/hr-moore

Follow @HR_Moore on TikTok

See what the world of *The Ancient Souls Series* looks like on Pinterest:
https://www.pinterest.com/authorhrmoore/nation-of-the-sun/

Like the HR Moore page on Facebook:
https://www.facebook.com/authorhrmoore

Follow HR Moore on Goodreads:
https://www.goodreads.com/author/show/7228761.H_R_Moore

TITLES BY HR MOORE

The Relic Trilogy:
Queen of Empire
Temple of Sand
Court of Crystal

In the Gleaming Light

The Ancient Souls Series:
Nation of the Sun
Nation of the Sword
Nation of the Stars

http://www.hrmoore.com

Printed in Great Britain
by Amazon

16177789R00185